# "This is what healing is about. This—"

She reached out and took his hand. Cradling it in hers, she rubbed her fingertips over his palm in a light circular motion, looking into his eyes with unflinching directness. "This is healing. It's the giving of strength and hope and—love."

Her last word came on a soft rush of breath, and Jake caught it with his own. They stood poised in twilight's embrace, his hand in hers, her touch kindling a slow heat. One motion, one word from her, and it would become wildfire in his blood.

She was taking him apart, making him burn inside.

Isabel gradually became aware of how near she stood to him. The realization came like a gentle change—the warm pressure of his hand in hers, the scent of him, the awareness of his size and strength. She tried to breathe easily, to achieve some measure of calm.

But the way he looked at her, his eyes darkening like storm clouds, quickened her heart and coursed a restless ache of longing through her veins.

Dear Reader,

The perfect complement to a hot summer day is a cool drink, some time off your feet and a good romance novel. And we have four terrific stories this month for you to choose from!

We are thrilled to welcome Nicole Foster to Harlequin Historical with her touching Western, *Jake's Angel*. Nicole Foster is actually the pen name for the writing team of Annette Chartier-Warren and Danette Fertig-Thompson. This duo has previously published several romances under various pseudonyms. *Jake's Angel* is the tender tale of an embittered—and wounded—Texas Ranger on the trail of a notorious outlaw; he winds up in a small New Mexican town and is healed, emotionally and physically, by a beautiful widow.

Jillian Hart brings us a wonderful Medieval, *Malcolm's Honor,* in which a ruthless knight discovers a lasting passion for the feisty noblewoman he is forced to marry for convenience. In *Lady of Lyonsbridge,* a superb story by Ana Seymour, a marriage-shy heiress uncharacteristically falls for the honorable knight who stays at her estate en route to pay a kidnapped king's ransom.

And don't miss Judith Stacy's darling new Western, *The Blushing Bride*, in which a young lady travels to a male-dominated logging camp to play matchmaker for a bevy of potential brides—only to find herself unexpectedly drawn to a certain mountain man of her own!

Enjoy! And come back again next month for four more choices of the best in historical romance.

Sincerely,

Tracy Farrell
Senior Editor

# JAKE'S ANGEL
# NICOLE FOSTER

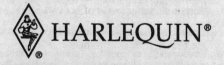

## HARLEQUIN®

TORONTO • NEW YORK • LONDON
AMSTERDAM • PARIS • SYDNEY • HAMBURG
STOCKHOLM • ATHENS • TOKYO • MILAN • MADRID
PRAGUE • WARSAW • BUDAPEST • AUCKLAND

ISBN 0-373-29122-1

JAKE'S ANGEL

Copyright © 2000 by Danette Fertig-Thompson and Annette Chartier-Warren

This edition published by arrangement with Harlequin Books S.A.

® and TM are trademarks of the publisher. Trademarks indicated with ® are registered in the United States Patent and Trademark Office, the Canadian Trade Marks Office and in other countries.

Visit us at www.eHarlequin.com

**Printed in U.S.A.**

Please address questions and book requests to:
Harlequin Reader Service
U.S.: 3010 Walden Ave., P.O. Box 1325, Buffalo, NY 14269
Canadian: P.O. Box 609, Fort Erie, Ont. L2A 5X3

For Jeff, always my hero.

For Ken, thanks for the memories of Paris, Rome, Amsterdam, London, Oxford, Copenhagen… but most of all Alassio.

# Chapter One

*Whispering Creek, New Mexico, 1874*

Jake Coulter limped up to the doors of the Silver Rose leaving a trail of blood and dust behind him. After two days of hard riding with a hole in his leg, no sleep, and nothing but a bottle of bad whiskey for solace, he felt mean enough to shoot the next man who crossed him.

He hadn't planned on dragging into Whispering Creek looking and feeling like something the vultures left behind; he hadn't planned on coming to Whispering Creek at all. But Jerico Grey had decided to run home to the New Mexico territory, and Jake hadn't spent nearly six months tracking him just to let him steal his freedom by crossing the border.

Jake tried to remember how much whiskey he'd drunk when he agreed to take on a job no one else wanted, deciding it was just what he needed to change his luck. His delusion lasted until he'd met up with three *bandidos* near Santa Fe. The encounter left him with a piece of lead in his thigh and a temper to rival the desert heat.

Pushing his way inside, Jake gave a quick, hard look around the saloon, almost sorry there wasn't anyone who invited trouble to take out his frustration on.

But with morning just turning to midday, the Silver Rose was nearly empty. Three old men, as brown and worn as old leather, sat hunched over a corner table dealing cards, and a stringy cowboy leaned backward against the bar, watching one of the saloon girls tempt with a swish of bright-yellow satin and a flash of dark eyes. Even the air felt lazy, baked hot and dry by the late morning sun and tasting of dust.

Jake limped up to the bar, tossed down a handful of coins, and from the shadow of his slouched hat glared at the man behind the long length of scarred and pitted wood. The cowboy glanced once at his face and the Colts riding low on his hips, then edged nearer to the end of the bar. A saloon girl sidled a step closer.

The bartender, polishing glasses with a rag as gray as his grizzled hair, took one look at Jake and grinned, showing a crooked row of yellowed teeth.

"Well, it looks like the devil comes a callin' and it ain't even my birthday." Without asking, he shoved a whiskey bottle and a smudged glass toward Jake. "You don't seem to have done too well fer yerself, friend. You're ugly enough to give a brave man a fright. But never let it be said that Elish Dodd turned away a payin' customer, no matter how ugly they get."

"Thanks for the welcome. I hope everyone in this town is as friendly as you."

"Depends on what day it is and why you're here."

Jake took a long pull from the bottle, ignoring the glass. "I need—help."

"I can see that. You're bleedin' all over my floor,"

Elish observed, leaning over the bar to glance at the pooling blood. "It ain't real good for business."

"Then I'll take my business upstairs. I need a room and someone who can cut out a bullet without taking off my leg in the process."

"And I need a bag full of gold and a good woman. This ain't a mission of mercy. Most of the girls couldn't patch up a skinned elbow without losin' their breakfast on your boots."

"I'm sure one of your girls is good enough to get me a doctor."

"Doctor! Too long in the sun's turned you *loco, amigo*. There ain't no doctor here. And the ones that have come through here pretendin' to be, why I'd as soon spit at a rattlesnake than let them get near enough to see the color of my hair."

Jake pulled himself upright, wincing as his weight settled on his bad leg, and, grabbing up the half-empty whiskey bottle, turned to the stairs leading to the second-floor rooms. "Just send up one of the girls. I'll figure out something."

"You please yourself. Take the room at the end of the hall, though I can only promise it to you if business is slow. This ain't a hotel."

"I noticed."

"I'll send Chessie along, then. Chessie don't like it rough, though, and I don't like the walls or the customers full of lead," Elish added, starting on the glasses again. "You remember that."

"You and Chessie don't have to worry." Jake threw his battered leather saddlebags over his shoulder as he dragged his bad leg up the uneven stairs. "Not tonight, anyway."

He heard Elish holler into the curtained room next

to the saloon for Chessie and the sound of it grated on
him. He didn't like having to depend on anyone for
help, no matter how little. But he didn't have much
choice at the moment.

The room Elish allotted him had the familiar feel of
old boots. Nothing fancy, but comfortable, and with the
advantage of being secluded from most of the noise of
the saloon. Someone had pulled the shades to ward off
the sun so the edges of everything looked eroded by
the diffused yellow light.

Putting down his bottle by the bed, Jake unbuckled
his gun belt and draped it over a chair, tossed his hat
and duster on top. He pulled up the shades, leaned
against the sill and looked out over the main street of
Whispering Creek.

In the valley, the heat warmed the shades of green
and brown, softening the outlines of the log-and-rock
buildings lining either side of the dirt street, muting the
sounds of the town so in a moment of stillness the
cicadas sang with the wind. Looking up to the jagged
evergreen peaks on either side of town, Jake imagined
he could smell the complex warm and sharp blend of
ponderosa pine, blue spruce, fireweed, and red clay
earth that belonged only to the rugged mountains of
the northern New Mexico territory.

If there had been any poetry in him, the moment
might have given him a sense of peace. But it only
agitated his restlessness, and made him more aware of
the ache in his thigh and the time he'd lost because he
hadn't been lucky enough this time to stay out of the
way of a bullet.

Jake hated the idea of having to stay in Whispering
Creek more than a day or two, but he reluctantly admitted it might be a week or longer before he'd be able

to ride so that he could track Grey and finish his business.

Not that Jake had any particular place in Texas to go back to; he'd left San Antonio long ago, forced out by the ghosts of his past. This wild, beautiful country was in his blood though, and that made it easier to keep moving, fast and often enough so he'd never come close to putting down roots. So he'd never make the mistake of calling any place home again.

A tentative knock at the door turned him from the window. A girl with rusty curls the color of Indian paintbrush stuck her head into the room, looking him over as if she expected him to fall down dead at any minute.

"You're not bleedin' everywhere, are you?"

"Probably. Get in here," Jake said, gesturing impatiently. "I need your help."

Chessie edged into the room and stood with her back pressed to the door. She was a tall girl, plump, with a generous mouth and eager eyes. He imagined that usually, she wasted no time in coming to the men who enjoyed her company. This time, she hung back as if he had the plague.

"I don't know anything about doctorin' and I ain't gonna touch anything that's bleedin'. I don't like anybody that much."

Jake glanced at her white face and decided she meant it.

"Just get me the doctor," he said, sitting down on the edge of the bed. He ran a hand over his hair, suddenly feeling tired and heavy.

"Doctor?" Her disbelief echoed Elish's. "A doctor that lives here?"

"Unless you're going to volunteer to dig this bullet out."

Chessie's eyes bulged. "Not me. But there ain't no doctor here and if there was, he wouldn't do you no good."

"You got a better idea?"

"Sure I do. I'll get the witch for you."

"You'll get *what?*"

"Isabel. The witch. She don't like bein' called a witch, and I suppose Elish might be right when he says she ain't really magic or nothin', but she can fix 'bout anything and she's a lot nicer than any doctor. Why, everyone tried to tell me the nettles and cedar Isabel gave me when I had the fever would more 'n likely kill me than cure me, but in just one day I was back workin'."

"Woman—" Jake lay back on the bed and slung an arm over his eyes, shutting out the sunlight and Chessie's jabbering about the so-called witch. "I don't believe in magic or witches. Just get me someone who can cut out a bullet without killing me."

Chessie looked at him a long moment, chewing on her lower lip. He'd tied a bandanna around midthigh, partly covering a jagged rip in his heavy pants, and she could see the dark patch staining both. Without saying anything, Chessie hurried out to find the witch.

The roadrunner lay quivering in the cradle of Isabel Bradshaw's palm, one wing hanging limply. Kneeling on the rocky ground, her worn cotton skirts bunched up around her, the hot dry breeze scattering wisps of dark-gold hair around her face, Isabel gently stroked her fingers over the bird's tiny body, soothing, judging its injuries with her touch.

"It's all right, I'm not going to hurt you," she murmured, her voice soft and soothing. She ran her fingertips over the roadrunner's wounded wing, her eyes never leaving the small bird.

"Don't be afraid, little friend. I only want to help you."

The roadrunner made a feeble attempt to flutter free and Isabel paused, practicing the way her grandmother had taught her so long ago of using the quiet rhythm of her own body and mind to reassure and calm frightened spirits.

"Mama? Is she all right?"

Turning her attention from the roadrunner, Isabel smiled at one of the two black-haired boys crouched at her side. Matthew looked up at her, his narrow face screwed up with concern, a tremble in his chin. He dragged the back of his hand against his nose, muffling a sniffle.

"Will it live? I knew you could help it so I brought it to you quick as I could. I didn't mean to hurt it."

"It's only because you're so clumsy with that slingshot, Matt," the older boy said, giving his brother a push on the arm.

"I'm not clumsy!"

"You are! You couldn't hit a whole barn if it was a foot in front of you!"

"Nate…" Isabel began, warning him off before a full-fledged battle could ensue.

"Oh, Matt, you're such a baby," Nate said, kicking at the dirt with the toe of his boot. "You just can't aim, that's all. But I knew you could heal it, Mama, so we ran all the way back home."

"You did just the right thing, Nate. Now both of

you, please be still while I finish or you'll startle this little one. Here, Matt, you can help me. Gently now…''

Fixing her eyes on the bird, Isabel reached into the basket at her side, being careful not to make any quick movements that would startle the small creature. She sensed its pain and fear, and, even more strongly, Matt's distress, and wanted to do something to quickly ease both.

In a worn leather pouch, she found a bit of lizard tail root. She spread it on a piece of cotton and added a dribble of water from a small bottle before folding the cloth into a square.

Then taking Matt's small hand in hers, she guided him to caress the bird's head and body while she bound the poultice to the bird's wing with a strip of cloth.

''Speak quietly to her. There…that's right…''

''You'll soon be well, little bird, and running with your friends again,'' Matt whispered. He began to hum softly to the roadrunner, one of his favorite bedtime lullabies.

Isabel smiled, watching him pet and soothe the bird. After a few minutes, she felt the timid creature settle easily into her hand, its heartbeat slowing, its eyes no longer frightened. Her greater reward, though, was seeing the beginning of hope on Matt's face.

''It looks better. Is it?''

''Much. She's only bruised. She just needs a little rest, that's all.''

''I think she likes me.''

''She likes your touch,'' Isabel said, watching Matt stroke the roadrunner's sleek feathers. ''And that's one of the most important parts of healing. You are doing it exactly right. In a few days, I promise you, she'll be running with the wind again.''

"Can we take her home until then? Please, Mama?"

"Matt, we have so many of your wounded animal friends at home we need another house just to keep them all." Isabel relented at the pleading on Matt's face, unable to deny him. "All right," she agreed, smoothing back an unruly lock of his hair, smiling. "She can stay a few days, until she's fully healed. Now, I should take this little one inside and you should get on to the meeting house before Aunt Katlyn misses you for lessons."

Making sure they had their books and lunch pails, Isabel hugged them both, then watched them scamper off in the direction of the rustic cabin that served as both community center and schoolhouse. She gathered up the roadrunner and rose to her feet, smiling a little at her boys' energy and their faith in her healing skills.

Matthew and Nathan were all she had left of her marriage—the best part, she'd decided.

Douglas Bradshaw hadn't left her much when he decided the promise of gold, whiskey and women in California appealed more than a series of failed prospecting ventures and raising a family in Whispering Creek. Isabel could admit now that her marriage to Douglas had been a farce from the beginning. He'd wanted someone to nurse him through a bad bout of influenza, to clean, cook and care for his stepsons after his wife died. And she'd longed for someone to love, to give her the complete family she'd never had.

She had trusted him with her dreams and he had lied to her.

But this past winter, with snow piled to the windows and the smokehouse and root cellar practically empty, when the high country was at its fiercest, the torn and smudged letter arrived telling her Douglas had died in a drunken fight with another miner.

In that moment she remembered very little of the caring she once felt for him. Regret, yes, that Matthew and Nathan had not only lost both their parents but a man they thought would be a father, and a lingering ache at Douglas's abandonment. But in her heart, Isabel had been a widow since the day just over a year ago when Douglas left suddenly after telling her he couldn't stomach the prospect of a lifetime stuck in Whispering Creek with her, her grandmother, and his late wife's children.

But of all the regrets she had about her marriage, Isabel never rued Douglas's leaving behind his two stepsons. She might not have birthed them, but in her heart Matt and Nate were no less her own. Along with her grandmother and her half sister Katlyn, they were part of her family now and she would do whatever it took to raise them right in the town where they had lived all their lives.

That was why after Douglas left, she'd decided to use part of the house she'd inherited for business, offering her skills as a healer and herbalist. The upstairs loft room she rented to boarders or used as a shelter to those needing a place to rest or recover from injury or illness, or to those who simply had nowhere else to go in Whispering Creek.

Overall, the rambling house was humble, but it afforded her a means to keep food on the table without the help of any man. And that, she determined after Douglas's leaving, was something she would never allow herself to need again.

Nothing would ever force her to give up her home.

And nothing would ever persuade her to risk her heart again for the sake of a dream.

Holding the roadrunner gently in the crook of her arm, Isabel walked around to the back of her cabin, to the small garden there, looking for one of the baskets she used for gathering herbs and vegetables that might serve as a temporary home for Matt's new boarder.

A harsh *cawk* greeted her and she looked up to where a large raven sat perched on the edge of the garden fence, eyeing her with an unblinking stare.

"Hello, Trouble," she called.

"Hello, hello!" the raven croaked. "Cookies, please!"

Isabel laughed, knowing Trouble had learned the phrase from Matt and Nate after following her boys into the kitchen so many times. In fact, his uncanny ability to sneak inside and wreak all manner of havoc had led Nate to give him his apt name.

"Ah, is Nana baking again? I promise, I'll save one for you and you can share with the boys this afternoon."

Isabel was still smiling a little to herself when she stepped in the door, lost in her thoughts, not expecting to find anyone in the kitchen at this time of the morning.

The moment the door closed behind her, though, her grandmother pounced on her with a triumphant cry.

"Isabel! At last!"

The old woman's sudden motion set the dozen strings of varied colored beads she wore swaying and clattering. Tall and scraggy with a snarl of black-and-silver hair, Esme Castillo looked as if her body and face had been roughly hewn from old wood. She gripped a long serving fork in one hand, brandishing it like a sword in Isabel's direction.

"What is that?" Esme asked flatly, stabbing the fork at the roadrunner. "No, no, no—do not tell me. It is another of Matthew's orphans. *Ay,* why do I ask? I should know we will never be rid of these creatures!"

"Oh, Nana, you know I can never say no to someone in need," Isabel said, laughing. She settled the roadrunner into a small basket by the stove. "Besides, there aren't that many creatures here."

"A lizard, a desert rat, a very ugly squirrel, a raven with the tongue of the devil, and now—this! Soon we will have no room for your human orphans."

"Oh, we'll find room. And you'll do as you always do with our guests, slip treats to each and every creature and human when you think no one is looking." Isabel smiled at Esme's scowl, then gave her grandmother a quick hug, kissing her cheek. The old woman huffed a bit, making a show of despising any kind of fuss over her, but Isabel saw the satisfied twinkle in her eyes.

"I could put her in Mr. Davis's room," she teased Esme, glancing at the roadrunner. "His arm has healed and he told me this morning he's moving out today to try his luck in Nevada." Isabel sighed then, her tone losing its humor. "I suppose it means looking for another boarder."

Esme shrugged. "It will not be difficult. Most of the prospectors would rather have something more than a bedroll and camp food. And *ay,* that food! I would as soon eat boiled owls and rat dung than the poison that man over at Lone Gulch mine who calls himself a cook prepares!"

"Well, you look as if you're preparing for a feast here."

Isabel waved a hand at the disarray of pots, serving vessels and utensils, various piles of half-readied corn and beans, and raw slabs of goat meat. A chaos of smells permeated the long, narrow room, from the sweet richness of chocolate, to the sharp burn of red and green chilies, combined with various scents of odd and familiar herbs.

Esme helped with the cooking for the family and the boarders as far as she was still able. But when she was angry or upset she attacked the kitchen with a vengeance, soothing her frayed temper by turning out large elaborate meals or concocting one of her seemingly endless potions or remedies.

Glancing at her grandmother, Isabel saw the expression in Esme's heavy-lidded eyes was shuttered, giving her her usual air of hoarding a great secret. Esme walked over to the black monstrosity of a stove and began vigorously stirring a pot of soup.

"Sheriff Reed, he comes here today to tell me about some robberies nearby. As close as the La Belle, Anchor and Midnight City mines he says. These robberies…" Esme drew a long breath. She turned from her cooking to look at Isabel, her face softening with concern. "The sheriff says they remind him of that man you knew as a girl."

Isabel shook her head, glancing away, not willing to see the questions in Esme's eyes. "Of course it isn't him. It's been so long, why would he ever come back here?"

"My child, we have all heard the stories that most of the gold he stole from the mining camps around Taos County is hidden in the mountains near here."

Esme hesitated then added, "And of course he always told everyone he cared for you, although I could never believe it of a man like that."

"Jerico only cared for himself," Isabel said, knowing it wasn't quite the truth. She and Jerico Grey had been childhood friends, and for a brief time Isabel imagined she loved him. It had been fleeting, a foolish feeling when she was still a girl and smitten with the wild, wicked attraction of an older boy who'd called her beautiful and promised her paradise.

Except Jerico Grey's idea of paradise was bought and paid for with someone else's gold.

"He would never come back here," Isabel said again, as much to reassure herself as her grandmother.

"Ah, well, I am sure you are right. Let us forget this foolishness. Cal Reed is growing old and *loco*. He should not be telling tales about robbers and ghosts of the past."

"I'm sure he was not telling tales. Cal knows his business. But you're right. We should forget it. I'll fix us some tea, shall I? One of your special mixes. And Trouble tells me you made cookies, too. Cinnamon, I hope."

"Cinnamon for you, and jam tarts for the boys. I had extra pastry that had to be used," Esme added quickly when Isabel smiled knowingly. "Cinnamon is very soothing, too. Just the thing for you, *pepita*."

The endearment, a relic from her childhood, only served to show Isabel how worried her grandmother was about the possibility of Jerico Grey touching their lives again. Shaking off a cold touch of uneasiness, she turned to warm the kettle and find the cups when Chessie, one of the girls from Elish Dodd's saloon, came rushing in, breathless, loudly banging the door behind her.

"Isabel, you have to come now. There's a man at the Silver Rose who wants a *doctor!*"

Isabel hid a smile and with a few gentle questions managed to elicit the facts that one of Chessie's would-be customers had been shot and needed healing. Leaving her grandmother to her frenzy of cooking, Isabel gathered up her basket of remedies and other supplies. "All right, Chessie, let's go see what the damage is."

As they approached the Silver Rose, Chessie paused. "Maybe you better come in the back door." The young woman slid a sideways glance at Isabel, as if not sure if it was a good idea to suggest such a thing.

Watching the shifting expressions on Chessie's face, Isabel easily read her thoughts. She suppressed a smile, knowing that Chessie, like some, thought she practiced some form of witchery passed down from her Spanish ancestors. It would be so easy to impress Chessie—a dark drape of shawl over her head, a sprinkle of powder and a few chanted words and Chessie would believe Isabel could raise the dead—or at least charm one of Chessie's admirers into an unlikely marriage.

On the other hand, Isabel knew Chessie truly fretted over anyone in trouble and was only trying to help in sneaking her up the back stairs so she could help a wounded man.

"Perhaps the back stairs would be best," Isabel said, making her voice and smile kind.

Chessie's face relaxed, and Isabel smiled to herself.

"There's a lot of blood," Chessie said, as she led the way to the second-floor rooms.

"Is there? It's all right, I've seen it before. Let's just hope your friend isn't faint from it."

Chessie stopped in front of the door at the farthest end of the hallway and looked at Isabel, biting her lower lip. "You ought to know something. He ain't gonna be too glad to see you. He asked me to get the doctor, but I knew you'd be better for him and besides I couldn't get somebody who ain't here. I hope you won't mind nothin' he says. He looks like the kind that's always one step from the noose, but he ain't gettin' around so good right now so I don't think he'll be too much trouble."

How comforting, Isabel thought, as she followed Chessie into the room.

Chessie's doubtful reassurance didn't improve the picture she had so far of this reluctant patient of hers. He was probably like every other man she'd met who used a gun to make a living, on one side of the law or the other. In the New Mexico high country it was hard to tell the difference between the two, most of the time anyway. But it didn't matter to her. She was here to heal his body, not his soul.

She did wonder, though, what Chessie had told him about her. Heaven knows, she thought, probably that I intend to heal him with chants and spells and boiled bat dung. And won't that impress him.

A foul combination of whiskey, blood and sweat assaulted Isabel the moment she stepped inside. If nothing else, Chessie's friend needed a bath and a night to become sober.

"Mister, it's me," Chessie called out. "You'll be feelin' yourself again soon, don't worry. I got just the person you need."

Something between a grumble and a growl answered her. "I hope you found a doctor."

"Oh, no, I told you I couldn't do that. I brought the witch."

# Chapter Two

Isabel glanced heavenward and shook her head. "Chessie—"

"Dammit, I told you to bring me a doctor."

The man lying on the bed half rose up on one elbow and looked Isabel over as if he expected her to have a broomstick and a peaked hat.

"She doesn't look like a witch," he said, falling back, one forearm covering his eyes. "She looks like a skinny woman carrying a basket who'd rather be picking flowers than traipsing around a whorehouse. Now, where the hell is the doctor?"

Isabel brushed by Chessie to the side of the bed. "There's no doctor and I'm not a witch, but if it pleases you, I can mutter a few chants and wave feathers over your head. Although no matter what I do, I'm probably wasting my time since you'll just walk out of here and get yourself shot up again."

She set her basket on the rickety oak nightstand next to a nearly empty whiskey bottle, noticing with a side-long glance the gun belt he'd draped over the bedpost within hand's reach. Probably another gambler or gun-slinger whose luck went sour over a card game or a woman. Deliberately ignoring the guns, she looked at him, appraising him with a long up and down gaze.

He was a big man, and older than she expected, mid-thirties she guessed, with a harshness around his eyes and mouth that looked permanently ingrained by experience and the elements. Hard lines shaped his face and body, giving her the impression there was no flesh to him, only tough brown skin covering honed muscle and bone.

The yellow wash of lamp glow did nothing to dispel the darkness of him. From his unkempt hair and beard to the heavy black denim and leather of his clothing to the look in the clouded eyes that glared at her when he pulled his arm back, nothing about him suggested he could or should be approached.

Isabel found herself holding her breath, staving off the chill his very presence seemed to evoke.

A pain-ridden groan escaped his throat. His dark brows drew together. "What are you still doing here? I don't want any crazy woman cutting me."

"I suppose you would rather bleed to death." Isabel ignored the gathering storm on his face and instead focused on the task at hand. She bent to gently pull away one end of the bloody bandanna. "Of course, if you have the strength, you may live long enough to die of lead poisoning."

His mind dulled by Elish's whiskey and two days' loss of blood, Jake tried to think of a nasty retort that would send her away. Nothing came to him and it made her seem all the more irritating.

"You must be a witch. You've only been here five minutes and I already feel cursed."

"Perhaps I am. And perhaps later I'll wave some essence of burnt toad over your head and make your leg disappear. Then it won't trouble you further. For now, you're going to find out that I can cut out a bullet as fast and clean as any so-called doctor.''

Before he could stop her, Isabel whipped a knife from the waistband of her skirt. With the skill of a surgeon she sliced through the bandanna in one clean swipe. The quick motion brought Jake halfway to his feet, his left hand slapping instinctively to his hip, his right reaching behind for the nearest Colt.

"Dammit, woman—"

She twisted the knife and pointed it at him, tip first.

"Be quiet and lie back. I don't expect your undying gratitude, but I won't fight you for the privilege of cutting a bullet out of your leg while you curse me for it."

From behind, Chessie let out a gasp, reminding Isabel she still lingered in the room.

"Don't worry," Isabel told her, flipping the knife blade back down, "I haven't killed anyone—yet." She gave Jake a hard-edged glance. "No matter how rude they are. Or perhaps you're just afraid of pain."

Jake studied her a moment, wondering why anyone would think she was a witch. The flush in her cheeks and the sting of her words made her look and sound far too real to be anything magical. He knew about Mexican women who used herbs and faith to doctor those who believed a handful of weeds and a touch could heal. But this Isabel didn't look Mexican, or even Spanish, with her pale hair and eyes the color of New Mexican turquoise.

"Who are you?" he heard himself ask, wondering why he cared.

"Isabel Bradshaw. I'm a healer."

"Bradshaw? That's not very Mexican."

"Considering my husband was an American, I wouldn't expect it to be. And you didn't answer my question. Are you afraid of pain?" She moved closer, still gripping the knife. "Or of me?"

"I'm afraid if I don't let you get this bullet out I'm going to bleed to death arguing with you." Jake fell back against the pillow, shading his eyes with his arm again. He wanted to argue, but a heavy lethargy weighing him down made the effort too much trouble. "Have you ever done this before?"

"A thousand times."

"You're probably lying, but what the hell. Get on with it. I'll pay you if I still have my leg in the morning."

"Your confidence inspires me," Isabel muttered.

She could sense Chessie's anticipation, yet she hesitated.

Isabel didn't like the look of him. She didn't want to be here, in Elish's saloon, with half of Whispering Creek downstairs and Chessie hovering. And she didn't want to touch him.

That feeling both surprised and disturbed her. It was like missing a step in the dark, a jarring sensation that momentarily threw her off balance and left her groping for a familiar feeling to steady herself. She'd never before felt an aversion to touching someone to heal.

It wasn't that he was so unique, either. She'd cut bullets out of many a man like him, men who killed as easily as they drank whiskey and bedded women. This time, though, some primitive instinct warned her of a danger she couldn't define.

Isabel pushed the feeling away, reminding herself why she had come. He was another wounded man, nothing more, nothing less. She reached for her basket, irritated to find her hand tremble as she picked out powdered willow leaves and bark and added them to a jar of pale amber liquid that enhanced the pain-killing benefits of the willow.

What was wrong with her that she couldn't do so simple a thing without behaving as if it meant her own life or death? Who was this man to her but another outlaw who had tangled with someone faster on the draw? Despite the undoubtedly ignoble cause of his injury, she wanted to help him. She'd never questioned her calling, even as a girl. She'd always cared for the sick and wounded, always sheltered those in need, just as her mother and grandmother before her.

She poured some of the elixir into a glass and held it out. "I don't know if you need this considering the amount of whiskey you've drunk, but it won't do you any harm, and it will help the pain and bleeding."

Jake moved his arm just enough to glare at her. "What is it?"

"Powdered toad and lizard spit. Drink it."

He hesitated then took the jar from her and drank it back in one draught. Almost immediately his face convulsed in a grimace. "That tastes like—"

"How would you know? Do you make a habit of dining on it?"

"You're starting to annoy me, woman."

"And I've only just begun. I'm sure you'll loathe me by the time I'm finished."

"It won't take that long," Jake muttered, covering his eyes again.

He heard rather than saw her rummage in her basket again and then felt the cold metal of the knife blade as she sliced away his pant leg. He tensed inside, waiting for the blade to cut into him, wishing he'd finished off

Elish's whiskey and asked for another bottle to follow it.

Instead, she touched him first. Her fingertips, cool and smooth, gently circled the hole in his thigh. He expected a painful probing. But she seemed more intent on simply touching, drawing long, gentle strokes on his skin.

At first it annoyed him. He wanted the bullet out of his leg, not a massage.

But gradually, the rhythm of her hands seduced him into focusing on what she was doing rather than the pain.

She began to speak, softly, in a cadence that almost became song. The words seemed to come from far away and Jake couldn't make any sense of them.

Coupled as they were with the stroke of her hands, it didn't matter. He could almost believe she was a witch because the combination worked a strange magic. The feel and sound of her might have been a caress—instead it was something deeper and stronger, something that soothed and made him vulnerable to a feeling perilously akin to contentment.

He didn't like it. It went too deep, forced him to accept an intimacy he didn't want, even if it was only for a few moments. Yet the rhythm of her voice, the feel of her touch became a seduction too tempting to resist.

When she finally cut into him with the knife, he felt a sharp pain. Then the dream induced by her touch and her herbs took him and there was nothing but darkness.

Isabel breathed a sigh when he passed out. She almost wished Chessie hadn't come to her about this one; he had an unnerving effect on her she didn't like one bit. But she hated hurting anyone, even a man who berated her for trying to help him.

She did what she had to do, digging out the imbedded piece of lead, cleaning the wound, applying a poultice of lizard tail to staunch the bleeding and prevent infection. When she'd finished, she straightened with one hand to her lower back, wiping damp tendrils away from her brow with the back of the other.

"You can look now," she said to Chessie. The young woman stood on the far side of the room, pressed close to the door, her nose practically squashed against it.

"You didn't cut off his leg, did you?"

"Of course not. Although I'll admit to being tempted. You're right—he's trouble."

Chessie turned around, casting a lingering glance at the man on the bed. "I suppose he is, but under all that blood and dirt, he's sure enough all man."

"I don't know about that but if you'd come to me any later, he would have been a dead man, whether he'll admit that or not."

"Well…I'm sorry about coming for you so sudden like, but I knew no doctor could do for him what you could." She looked up at Isabel, chewing her lower lip. "I hope you ain't mad."

"No, I'm glad you did. You know I can't refuse when someone's hurting. Although this once I might have been tempted because I've probably wasted my time here. Look at him and tell me he's not the kind to go right back out and get himself shot up again."

"I hope you're wrong about that." Chessie moved over to the bed and brushed her fingertips over the man's rough stubble. "He's one fine man, I can tell.

Losin' him'd be a waste. And besides, I ain't sure he's that kind, though he does look it."

"Oh, he's *that kind* all right. I'd put money on it. But—" Isabel shrugged and began to gather up bloody cloths and her pouches of herbs "—with the grace of God and any luck, he'll be back on his feet and out of town before we find out."

Chessie watched her, anxious again. "Will you be all right, Isabel? I mean leavin' here alone. You bein' a decent woman, I know some people, well…"

"Don't worry about me." A mischievous grin twisted the corner of her mouth. "The women in my family stopped caring what people said about us a long time ago."

She looked once more to the bed. The man lay still in the grip of deep sleep, yet even in this rest he didn't look peaceful. She thought she had been right in guessing his character, but she also could understand Chessie's admiration. Without the grime and the blood and the ragged beard, he would be compelling, if not handsome. And that combined with his aura of danger and mystery had no doubt been the downfall of more than one woman.

But not her. Never her. Never again.

"He should sleep until morning," she told Chessie. "I'll come back then and bring something for the pain and to prevent infection. He should be fine in a few weeks, perhaps sooner."

"I sure hope it's sooner. I don't think he's the kind to be happy sittin' around waitin' to get well."

He probably isn't, Isabel thought, and it's just as well. The sooner he leaves Whispering Creek, the better."

* * *

Isabel pushed open the kitchen door and swung her basket onto the counter, the savory scent of a hearty beef stew reminding her she'd scarcely eaten since dawn. The door, hanging slightly askew on its rusted hinges, slapped against its wooden frame several times in her wake.

"Ah, *pepita*," Esme said, turning from the stove, "I was beginning to worry."

"It took longer than I expected. Chessie's man turned out to be a gunslinger with a bullet in his leg."

Esme went back to stirring the pot on the black cast-iron cookstove, clicking her tongue in distaste.

Isabel moved to put an arm around her grandmother's shoulders, giving her a quick hug. "Now don't start, Nana. You'd have done the same thing. You *have* done the same thing."

The old woman's expression softened. "*Sí*, but I did not set foot in a place like Elish Dodd's saloon. Every devil who comes to Whispering Creek beds there."

"Yes, well, I don't think you would have wanted Elish to bring this particular devil here." An image of wild black hair, the scent of leather and denim, the feel of hard muscle, flashed through Isabel's mind. The vision provoked a shivery feeling in her, something akin to uneasiness, except darker, more complex.

Shaking her head to rid herself of the image, she pulled out a chair and sank into it, resting her elbows on the smooth pine table in front of her.

"You must be starving, child." Esme grabbed a bowl and ladled out a liberal portion of the succulent stew, holding up a hand to stop Isabel's protest at the large helping. "You did not eat breakfast."

"Oh...Nate split a seam on his shirt and then Matt needed help with his sums, and Mr. Davis—"

"*Sí, sí*, I know." Esme poured herself a cup of coffee and sat down across from Isabel. She stared at her granddaughter a moment in silence then shook her head. "You take too much on yourself."

Isabel swallowed a spoonful of stew. She knew she was practically inhaling it, but the morning's excitement had left her famished. "No more than any woman with a family to care for."

"You are young, beautiful, but so often the jewel you are is buried deep behind your tired eyes."

Isabel laughed. "This *jewel* has no desire to come out and be polished for some man's pleasure, if that's what you're hinting at, Nana. I was a wife once, I can't imagine ever meeting another man with the power to convince me to become one again."

"You can hardly call yourself a wife, you were married for so short a time. You are not an old woman, nor are you blind and deaf. You cannot truly be so uninterested in what a true man can give you."

"And what is that? A home? I have that, and my children and you and now Katlyn as well. What else is there?"

"You know there is more. Much more. In your heart, you yearn for it. Yet you deny yourself because that man you called a husband broke your heart."

"He didn't…it was never like that." Isabel glanced down at her bowl, not quite able to face the disbelief on Esme's face. "He taught me that my dreams of building a home with a husband were something I could live without if I had to."

"Perhaps, but it was not always that way, no matter what you tell me. Your heart is too tender. You will never prize freedom above loving."

Isabel smiled a little. "Well, I will certainly never

find a man who will give me the freedom I have now. What man would want to be husband to a woman who leaves his bed because she must go to a saloon to cut a bullet out of another's man's leg?''

"The man who loves you above all else. But if you refuse to see him, you will never find him.''

"I hardly think I'll find him in this town whether I'm looking or not," Isabel said, laughing. "You wouldn't want me looking too closely at the kind of man I usually see.''

"And what kind is that? The man you went to help today?''

For some reason, Isabel felt her face flush. "Don't start spinning any romantic dreams of him as a potential husband. He's more the kind to bed all of Elish's girls in a night, drink down most of his whiskey, shoot up the bar, then throw on his boots and ride out of town, bad leg or not.''

Esme swallowed the last of her coffee and shoved back from the table. "A dangerous man. *Sí,* you are right to stay away from that one then." She said nothing more, but gave Isabel an appraising look.

Isabel got up quickly and took her bowl to the sink to rinse. "I must go to the shop for a few hours. Will you need help with dinner?''

"Of course not. Go then, since you are determined to listen to no one but yourself.''

"I always listen to you, Nana," Isabel murmured, giving her grandmother a quick kiss on the cheek. "But all I have is enough. I don't need the complication of another man in my life.''

Enough. Of course I have enough, Isabel told herself as she let herself into the front room of her house where she kept her shop. Her boys were enough. Esme and

her newfound sister Katlyn were enough. Her borders
were enough. Her work helping people was enough.
The house was more than enough! Besides, if something—or someone—were missing in her life, it—or
he—would have to have a lot more to offer than one
of Elish Dodd's reckless wanderers.

She knew that breed, and she'd had more than
enough of them!

Isabel awoke early the next morning, determined to
get to the Silver Rose, pay her obligatory call on Chessie's wounded outlaw, and be done with him. Especially him. She rose before the boys, washed and
dressed quickly, packed their lunch pails, and put a
batch of cinnamon-and-raisin biscuits in the oven.

Just as she closed the heavy cast-iron oven door,
Matt followed Nate into the kitchen.

Katlyn hurried in after them, looking, as usual, unsettled by the early daylight. It was later, fortified by
breakfast and copious amounts of cold water, that Katlyn came alive in a burst of restless, infectious energy
which often earned her raised eyebrows and disapproving frowns from Whispering Creek's more staid residents.

But Katlyn, with a toss of her tumbled red curls and
a flash of those lovely blue eyes, managed to charm
them all and earn their indulgence for even her most
outrageous acts.

"Oh, coffee," she breathed in delight as Isabel offered her a mug. She tossed her haphazard pile of
books and papers on the kitchen table and sniffed appreciatively at the steaming brew. "Cream and honey,
too. You are an angel, Isabel. And you've made those
wonderful biscuits."

Nate rubbed his palm to his stomach. "Yum-my, does that smell good. My stomach's aching this morning."

"You have to save more for me this time," Matt said, shoving past his brother. "Mama, he always gets more."

"That's 'cause I'm older and bigger."

"It's not fair!"

Isabel laughed. "Don't I get a hug and a good-morning kiss?"

Both boys ran to embrace her, and she hugged them close, cherishing the warmth of the moment.

"Are you goin' back to the Silver Rose again today, Mama?" Nate asked as he took his seat at the head of the small table.

"Yes, I have to check on the man I told you about, the one with the injured leg."

"He sounds dark and mysterious to me," Katlyn said around a mouthful of biscuit. "My kind of man," she added, laughing when Isabel shook her head and shot her a disapproving look.

Esme came into the kitchen rubbing at the arthritis knotting her thin hands. "Good morning. I am glad you lit the stove so early, Isabel, there is a chill in the air today."

Matt moved from Isabel to Esme. "Mornin', Nana. It's not cold, you're just always cold."

"That I am. It is because I am an old woman."

"I like you old."

Nate rolled his eyes at his brother. "That's 'cause you never knew her any other way," Nate interjected. "Mama says Nana was a real beauty when she was a girl. Isn't that right, Mama?"

"Of course it is right," Esme answered for Isabel.

"That's why your Mama is so beautiful. When she takes time to brush her hair and change her dress, that is."

Instinctively, Isabel tried to smooth her wayward mass of hair. She realized in her rush to get up and dressed this morning she'd forgotten to braid her hair. Deftly, she twined heavy locks into a long braid and tied it with a bit of ribbon she kept in her apron pocket.

"Better?"

Esme answered with an ambiguous shrug.

Katlyn stifled a giggle, smiling back ruefully at Isabel as she put a hand to her own wayward hair. Though they looked very different—Isabel favoring their father and Katlyn her mother—they both laughed often over their shared inability to ever look neatly polished.

While the boys and Katlyn devoured the biscuits, Isabel organized her thoughts, deciding what medicines to take to the Silver Rose. She glanced outside, looking over the bunches of herbs, withered and faded by the sun, swinging on the long poles outside her windows. A dozen chimes, made from broken glass, bones, and stones, hung from the eaves and sang odd faraway music in cadence with the wind. The air smelled like pine and wood smoke and the scent of the drying herbs.

The chimes sang, a lark called, and Isabel suddenly felt fiercely glad to be here. This was her home, her family, and nothing and no one could take them from her.

Intending to take care of her chore at the Silver Rose before the town was in full swing, she packed up her basket. She then quickly did the dishes, and scurried the boys out the door with her, watching them until they disappeared around the corner on their way to lessons with Katlyn.

At this time of the morning, there was no one about to care whether she came or went or what business she had at the saloon. Isabel walked straight in the front door. Three cowboys and a man she recognized as a fur trader, drinking Elish's dubious coffee and laughing with Chessie and Anita over the night's escapades, barely glanced her way. Elish, unpacking a crate of whiskey bottles, looked up and grinned when the slatted wooden doors swung shut behind her.

"Well, if it ain't our angel of mercy. You must be here to tend to our one-legged guest. I hope he's still livin'. I hate it when they breathe their last in one of our beds."

Isabel smiled. "I don't think you have to worry about this one dying. He seems to me the kind of man who'll live just to spite everyone."

"Even you? From the way Chessie tells it, it was even odds whether you was gonna cut out that bullet or his heart."

"He wasn't particularly glad to see me, but he doesn't have a choice."

Isabel climbed the stairs and, at the top, didn't hesitate in going to the man's room. She knocked lightly at his door and, getting no reply, pushed it open and went in.

He lay sprawled out on the narrow bed, half covered by the thin quilt, his clothes in a heap on the floor, one arm flung over his head. He looked asleep but when she moved beside him and laid down her basket, his eyes snapped open and he half rose up. They stared at each other, his wary dark eyes meeting her cool blue ones.

For a moment, Isabel had the uncomfortable feeling of being stripped bare, from skin to soul. His eyes, she noticed, weren't brown, but a deep gray, and from the look in them she got the impression he was a man who kept secrets, and who guessed them in others. Nana was right. A dangerous man.

Several beats of silence ticked off before he ended the standoff between them, flopping back down against the pillow, not bothering to pull up the quilt bunched around his waist. The morning light gilded his skin, defining the planes and valleys of his bared body, and picking out a scar running diagonally from shoulder to collarbone, and another slashed horizontally, just under his rib cage.

"You again. I thought you were a bad dream."

"Did you also dream the bullet out of your leg? If so, I wish you would teach me the trick. It would make my work so much easier."

"What are you doing here?"

"I came to make sure you hadn't died in Elish's bed. He hates that."

"Then you've done your duty. You can leave me to suffer in peace."

Isabel ignored his nasty expression. "I fully intend to, after I take a look at that leg." She rummaged in her basket for a jar of salve and the ingredients for a new poultice. Without asking his permission, she pulled back the quilt enough to bare his leg to her scrutiny.

"Anything else you'd like to see while you're down there?" Jake asked, annoyed when she didn't so much as bat an eyelash.

"Nothing I haven't seen before. Are you still in pain?"

"It's nothing a bottle of whiskey won't cure. Look, lady—" Jake propped up on one elbow and trapped her wrist with his free hand "—I'm sure you do a real nice job soothing stomachaches and curing skinned elbows, and you did get the bullet out of my leg. For that I'm much obliged. But your weeds are more likely to kill me than do any good and I'm not anxious to be knocking on hell's door any earlier than necessary. I'll send one of the girls along to pay you for your trouble."

"Mister, for what I've been through trying to help you, you can't afford my trouble. Now let go of me or I'll yell loud enough to bring Elish and every cowboy in the saloon up here with guns drawn."

He held on hard for a moment, his pulse thrumming against her skin. Isabel knew he sized her up with his eyes before releasing her wrist. She resisted the urge to rub at her skin, feeling the impression of his strength long after his physical touch.

"I'll give you one thing, lady, nothing much seems to rattle you. Remind me to never play poker with you."

"I'm not interested in playing any game with you. I came here to check your wound and that's what I'm going to do. Now be still. Is this tender?" Isabel ran her fingers over the wound, probing gently.

Jake started at the touch of her, jolted more by her tenderness than the pain. "It hurts like hell. Did you bring any whiskey?"

"No, Mr.-whatever-your-name-is—I didn't. I'm not a saloon keeper." She thrust the jar of salve at him. "Here, put this on it daily for the next few weeks, if you have any desire to keep your leg from rotting off, that is."

Jake eyed the thick, yellow-colored grease warily, then sniffed at it, drawing back with a grimace.

"It's Coulter, Jake Coulter, and what is this stuff? It smells like horse dung."

"Mouse."

"Mouse what?"

"It's mouse dung," Isabel said matter-of-factly. "Mixed with butter, horsetail and a little turpentine. It's quite useful."

Jake stared at her, wondering if she meant it or if she were trying to bait him into asking a dumb question. "You're not serious."

"Of course I am. I use it often."

"To attract flies? Do you have a jar of leeches around somewhere as well? No—don't answer that. Whatever this is, I sure as hell don't want it smeared on me. Look, I've no doubt you mean well, you did a fair job cutting that bullet out—"

"Such generous praise. And I'm overwhelmed by your gratitude."

"—but my leg probably needs stitches and definitely a good dose of sulfur powder and someone who knows how to administer both without a shaking hand."

"Ah, I see. And did you gain this knowledge from some drunken fool who's only claim to being a doctor is that he can cut off limbs and pour whiskey faster than the man before him?"

"And where did you get yours? From a vision after chewing peyote?"

"Well, if I did, it's too late for you now. You've drunk my potion. Perhaps you're already under my spell."

The look she gave him, a little mysterious smile, a flash of laughter, roused in Jake a sudden, sharp aware-

ness of her nearness. He could smell the wildflower
scent of her, feel her warmth almost as a touch. It had
been a long time since he'd let a woman get close to
him.

This woman... He shook his head, trying to clear it.

"Am I?" he said, his voice rough-edged.

Piercing gray eyes locked with hers and for a moment, Isabel could think of nothing to say in reply.

She realized she hadn't taken time to study him fully
yesterday. There was certainly an almost frightening
strength in him, and an unflinching directness in his
eyes. But there were also lines in his face left by an
experience of bitterness or suffering, she didn't know
which. It left her intrigued, wondering exactly what he
was and why he was here. It also left her disconcerted,
questioning her reaction to him.

Feeling shaken, Isabel took her jar of salve from him
and jerked the quilt back up over his leg. "Since you
don't want my help, I'll go."

She started to gather up her basket and Jake watched
her hands move over the jar and cloths, efficient, graceful. She riled him to the point of fury, but he liked
looking at her, though he couldn't have said why. He
preferred his women lush and pliant, but with her delicate fairy face and her quick tongue she was neither.
She didn't even go out of her way to make herself
particularly attractive the way most women did.

Her hair hung in a loose braid down her back and,
as far as he could tell, she wore nothing but a thin
cotton dress that looked as if the sun had scorched all
the color out of it. There was nothing deliberately provocative about her. She seemed indifferent to the way
she moved, except when she plied her dubious trade

and then all the sensuality was in her hands, the intimacy in her touch.

"You aren't coming back, are you?" he asked suddenly, surprising them both.

"I'm not a glutton for punishment. If you're bored, I'm sure Chessie or Anita can find some way to amuse you."

"Maybe I should have been more careful. I'll be wondering now what spell you have cast over me."

"I wouldn't let it trouble you. I'm not adept enough to charm serpents into your room. Yet."

She walked to the door and turned to give him a tight smile. "Goodbye, Mr. Coulter. I promise you, the only sorcery you'll find here will come from the hands of one of Elish's girls."

Jake stared after her, torn between following her just to take away her advantage of getting the last word or trying to forget she ever lived to annoy him. Before he could decide, Elish Dodd appeared in the doorway, stopping Isabel from leaving.

"If you're lookin' for magic, you're gonna have to find it somewhere else," he said, stepping past Isabel to face Jake. "I just got word a dozen or more men finishin' a cattle drive will be ridin' in tonight lookin' for whiskey and girls and I'm gonna need all the rooms I have. Since you ain't in no condition to be takin' advantage of the amenities here, you might want to consider a room in the nearest thing we got here to a hospital."

"And where might that be?" Jake asked, already suspecting he knew the answer and not wanting to hear it.

"Why, in Mrs. Bradshaw's house," Elish said, flashing a grin between Jake and Isabel. "You know, the woman you've managed to rile enough for her to turn a knife on you. I'm sure she'll take you in, she has this fondness for strays no matter how ornery they are.'' Before he left, Elish winked at Isabel then turned to Jake. ''But if I was you, friend, I'd sleep with one eye open 'til you get back on her good side.''

# *Chapter Three*

"**I**'ll make room for you, cowboy."

The purr of Anita Devine's voice broke the awkward silence between Isabel and Jake. Caught in the moment of suspended tension, Isabel jumped at the sound, jerking around toward the doorway.

Anita posed there, her dark eyes roving over Jake with slow deliberation. Raven tresses spilled over her bare shoulders, a few spiral curls catching in the lace at her low-cut bodice. As her gaze slid over Jake's body, a satisfied smile curved the edges of her painted mouth.

She sauntered into the room, petticoats swishing at her ankles, brushing past Isabel as though she didn't exist, heading straight to the edge of the bed. Bending down far enough for her ample bosom to spill over the black lace at the scooped neckline of her dress, she smoothed a heavy wave from Jake's brow.

"Elish told me about your dilemma, Mr. Coulter. And I've come to offer a solution. I'd be quite happy to make room so you can stay with me while you recover."

Isabel stood to the side, caught off guard by Anita's

brazen proposition, though she didn't know why she should be. Anita's reputation was well-known all over the high country towns surrounding Whispering Creek. Women around town called her the Black Widow because she had a way of seducing a handsome man and using him up, leaving him with little more than his boots when she sent him walking.

Isabel tried to judge Jake's response, but his expression gave nothing away. Only his eyes showed any reaction and the coldness there almost forced her back a step.

"What a generous offer," he drawled, raking Anita with a dismissing glance that was far from flattering.

Anita's eyes narrowed, but her smile stayed in place. "I'm part owner in this place, so my offer is sincere, I assure you."

"Oh, I'm sure it is." Jake shifted and looked directly at Isabel.

The moment his eyes settled on her, Isabel itched to turn her back on both of them and leave them to haggle over the living arrangements without her witness.

What did he want? For her to make him a better offer? Did he expect her to beg for his company?

Perversely, part of her wanted to insist he return home with her. She supposed the ridiculous urge was nothing more than instinctive feminine competition though normally she wasn't at all given to that sort of nonsense.

Especially when Jake Coulter was the last man she should want sleeping under her roof.

Still, he looked at her with that faintly challenging glint in his eyes and she felt herself responding even while common sense called her a fool. He'd done noth-

ing to indicate he needed or wanted her help, in fact
he'd practically thrown her out when she offered.

Then again, she did have a vacant room and heaven
only knew how long she might have to wait to find a
new boarder. And she could ill afford a long spell with
no rent on that room. Even with her shop, she barely
made ends meet.

Aware both Jake and Anita now stared at her, Isabel
drew herself up. "Well, Mr. Coulter, I was going to
tell you I did have a room open up yesterday, but it
sounds as though you have a fine offer for a very comfortable room right here—"

"I'll take it."

"What?" Isabel and Anita blurted out in unison.

Anita slapped her hands to her tightly cinched-in
waist. "Are you sayin' you'd rather go and stay with
the *witch* and her brats than here with me? I'll have
you know I don't make a habit of offerin' to share my
room with just *anyone!*"

"Oh, I don't doubt it," Jake said. "A man's got to
be willing to pay the price and I'm sure your price is
high."

"I'll make an exception for you, darlin'."

"No, thanks."

"No—!"

"I want someplace private, where I can find a little
peace and quiet." He looked back to Isabel. "You can
promise that much, Mrs. Bradshaw, can't you?"

"Not particularly," Isabel said lightly. "I can offer
you a measure of privacy. As for peace and quiet, once
my boys get home from their lessons, the noise in my
house could easily rival with a raucous crowd on a
good night at the Silver Rose."

"See there." Anita leaned a little farther over, ma-

neuvering closer to give Jake the best view of her vo-
luptuous body. "Now is *that* what you call peace and
quiet?"

Jake scowled at Isabel. "Can you give me a room
or not?"

"I'll *rent* you a room."

"Then it's settled. I'll move in today."

Anita stood up straight and squared her shoulders.
"Suit yourself, but don't come back here knocking on
my door when you find out you've moved into a hor-
net's nest." Her eyes narrowed to catlike slits. "I won't
forget this insult, *Mr. Coulter.*"

Isabel couldn't suppress a small grin as Anita
flounced out of the room in a snit.

"You look pleased with yourself. Did you want me
that bad?"

Jake nearly regretted the jibe when her smile up-
ended and she frowned. He'd surprised himself in flatly
turning down Anita Devine. He'd done it not because
of the obvious services she offered in his recovery, or
because Isabel could get him on his feet faster than
anyone, but out of some instinctive reaction to protect
Isabel Bradshaw.

Why she provoked that reaction he couldn't say. She
didn't seem the type to want or need a man's shelter.
Yet he sensed some unseen vulnerability in her. Despite himself, she'd inspired a response even he didn't
expect.

Now he found himself enjoying the fire he'd sparked
in her.

"Want you?" she sputtered. "Don't flatter yourself,
Mr. Coulter. You were practically begging me to rent
you that room."

"Dodd says you have the only place in town that takes wounded strays."

"I'm sure Anita would have given you her undivided attention."

"I don't want her attention. I want yours."

"Really? I can't imagine why. You haven't missed an opportunity to insult me. And I can hardly offer you the same amenities as Anita."

Jake let his eyes rove over her in deliberate suggestion. To her credit, she didn't flinch away, but gave his bold appraisal back in full measure. "Oh, I wouldn't say that. You've got those wonderful weeds."

"I'm tempted to give you a double dose of them and have you hauled off to my house, with or without your blessing," Isabel said, not really understanding his sudden faith in her healing ability and not certain whether she should be flattered or good and riled at him.

"You're the only one in this town who can tell if this wound's getting better or worse," he reasoned. "And I'll be helping you out by keeping your room rented until a more permanent border comes along."

"So you're doing me a favor now. I see. How kind of you, sir."

"Let's just say we can help each other out for the time being, okay? I have business here and I don't want to get it done from a saloon."

Isabel immediately stiffened. She'd been afraid of this. Still it was better to face the truth about Jake Coulter now. "Business? What business, may I ask?"

The look he gave her might have daunted a strong man, let alone a woman armed only with her wits and a single knife. Isabel, though, refused to back down. If she planned on taking Jake Coulter into her house, she needed to know who might come looking for him, guns drawn.

"You can ask," Jake said. "I don't have any answers for you right now. Don't worry though, in this condition, I'm not too dangerous."

"That's not good enough." What was he hiding, and more importantly, why? Her eyes strayed to the gun belt looped over the bedpost. "I have a family to think of."

Jake followed her gaze but said nothing, only smiled, a faint, sardonic twist of his lips that made Isabel shiver and at the same time roused her irritation.

"I'll be long gone before I'd put your family in harm's way. Now, I could use another shot of that magic potion of yours. I don't think I can get down the stairs without it and a large bottle of whiskey."

"You won't be able to get down the stairs *with* that combination, I guarantee it."

"You have a better idea?"

Isabel had several, but she kept them to herself. *I'll learn your secrets, Jake Coulter,* she told him silently, *one way or the other.*

Out loud, she told him, "I'll give you something that'll put you to sleep for several hours and from the look in your eyes, that will be a relief to both of us."

Not waiting for his retort, she plunged ahead, taking refuge from his disturbing presence by organizing his release from the Silver Rose. "Besides, you're going to need something for the ride home. I'll ask Elish to help move you to his cart, but it's a rough ride to my place."

"So's life," Jake said with a short, mirthless laugh. "Go ahead and bring me my poison, witch."

* * *

Jake woke to the voice of an angel singing and wondered if he'd died in one of Elish Dodd's beds after all. Heaven, though, surely must be a lot less painful, he decided as he shifted a little in the direction of the sound. His leg ached and when he forced open his eyes, the glare of afternoon sunlight through an open window knifed his head. Wincing, he turned away, focusing instead on the unfamiliar room.

Heaven or hell, it was definitely not the Silver Rose. The high-pitched ceiling of the upstairs log cabin loft reflected a woman's touch, from the woven, multicolored rug on the pine plank floor and the lace curtains at the window, to the earthenware jar of rosemary and lavender on the dresser. *Her* touch. Chessie's witch; his angel of mercy.

She meant it, he thought, remembering Isabel Bradshaw's threat to pack him off to her "hospital" with or without his permission. He didn't know whether to be impressed or annoyed that she'd pulled it off.

Before he could decide, a hot drift of breeze carried the angel's song into the room again, a clear, pure voice raised in a soulful Spanish ballad. Ignoring the wash of pain and dizziness, Jake flung back the quilt and limped to the window to look down on the garden below.

Isabel was there, singing to herself and a large raven perched on the rock wall beside her. As he watched, she bent to pluck a few sprigs from some leafy plant. She rubbed them gently between her fingertips, then cupped the leaves to inhale their scent before adding them to the collection in the basket looped over her arm.

Sunlight washed her dark-golden hair and Jake found

himself wondering what it would look like, freed from its confining braid, spread over her shoulders and—

He cut short the thought, shaking his head to clear it. Whatever potion she'd given him was clouding his thoughts, making him crazy. He turned to move away from the window and shut out her vision. The stiffness in his leg made him awkward and he knocked against a small table, rattling the pitcher and bowl there.

The clatter, in the late day stillness, brought Isabel's head up and for a moment, their gazes locked. Jake could almost hear her catch her breath and he felt himself holding his.

"What are you doing on your feet?" she called up, breaking the spell. She shook her head, giving an exasperated sigh. "I hope you aren't going to be this stubborn over everything or I'll never be rid of you. Get back into bed, I'm coming up."

"Now there's an invitation I can't refuse," Jake said, unable to resist baiting her.

Isabel only glared at him then quickened her step to the door below his window. Jake heard it slam behind her and smiled.

She found him propped up against the pillows, the quilt pulled carelessly up to his waist as if he'd just tossed it there after hearing her footsteps. He'd flung his shirt and it lay in a heap in the corner. She chose to ignore the reality he now wore nothing but the quilt.

Putting down the tray she'd carried up on the dresser top, Isabel turned to face him, determined not to give him the upper hand.

"If you're going to lecture me about staying in bed, save your breath," Jake said before she could open her mouth. "I'm beginning to regret even opening my eyes."

"I'm not surprised. Do you always make a habit of acting before you think, Mr. Coulter?"

"Usually I don't have the luxury of time to think."

"Does that mean you're usually on the run?" Isabel could see her bluntness surprised him. But it was obvious he wasn't going to volunteer the information.

"I see subtlety is one art you don't practice. And no, ma'am, I'm not usually on the run, although I'll confess I've worn out a few saddles in the past years."

"I see," Isabel said, although she didn't. She studied him a moment, then from the tray picked up a pile of fresh cloths and a new poultice she'd made. Setting them down on the bedside table, she poured water from the pitcher into the bowl, then turned to him again. "I need to look at your leg."

"It's becoming a habit with you. Do you enjoy it that much?"

Isabel smiled. "Don't flatter yourself." Flipping back the edge of the quilt, she busied herself removing the old bandages. When she'd finished, she ran her fingers lightly over the bullet wound.

Jake flinched at the gentleness of her touch and she glanced at him in concern. "Is it that painful?"

"No—no. It's—I'm not used to being touched like that."

"That I can believe. You have more scars than my furniture and believe me, with two boys in the house, that's saying a lot."

"You said you had children."

She nodded, her attention fixed on cleaning his wound and reapplying a poultice and bandage. Her hands moved deftly over him, warm and sure, more soothing than the herbs she used to ease his pain. "My grandmother and sister live here, too. You're my only boarder.''

"And your husband?"

"Is dead," she said shortly. She kept her eyes down, not because of any pretense of modesty, Jake guessed, but because she wanted to guard her feelings from him.

"Don't get any ideas that I can't protect myself and my own," Isabel said when he let the silence stretch between them. She yanked the quilt back over him, her stance defiant. "I'm used to doing it and it'll take more than a down-on-his-luck outlaw to give me trouble."

"That, I don't doubt."

"And what about you?"

"What about me?"

"Why are you in Whispering Creek?" With her family to protect, she had to know. Obviously, Jake Coulter was no miner, and he didn't have the smooth charm of a gambler, nor the rough edges of a cowboy.

He reminded her, instead, of a hunter, dark and dangerous, and not quite civilized.

"I'm here because I can't ride out on my own," Jake answered. "But you don't have to worry. You're not going to find my face on any of the sheriff's wanted posters. No one will be looking for me here."

"I see," she said, unsatisfied. She decided to try another approach. "Where are you from, Mr. Coulter?"

"Jake. And where I'm from depends on what day it is. Yesterday I came from Taos. Does it matter?"

"I don't know," Isabel said slowly. "Perhaps it should."

"It doesn't to me, not anymore."

The words were heavy with weariness and he closed his eyes against them, rousing both concern and curiosity in Isabel. Something had hurt Jake Coulter and it was more than a bullet. The healer in her wanted to know what it was. The woman in her warned against finding the answer.

"Mr. Coulter…Jake—"

The sound of a downstairs door slamming and a clatter of footsteps up the stairs stopped whatever Isabel intended to say.

There was a scuffling noise outside Jake's door, and a flurry of whispering before Nate poked his head inside. He darted a quick curious glance at Jake, then looked at Isabel, his face suspiciously innocent.

"We wanted to know if we could have jam tarts. Nana made them, but she's visiting Mrs. Parker, and well…we thought we'd ask."

"Did you now?" Isabel shook her head, unable to hide her smile. "It sounds to me as if you needed a reason to come upstairs and meet our new guest."

"It was Nate's idea," Matt piped up behind him. "He wanted to see the gunfighter." He peeked around the corner, wide-eyed. "But we would like jam tarts, too."

"Ah, I see. Matt, Nate…" She took their hands and led them just inside the room. "This is Mr. Coulter. He's not a gunfighter," she said, praying she didn't lie, "and he's going to be staying with us until his leg is healed. He's not feeling very well, so he won't be up to having any visitors for a while. Now go downstairs to the kitchen. I'll be along in a minute and I'll help you eat those jam tarts Nana left for you."

Before Jake could respond, Isabel shooed her sons out the door and the boys scampered off, clattering noisily down the stairs. "You didn't tell me I was contagious," he said, watching after them.

"They're very impressionable," she said, not quite meeting his gaze. She quickly gathered up her supplies and put them back on the tray. "They've already decided you're a dangerous outlaw and that you can tell them all sorts of exciting stories about gunfights and stolen gold. I don't want to encourage them."

"I don't know any stories about stolen gold."

"At least you don't deny the gunfights."

"You wouldn't believe me if I did."

"No, I wouldn't. Unless you want to confess you shot yourself in the leg." Returning to his bedside, Isabel handed him a cup. "Drink this. It will help the pain."

Jake sniffed warily at it, not liking the smell or the look of the pale-green liquid. "By the time you're through with me, I'll have tried every weed in the territory. Whiskey would be kinder."

"Not to your head." She waited until he'd downed the herbal brew, then gently pushed him back on the pillows. Her fingers brushed his forehead, pushing aside a heavy dark wave of hair that stubbornly refused to stay aside. "No fever. I think you'll do, Mr. Coulter. A week or so and you'll be up and around again."

Her fingers lingered for a moment on his skin and Jake captured them with his own, absently rubbing her hand, enjoying the smooth feel of her. "Is that a promise, ma'am, or a threat to throw me out then?" he asked, his voice low and dark, teasing her.

"Perhaps both," Isabel said, freeing her hand from his disturbing touch. "I must go. The boys will be waiting, and you need to rest. I'll be back in a few hours with supper."

Jake stared after her, wondering what had caused the

crack in her cool facade, and why he found it so pleasing to know he'd played a part in it.

Isabel had just finished cleaning up the kitchen after dinner, and was getting ready to make certain the boys had fed and watered all their animal boarders for the night when a loud rapping sounded at the front door. Pushing her hands down her skirts to dry them, she hurried to answer it.

"Cal," she said, opening the door to a tall, squarely built man holding a battered hat between his hands. "What brings you here this time of day?"

Isabel forced herself to sound casual, but she'd known Calvin Reed all her life, even before he'd taken over as sheriff in Whispering Creek, and knew he wouldn't be stopping by twice in two days simply to chat. She remembered her grandmother's talk about Jerico Grey and wondered just how much of it had been rumor.

"Wearin' out my welcome, am I, Belle?" Cal asked.

Isabel smiled a little over the familiar nickname, one only Cal used. He'd taken to calling her that ever since she was a little girl and Calvin Reed had been a young deputy, paying court to her mama after her papa had abandoned them.

"Of course not," she said, leading him inside with a hand on his arm. "Come inside and I'll get you some coffee."

Cal ran a hand over his graying hair. The lines in his face seemed deeper, and his eyes sober, telling Isabel more than any words he was worried over something.

"I hate to turn it down, but I'd best get my business out of the way first. I need to speak to your new boarder, if he's in any shape to have a conversation. Elish tells me you slipped him one of your fine elixirs to get him out of the Silver Rose this mornin'.''

"He's well enough to talk to you." Isabel hesitated, then started, "Cal…"

"Now don't you worry, honey. I just want to see what his business here is. With this recent string of robberies at the mines around here, I can't be too careful."

"Do you think…" Isabel stopped, not certain if she wanted to put her fears into words. But it would be better to know. "Is it Jerico?"

"Now Belle—"

"Is it? He did it before. He was robbing camps all over these mountains before he fled the territory."

"Don't you worry, now. I know you were sweet on him once. Don't bother to tell me it's not true," he said, holding up a hand to ward off her protest.

"I was a girl, in love with the idea of loving a dangerous man. You can trust my illusions about Jerico faded quickly. If you're thinking he'd come back to Whispering Creek for me, you're mistaken."

"You're probably right. I suspect his reasons for headin' this way have more to do with him havin' the law on his tail in Texas."

Isabel saw a shadow of doubt in Cal's eyes and put her hand on his arm, looking straight at him. "If I knew anything, I would tell you. The thought of Jerico coming back here, after all these years—" She shook her head, trying to rid herself of her uneasiness. "I seem to have a knack for attracting the wrong kind of man," she said with a small smile.

"Like your new boarder? Well, now, he's probably just what he appears to be, one of them thorns in a sheriff's side whose luck's run a little muddy. I'll have a talk with him, but I doubt he's too dangerous.''

"I wouldn't be so sure of that," Isabel said more to herself than Cal as she turned and led him up the stair-case, to the loft.

She knocked once at Jake's door then opened it half-way and looked inside. Slouched in the rocker he'd shoved next to the window, he was looking out at the deepening evening, a slight frown tensing his face. He'd pulled on a man's robe he'd found draped over the bed, loosely tying it at the waist.

He turned slightly when he heard Isabel step into the room, and then looked back to the window with a view of the rear garden. "Back again with your weeds so soon?"

"No," Isabel said, watching him carefully for his reaction. "You have a visitor. Sheriff Reed wants to meet you."

"Yeah, I'll just bet he does," Jake drawled.

He shifted to look at Cal and surprised Isabel by grinning. "I suppose you've decided I'm responsible for robbing every mining office between here and the Texas Panhandle." Rubbing a hand through his hair, he gave a wry shrug. "Can't say that I blame you."

"Then maybe you can tell me why you are here in Whispering Creek, and we can get this settled and leave Mrs. Bradshaw with some peace of mind."

"I don't know if it'll give her any peace of mind but I'll tell you why I'm here. Jerico Grey."

Isabel caught her breath and the slight sound caused Jake's gaze to shift sharply to her. She tried to keep her expression blank, to conceal the twist of emotion she felt hearing Jerico's name over again after not even thinking it for so many years, and this time hearing it from a stranger.

"What's your business with Grey?" Cal asked, his expression wooden.

"The same business I've had for over six months, only now I intend to finish it." Pushing himself up out of the rocker, Jake limped over to the corner where Isabel had propped his saddlebag and fished out a mud-spattered badge. He turned and handed it to Cal.

Cal rubbed away the dirt and shook his head. "Well, I'll be damned." Answering the question on Isabel's face, he smiled broadly and said, "It looks as if we were paintin' us a devil's face on an angel, Belle. Mr. Coulter here is a Texas Ranger."

"He's a…" Isabel stared at Cal a moment, trying to decide if she felt relieved Jake Coulter wasn't an out-law or angry for how thoroughly she'd been taken in by his appearance.

As Cal's words sank in fully, she whirled on Jake, her eyes blazing. "I suppose you enjoyed playing the wounded gunslinger, letting me believe I'd let an out-law into my house, around my boys. You have a strange way of amusing yourself, Mr. Coulter."

"If I wanted entertainment, I'd have stayed at the Silver Rose, Mrs. Bradshaw. I came here for rest and privacy. I'd just as soon Grey didn't hear that I'm laid up. None of us want him to come looking for me under your roof. I don't know how much you know about Jerico Grey, but you can trust me when I say he's not the kind of man you'd ever turn your back on."

All traces of warmth had vanished from his face as if they'd never been there and Isabel felt a shiver up her spine looking at the ice in its place.

Jake Coulter might be one step on the right side of

the law, but Cal was wrong. He was dangerous, maybe even more so than the man he vowed to bring to justice.

Jake watched her, trying to decipher the odd play of emotions on her face. Anger, worry, he could understand. What confused him was the strong sense that Isabel Bradshaw's interest in Jerico Grey was more than concern a woman alone would have for herself and her family knowing an outlaw was somewhere in the area.

She seemed strong-willed enough to face down the devil if necessary to protect her own. Yet one name washed the color from her face and put fear in her eyes. At least he thought it was fear.

He didn't realize he'd been staring at her, trying to figure her out, until the sheriff cleared his throat.

"I'd like to talk to you more about this, when you're feelin' up to a walk to my office," Cal said. "Until then, you're right, it's probably best everyone in town thinks you're another drifter Belle's taken under her wing for a spell."

He said something else but Isabel didn't hear the rest of the conversation between the two men. Jerico was coming back to Whispering Creek and Jake Coulter wanted him dead. What kind of man had she taken into her home? Yet how could she turn him out when he was wounded?

"...you tomorrow, Belle."

She started, realizing Cal was talking to her. "Yes, yes of course."

"I'll see myself out, let you get back to your business." Shoving his hat back on, he nodded to Jake and gave Isabel's arm a reassuring pat before clomping back down the stairs.

As his footsteps receded Isabel turned to look fully at Jake.

"I'll leave. Tonight if possible." He limped toward the bed and shoved the badge back into his saddlebag. "I'll see if I can sweet-talk my way into Anita's room at the Silver Rose."

"Don't be ridiculous. You can't go walking around town in your condition. Lie down before you fall down," she commanded, coming to him and pushing a hand flat against his chest.

"I'm going. I had to tell the sheriff the truth. But now that he knows why I'm here, word's bound to get back to Jerico. I can't guarantee your safety."

"I don't recall asking you to be my protector. You're hurt, I can help you. That's the end of it."

"Is it? Well, I don't recall asking for your help. In fact, I distinctly remember telling you to stay out of my life. Yet, here you are." He gestured to her hand, still pressed against his bare chest.

Isabel suddenly became acutely aware of the hard wall of muscle under her palm, and that she stood close enough to him to feel the heat and tension in him.

"Get back into bed," she said, jerking her hand away. "I refuse to let you go wandering around Whispering Creek, making yourself an easy target for any drunk with a gun. A dead patient isn't good for business."

Jake said nothing and for a moment, Isabel thought he would ignore her and limp away anyhow. But finally, he sat down heavily on the bed, raking his fingers through his hair. "Just don't count on me."

"For what?"

"For anything. Anything at all. I'm here to do this

job and then I'll be moving on to the next one. That's all I can promise.''

''Do you think I'm so desperate for male companionship I'll be begging for your attention by week's end?'' Isabel nearly laughed at his arrogance except the shuttered look on his face stopped her. His expression told her he hadn't made the comment lightly and she wondered what meaning she was supposed to find in it.

''Let me assure you, the only promise I want from you is that you'll pay your rent on time. Five dollars a week for the room, breakfast and supper. I do laundry and linens once a week.''

''Does that include your weed potions, too?'' he asked, a hint of a smile playing with a corner of his mouth.

''Those are on the house. I couldn't charge for anything you take so much pleasure in.''

There seemed to be nothing else to say, but in the hush that suddenly fell between them, Isabel sensed there was much more, yet neither of them knew how to give it voice. She finally forced herself to end the strange, tense silence, and, murmuring a quick goodnight, left him alone.

Jake leaned back against the pillows. He felt completely thrown off center by her. It was a disarming, unsettling feeling unlike any he'd ever known with any other woman.

Not even his wife. It irritated him, like a splinter just under the skin. And it annoyed him even more that he had to depend on her to get back on his feet.

Nothing about Isabel Bradshaw was easy, he was discovering. Except the way she touched him. And that, if he was honest, disturbed him most of all.

# Chapter Four

Golden-yellow afternoon sunlight streamed down between snowy clouds, and Matt danced a hopscotch path on the patches of light and shadow across the backyard.

"I get to do it! I found her!" he cried, glancing over his shoulder and picking up his pace as he heard Nate catching up behind him.

Lagging in their wake, Isabel glanced across the stone path to her rose garden and sighed. She had planted the bushes shortly after her marriage, her one indulgence. Some years roses flourished in the high country; other times the extremes of hot days and cold nights, fierce sometimes even here in the valley, drained the life from their fragile petals.

Better to be sturdy than beautiful in this wild place, she thought, looking at several tender new pink and silver blossoms and wondering if they'd have the stamina to survive.

"Mama, hurry!" Matt yelled over his shoulder. "Nate is going to let the roadrunner loose before I even have a chance to say goodbye to her."

Nate gave a disgusted snort. "Am not! You're just trying to get me in trouble."

"I think this is something we can all share," Isabel said, ruffling Matt's hair and rubbing Nate's shoulder. She moved up directly between them and released the wire latch on the cage. "Go ahead, Nate. You can take her out. Gently now."

Gingerly, Nate reached into the cage and cupped his hands around the bird's wings so the small creature wouldn't panic. He spoke softly to it as he eased it into his arms, stroking its tiny head.

"Come on, little one. You can go home today."

Pride surged through Isabel as she watched him. He was learning. Learning as she had from her mother and Nana that healing was more than medicine; it was also touch and the power and music of the voice. Learning that sharing another's pain meant sharing their hopes and also rejoicing in their recovery.

An image of her new reluctant patient flashed across her mind. Absently, she glanced upward to where the white lace curtains fluttered in the open window of the room where Jake slept. She'd given him another dose of a willow powder elixir for pain, and had started applying hourly mashes of blue corn to his leg. Despite her care, the wound seemed to want to fester and she worried infection and fever might set in, delaying his recovery, possibly jeopardizing his leg.

And having Jake Coulter under her roof longer than necessary wasn't something either of them wanted, she reminded herself.

"My turn. My turn," Matt insisted beside Nate, wriggling with his eagerness to hold the roadrunner.

"Slowly, now," Isabel encouraged. "Hold her firmly."

As though lifting a priceless treasure, Matt wrapped

his small, sun-browned fingers around the bird and squatted to set it on the earth beneath them.

"Adios, *amiga,*" he whispered. "Come visit us again one day."

As soon as he released the long-legged bird, its head darted up at one end, its tail perked at the other. With a quick twist of its neck to look back at his caretakers, it shot away, dashing across the yard toward the evergreen mountains beyond.

"I'm going to miss her." Matt snuggled close to Isabel. "I wish she could have stayed with us."

Isabel hugged him to her side. "She's a wild creature, and she doesn't need us any longer. But don't worry, darling, you'll find another lost or wounded creature who needs a home before you even have this cage cleaned out. Which by the way, you can do after dinner tonight. For now, I need you two to run out to the shed and get a hammer and nails and go up and knock on Mr. Coulter's door. He may need that dresser space, but the drawer has to be fixed before he can use it."

"Yes, ma'am. C'mon, Matt, I'll get the hammer and you can take the nails."

"I want to hammer! You always get to do the fun part," Matt grumbled, hopping again from light patch to light patch across the yard after his brother.

Isabel laughed to herself as she turned to head back up the path to the back kitchen door. Those boys…my boys, best friends, worst enemies. At least they have each other, she mused, recalling how all her life she'd longed for a brother or a sister, until Katlyn had come unexpectedly into her life.

She wished she'd known about her half-sister earlier. But their father, a gambler who never stayed in one place longer than his luck held out, left Isabel's mother before Isabel was born. Five years later, he found his way to Missouri and charmed a vivacious riverboat singer into his bed, leaving her with three-month-old Katlyn.

Something, perhaps guilt, had finally motivated Katlyn's mother to tell her daughter about her half-sister in Whispering Creek. Shortly thereafter, Katlyn appeared on the doorstep at a time Isabel most needed a sister. She recalled with warmth how Katlyn's spunk and vigor had been tremendously cheering to her and to the boys when the news came that Douglas wouldn't be coming back.

As Isabel pushed open the back door, she saw Esme had already begun to set out the simple blue-and-white floral-patterned china on the kitchen worktable for dinner.

Isabel took a brightly painted pottery vase from a shelf on the kitchen wall and arranged a handful of yellow-and-white daises in it she'd plucked on the way back to the house.

"I'll get the white tablecloth with the little yellow tulips around the edges to go with these," she told Esme. "Katlyn loves that old thing. I don't even think she sees all of the stains. She's always the optimist."

Esme held a spoon up to the light then wiped a spot from it with the corner of her apron. "Katlyn is too restless to see what is in front of her eyes. She is always looking to the horizon, seeking something she cannot even name."

"Oh, Nana, I'm sure you said the same about Mama and about me at one time." As soon as she said the words, Isabel regretted them. It would only give Nana

an opening to talk about husbands and Isabel's refusal
to consider another one.

"No, my daughter was not restless, not like Katlyn
is. Sonalda dreamed of family, a place for her spirit to
rest. My daughter always trusted a man would bring
her that happiness." Esme shook her head. "I warned
her, but she could hear nothing but that gambler's
pretty words. He left her before he ever saw you. And
you were no different when I told you Douglas Bradshaw and that devil Jerico Grey would do the same."

Isabel started at the name. She certainly didn't intend
for Esme to bring *that* up. She stepped over to a simply
crafted pine dry sink and pulled open the latch to the
shelves beneath to rummage through the linens for the
tablecloth. "Yes, well, I can't say I listened to you
about either of them, but Jerico at least was never more
than a girlish crush for me. He always frightened me,
even then."

Esme followed Isabel into the dining area and helped
her smooth out the cloth on the scuffed pine table,
perked up with a good rubdown and a thick coat of
beeswax.

"And with good reason," Esme said, clicking her
tongue in disgust. "*Ay,* that one is more wicked at heart
than any I have seen."

"Well, our new boarder seems determined to find
him, one way or the other," Isabel said lightly. She
brought the vase in and centered it on the table, giving
her hands something to do as a distraction for her trou-
bled thoughts.

"I do not approve of renting our rooms to such a
man."

Isabel shrugged. "The money will help. Besides,
he's a Texas Ranger, not an outlaw."

"You would not believe it by the look of him. He may call himself a lawman but believe me when I tell you he is only one step from being an outlaw. It is not safe for the boys to be upstairs with him alone."

"Of course it is," Isabel said firmly, to reassure herself as much as her grandmother. "Mr. Coulter's in no shape to draw a gun on anyone, least of all two little boys."

Esme plopped a fork down next to a plate, muttering something in Spanish, then added, "We will see about that."

"Nana," Isabel began warningly, "I know that look. Don't get any ideas about practicing your magic on Mr. Coulter."

"Ah, but you say you do not believe in my magic, *pepita.*"

Esme's carefully innocent expression didn't fool Isabel. While she had learned much about herbal healing from her grandmother, she had, from the time she could understand, steadfastly refused to become tutored in the ways of a *curandera.* Witch magic, many in the territory called it.

And Isabel put no faith in magic or spirits or an ephemeral power conjured to vanquish evil curses.

Esme, though, continued to practice her spells and incantations, and had a small, but steady trade among the Mexican and Spanish families in and around Whispering Creek.

"Leave Mr. Coulter alone," Isabel told her, trying to look sufficiently stern.

Esme lifted one shoulder and went back to setting the table, a small smile lifting her mouth. "But of course, my granddaughter. Of course."

* * *

Jake saw black spots. Big black circles, bobbing over his face. How many? He tried to count, but found he'd forgotten how. The spots faded. Then he realized his eyes were closed. With a concentrated effort he lifted first one, then the other leaded eyelid. The spots were back. And they were making noises.

"What the…" he groaned.

Nate backed a little away from the bruised and bearded man making strange faces at him. "We tried to knock, sir—Mr. Coulter."

"Yes, sir, but you didn't answer," Matt piped in. "And Mama says we have to fix the broken dresser drawer for you."

"Mama?"

"Mrs. Bradshaw," Nate clarified.

"Oh," Jake groaned. "The witch."

Both boys slapped their hands to their mouths, trying to smother their laughter.

"You think it's funny, do you? She did this to me again with those weeds of hers. I feel like I was dragged here from Texas under the wheels of a wagon train."

"Mama said you might be sleepy, but that you needed to be stirred up."

Nate shoved his little brother's shoulder. "That's not what she said. She said you needed to wake up and move a little else your leg will stiffen up. And she said to put the robe she left you or some clothes on, 'cause she's gonna bring your dinner up soon."

Jake heard what the boys were saying, but he was having trouble making much sense of anything. That damned potion she'd given him left him feeling worse than a week's worth of hard drinking.

He reached halfheartedly under the covers to see if

he had any clothes on and found he hadn't. Vaguely, he remembered tossing them off.

"I'm going to need a change of clothes."

Nate pointed across the room. "They're still in your saddle bags. As soon as we fix the dresser drawer you can unload them in there."

"I brought the nails. See?" Matt thrust a palmful of what looked more like tacks into Jake's face.

Despite the fact he'd awakened to the boys studying him like an exhibit at a traveling sideshow, they seemed harmless enough.

Jake hauled himself to a sitting position against the pillows, regretting it as pain stabbed his temples. "Tell you what," he said, rubbing at his jaw. "If one of you would bring me a pitcher of water and a towel, I might be able to shake off your Mama's evil brew enough to give you a hand."

"Matt'll do it."

"What? Will not. You go. I want to talk to Mr. Coulter."

"I'm the oldest and I say you go."

Jake's head began to pound. "Whoa there, this isn't gonna help get me on my feet. Now one of you—you, Nate, is it? Go on over to my pants hanging on that chair over there and pull out a penny from that front pocket."

"Are you going to flip a coin?" Matt sounded hopeful. At least he'd have a fair chance of winning instead of having to automatically obey his brother. "I call heads."

"Okay, fair and square and no more squabbling."

Nate brought the coin over and Jake shifted enough to shake the coin in one hand and flop it atop the back of the other. "Tails all right with you, Nate?"

Nate shrugged. "I guess."

Jake lifted his hand. "Tails it is. Sorry, Matt, better luck next time."

Matt scuffed his toe against the hardwood floor, frowning.

"I'll tell you what though, you can keep the penny for your trouble."

"I can?" He beamed up at Nate. "I'll be right back with soap, water and a towel, then."

Jake rubbed his beard. "And a razor, if you can round one up."

Nate shook his head as his brother scampered out of the room and down the back stairs to the pump outside. "You didn't have to do that."

"Your Mama didn't have to cut that bullet out of my leg, either."

"Oh, she likes doing that."

Jake smiled a little, though he was certain Nate had no idea the humor he found had nothing to do with Isabel's charity. He was wondering if it was taking a knife to a man she liked, or if she liked the danger, the risk.

The fog from his drugged sleep began to fade a little, and he looked around the room. Despite the touches of Isabel's warmth he'd noticed yesterday, it was sparse to be sure. But it was clean and had all he needed for the time being: a bed, a lamp, a table and a dresser. A dresser with the front of the bottom drawer lying on the floor beside it.

Nate followed Jake's eyes. "That's what we came to fix."

"Well, I appreciate the gesture, but if you think those scrawny little nails your brother had are going to hold that together, you're mistaken. Don't you have anything bigger?''

"I—well, we sometimes don't have all the right tools around here." He didn't quite meet Jake's eyes.

"Why's that?"

"Well…" Nate shifted uncomfortably, still studying his boots. "Mr. Bradshaw, he married my first mama after Pa died. But I don't think he liked us much. He brought us here when she died and married Mama, then he took off. And Mama, well, she's a girl, you know. She does the best she can, but she's not…she doesn't know much about— Well, she's real good at healing people and animals anyway!" he finished defiantly.

"I'm sure she is," Jake said, half to himself. The boy's reluctant story explained a lot about the house and Isabel herself. And despite himself, it roused his curiosity.

"Look," he said to Nate, "why don't you go look once more for some longer, thicker nails wherever you keep your tools and such while I get cleaned up. By the time you get back, I'll be up and dressed and ready to help you with that drawer."

"Thanks, Mr. Coulter. Gee, you sure don't act like an outlaw."

"You almost sound disappointed. Is that what your mama told you I am?"

"Naw, Mama said you were a lawman, but I just thought with you being all shot up when you came to town, you were probably really a dangerous gunslinger who got himself into a heap of trouble with the wrong gang. Nana—that's my grandma—thinks so, too. She says you look wicked."

Jake laughed. "Does she now? Well, I wish I were

more exciting. Look over there on the dresser, though, you'll see I'm on the right side of the law."

Nate saw the shiny badge at once. "Wow! You really are a Ranger. I never met a real one before you, but I heard plenty about 'em."

"Well, don't believe everything you hear, son. Trouble with all that gunslinger glory is that if your mama found out it was true, she wouldn't have let me stay under her roof."

"Oh, I don't know about that," Nate said, grinning. "You never know what my Mama'll do."

Isabel hefted the heavy iron skillet of corn bread away from the stove and set it on the worktable, quickly cutting the bread into wedges and arranging them on a platter. That finished, she glanced around to assure herself she hadn't forgotten anything for the evening meal. The mingled sounds of the boys chattering to Esme, the scuffling of chairs and the clink of dishes and silverware in the dining area hurried her step.

She wanted to get her family settled and eating and then take a tray up to Jake. Although he'd gotten out of bed, Isabel didn't expect he would be ready to trot up and down stairs several times a day to take his meals with the family. Even if he was, he hardly seemed the kind to engage in light dinner conversation. He had no ties to Whispering Creek, or anywhere it seemed, and his business in town wasn't something she wanted discussed freely around her boys.

Distracted by her thoughts, Isabel rushed into the dining area, turned and nearly dropped the platter.

Jake was there, one hand leaning on the back of a chair for support. Upright, clean-shaven, fully dressed, and without a gun within easy reach, he scarcely resembled the man Elish had half-dragged into her home yesterday. Instead, seeing him vividly recalled Chessie's declaration he was all man.

Nana was right. He did look wicked. But it was the kind of danger that roused a breathless excitement in her, a feeling both provocative and unwelcome.

"Here—give that to me before it becomes a part of the rug," Esme said, taking the platter from her hands.

Flushing, Isabel let her take it, realizing she'd been staring at Jake and that everyone in the room was now staring at her.

"I—I wasn't expecting you, Mr. Coulter. Your leg—"

"Hasn't fallen off yet," he finished for her, smiling a little.

"Of course it hasn't!" Matt said. "Mama knows how to heal everything. We told you that."

"Sit here, Mr. Coulter. I made sure Nana set out a plate for you." Nate pulled out the chair next to his own, giving Jake the place between him and Matthew.

Isabel frowned a little at the familiarity between her boys and her new boarder, watching all three as Jake sat down. When had that happened?

"You said I wasn't contagious," Jake said, his tone lightly mocking. "And you did promise me breakfast and supper."

"Yes…well, I'm glad you're well enough to join us. My mouse dung and weeds seem to have done you some good."

"As incentive to stay out of bed. That last one nearly did me in. I hope your potions aren't on the menu tonight."

"No, Mama made chicken," Matt piped up, "and corn bread. My favorites."

"And they are getting cold," Esme said. She glanced away from Isabel as Katlyn hurried into the dining room. "Ah, here is Katlyn. No, no, do not say you are sorry for being late again. We would not start without you. Sit down, Isabel, and now you can give the blessing, Nate."

Isabel distracted herself for the next few minutes getting supper underway, and introducing Katlyn to Jake. The tension that leaped up as soon as they looked at each other made Isabel glad they wouldn't be seeing much of each other.

Katlyn eyed Jake almost defiantly, as if she expected to do battle with him at any moment, and Isabel once noticed Jake studying her, as if she evoked an unwanted memory of someone for him.

She's probably just the type of woman he admires, Isabel thought, shoving a lank strand of hair from her brow. The heat of cooking had practically melted her hair to her head. Suddenly aware of how she must look from her neck down as well, she made a vague and useless attempt to smooth her well-worn housedress. While Katlyn, five years younger at just twenty, pretty, feminine, looked as fresh as a morning glory.

"I have some news for you all," Katlyn said as they started dinner. "Daniel and I have decided to get married in October."

"You've set a date already? But you scarcely know him. You've only been here a few months." Isabel reached across the table to give Katlyn's hand a squeeze. "Besides, you're going to disappoint every young man in Whispering Creek."

Isabel turned to Jake to explain. "Daniel works on

the Parkers' ranch, a few miles from here, and Katlyn is giving the children their lessons while our school-teacher gets ready for her first baby. Of course, in due time I want nothing more than for Katlyn to marry and settle in Whispering Creek.'' Catching Katlyn's attention in the corner of her eye, she winked at her sister. ''That way I can see to it she doesn't run off to do something outrageous.''

''You mean like join the circus?'' Katlyn teased.

Jake watched the two sisters but said nothing. Courtesy dictated he say some words of congratulations, or at least well wishes. But looking at Katlyn McLain, he saw his wife, five years ago, assuring him she wanted nothing more than a life with him in the Texas wilderness, but yearning for something else in her heart, and so unprepared for what that life turned out to be.

''Don't you approve of marriage, Mr. Coulter? You're scowling.''

Isabel's voice snapped Jake from his thoughts. He focused on filling his plate with the delectable-looking meal, accepting the hot corn bread Matt passed him instead of answering Isabel's blunt question.

The sweetness of her tone didn't fool him. The woman wanted to get behind his guard, probably with some crazy idea of healing more than his leg. But he'd spent too many years outriding his past to let a woman's smile and sweet words slow him down enough for them to catch up with him.

''It depends,'' he drawled at last. ''I've seen enough women who, away from town, can't abide the loneliness of frontier life. No offense, Miss McLain, but not many gently bred women can stand up to it, especially if inside, it's not what they really want.''

''You have no idea what I want, Mr. Coulter!'' Kat-

lyn snapped. She slammed down her fork on her half-
eaten meal, her mouth a mutinous line, that just as
quickly transformed into a smile. She laughed aloud.
"And I wouldn't exactly call my breeding *gentle.*
Would you, sister?"

"Growing up on riverboats, the daughter of a saloon
singer? Pampered, perhaps, but no, I wouldn't call your
upbringing gentle." Isabel watched Jake's reaction intently, wondering if she and Katlyn had managed to
unseat his confidence a little.

Jake didn't even flinch. "Still, I'd bet a hand of aces
you know nothing about frontier life. My guess is a
woman like you, delicate, pretty, is used to plenty of
comfort. You adjusting to the West is like trying to
grow a rose in the desert."

Isabel found his analysis of her sister surprisingly
accurate. "Roses can grow here, with a lot of nurturing."

"And Daniel is a wonderful, stable man," Katlyn
said, tossing her curls. "That will be enough for me. I
don't know much about ranching, but I'm sure I'll
learn quickly. Now, if you all will excuse me, I have
some grading to do."

"You will starve to death, child," Esme scolded.

Katlyn smiled at Esme. "I had plenty. And it was
delicious as always. But I'll be glad when Mrs. O'Neal
comes back. All these books and papers are making me
cross-eyed!" Waving her goodbyes, she left the room.

As soon as the boys finished eating, Esme insisted
on taking them in the kitchen to do their sums. "We
will clean up tonight. You two have not had time yet
to discuss the rules here." She shot Isabel a pointed
look then ushered the boys out, leaving Jake and Isabel
to linger over their coffee.

Isabel knew Esme's intention was to make certain her granddaughter told Jake Coulter right up front what would and would not be acceptable behavior under her roof and in front of her boys. But for the moment, Isabel was far more interested in understanding what had spurred her new boarder to get his fur up over Katlyn's impending marriage.

"You've annoyed Katlyn," Isabel said.

Jake set his coffee cup aside and propped his leg up on a nearby chair. "I think it's more I challenged her illusions. But I promise to be more civilized at breakfast and apologize, if that will please you."

The glint in his eyes and the smile tugging at a corner of his mouth raised Isabel's doubts he would keep that promise. At least the part about being civilized. She lifted a brow, eyeing him with challenge. "Maybe if you stayed in one place longer than a day you'd remember a few manners."

"I doubt it."

"So do I."

"Well, Mrs. Bradshaw, at least you can count on your new boarder for lively dinner conversation."

Isabel laughed, unable to help herself. "Lively is one way to describe it."

"Does that count as a redeeming quality?" Jake leaned back, stretching out his injured leg in front of him, rubbing his hand up and down his thigh to ease the ache. "Does it make up for irritating you?"

"I'm not irritated."

Yet she realized he had irritated her, not with his comments about women on the frontier, or the fact he was a wanderer never content with ordinary living, but inexplicably by his description of Katlyn. By comparison, she knew he wouldn't call her delicate or lovely, or say she needed attention or comforts.

She didn't want him to think of her that way, of course. But the idea he didn't consider her in any way a feminine creature, worthy of sheltering and nurturing, rankled.

Then in the next instant, Isabel realized how ridiculous she was for being irked by a few pretty words from a stranger to Katlyn. Why should his opinions about anything matter to her?

Jake watched her, and the emotions playing across her face, so easy to read. He wondered why she intrigued him. He knew the attraction of a woman like Katlyn McLain: violet perfume, teasing laughter, that flirting smile that promised sweet reward.

Isabel—he didn't know. Strong, tough enough to make her own way and provide for her grandmother and sister, tender enough to heal others and nurture two sons. She was nothing he had ever before considered appealing, but he couldn't look away from that soft mouth with its suggestion of passion and laughter in the delicate curves.

Yet, now and then something in her eyes, something in her touch, something in the gentle music of her voice hinted at vulnerability she had obviously buried deep inside herself.

"Are you going to share the joke?" he asked, wanting to hear her voice more than her answer.

"It's nothing, I was only laughing at how from the first, even when you were barely conscious, you've tried to have things your way."

"Tried?"

"You're here, aren't you? I think those honors go

to me. You barely knew what happened until you woke up in my bed.''

"An interesting thought," Jake said slowly, making her blush.

"You should be there now," Isabel said, determined not to let him rattle her, or at least show him how he disturbed her equilibrium with that dark, rough-edged voice that seemed to graze her skin like a physical touch. "It's too soon for you to be up on that leg for more than a few hours at a time."

"I'm not paying to have you fuss over me. Besides, I wanted to talk to you—about Jerico Grey."

Isabel started. "Jerico? Why do you think I know anything about him?"

"Your reaction every time someone says his name. You look as if there's a ghost in the room."

She hesitated for so long Jake was about to repeat his question. At last she said quietly, "I knew Jerico, a lifetime ago." Her chin came up. "I know what kind of man he is."

She got to her feet and started to reach for the coffee cups to give herself a reason to leave the room and the conversation she wanted to end. Jake's hand on hers made her pause.

He held fast, looking at her as if he were memorizing the shape and texture of her face, trying to learn her secret feelings. Finally, he released her, slowly, leaving lingering warmth where his callused palm had rubbed her tender skin.

"I planned to have Grey shackled and headed back to Texas to stand trial before he got near enough to Whispering Creek to cause any trouble," he said, the hardened expression in his eyes leaving her no doubt he meant every word. "This leg has put a rock in my stream, but I will take him back to Texas and see him to the end of a noose. You can trust that.''

''After you told me never to count on you?'' Isabel asked, smiling a little. ''You don't seem like a very good gamble, Mr. Coulter.''

''I'm not and my name is Jake. You've seen me undressed, pointed a knife in my face, drugged me with your witch's potions and now I'm sleeping under your roof. Seems there's no reason to be so formal now.''

''As I recall, it was you who jumped at the chance to have a room in my house. Besides, if I were a witch, I'd have turned you into something a bit more tame by now.''

''There's no magic strong enough for that. Although, I believe your grandmother is already working on a spell to make me vanish from your life. I'm convinced *she* really is a witch.''

Isabel laughed outright. ''She's convinced as well, I think. I wouldn't worry though, Nana's interests run more to love potions. Except maybe in your case. She thinks you're dangerous.''

''Well, I'm not feeling too dangerous right now,'' Jake said, rubbing his palm over his injured leg again and grimacing. ''Those stairs are beginning to look pretty daunting.''

''I told you, you should have stayed in bed. Here—'' Isabel went to him, offering her arm as help in standing. When he was on his feet, she braced herself to offer herself as support. ''You can lean on me, I'm not a gently bred delicate flower.''

Before heading up, he caught and held her gaze. ''No, you're not,'' he said softly. ''You're something much more.''

Jake smiled, but reached for the stairwell instead of her arm.

# *Chapter Five*

Isabel finished sweeping the last of the dust from the shop floor out onto the road. Surveying her work, she laid both hands atop the broom handle and rested her chin on them.

Glancing down the dusty street she could just make out the figures of a few shopkeepers locking up for the day and an old man driving a wagon heaped with whiskey barrels headed toward the Silver Rose.

She breathed in the soft, slightly spicy scent of wildflowers that caught on a breeze from the meadow. The grassy expanse, dotted with red, pink, orange and lavender, stretched wide and open beneath the green-and-purple silhouette of the Sangre de Cristo Mountains. Late-day sun slanted over the rugged peaks, washing the vista a mellow gold, leaving behind lingering warmth.

Though the familiar view from her front porch looked serene, it failed to calm her spirits. She felt restless, stirred up inside by something she had no name for. She'd worked intently throughout the day, trying to rid herself of her discontent. It made no sense. She had everything she wanted: family, home, work.

Why, suddenly, should she be struck by an undefinable longing for something more, something she couldn't even name?

Except she feared the source of her uneasiness did have a name and she didn't want to admit that it might be Jake Coulter.

Shaking herself free of her reverie, Isabel straightened, determined to put her odd mood behind her and finish closing the shop so she could start supper.

"Wait! Don't shut the door, these are heavy!" Isabel held the door open as Katlyn burst into her shop, arms laden with books she promptly dropped on Isabel's counter. "Guess what?"

"And hello to you, too."

"There's going to be a street dance tonight outside the Silver Rose and I thought you might want to go. It's time you had some fun," Katlyn said, reaching under the counter to Isabel's stash of hard peppermint candy and helping herself. "I heard a fiddler called Jimmy Briggs and his brother came into town with the cattle drive. Elish convinced them to play outside his place tonight."

"I can already see you've made plans to go." Isabel was rapidly learning her sister would sooner die in the desert sun than miss a single social or dance.

"Of course! I just love good music, and anything's got to be better than that wretched piano of Elish's."

"And what would you know about Elish Dodd's piano?"

"Oh, don't look at me like that. I'm not the one who's been taking in dangerous, handsome strangers from the Silver Rose." Katlyn laughed at Isabel's scowl. "Besides, *I've* never been in that place in my life—yet. I just like to stand outside and sing along."

With that she slid off the chair, grabbed up her books and kissed her sister on the cheek. "Go kick up your heels for a change. Who knows what might happen!"

Unable to help a smile at Katlyn's exuberance, Isabel considered her invitation after her sister had gone. It would be nice not to cook and clean one night, and instead indulge herself in laughing and talking with friends. Katlyn was right, Isabel couldn't recall when she'd last spent an evening away from home having fun.

At the same time, an odd reluctance tugged at her. She would be leaving her wounded boarder alone. Esme, of course, would be there. But Isabel felt a twinge of guilt at abandoning him, even for a few hours.

*You're being foolish,* she told herself. Jake is used to being alone. He doesn't need you standing watch over him.

And she didn't need to begin, in any way, to have feelings beyond a healer's concern for him. Once his leg healed, he'd be gone. She couldn't forget that. Not if she wanted to protect the life she'd built.

Not if she wanted to protect her heart.

A couple of hours later, after waving Matt and Nate off on their adventure at the Parkers', Esme practically pushed Isabel out of the kitchen to go change her clothes. As there was nothing too formal about the evening's plans, she didn't bother to do more than replace her soiled dress with one the color of saffron and unbraid her hair, letting it hang loose. Her only addition was a pair of silver earrings her mother had left her.

The music had already started by the time she reached the town square. A little self-conscious at be-

ing alone, she wandered out to join other townsfolk
who'd gathered on porches and in the street to listen
to Jimmy and Joey Briggs spin out their music on two
lively fiddles.

Several other musicians from among the miners and
residents had joined them, and the street was alive with
the sound of the fiddles, guitars, a harmonica and even
a drum, singing and gossiping, laughing and dancing.
As soon as Isabel reached the edge of the revelry, she
caught the attention of one of the miners she'd once
treated for a sprained ankle.

"You're missin' all the fun, Mrs. Bradshaw."

"Oh no, I'm enjoying the music."

"Well, you'll like it a lot better if you're dancin' to
it," he cajoled. Laughing, and not taking no for an
answer, he coaxed her into the center of the dancing.

Swept into the lively rhythm of the jig, Isabel let
pleasure take command. She'd almost forgotten the
wild, free days of her girlhood, this feeling of being
young and alive and unfettered by worry or care.

The heat of the dance slicked her skin with a fine
dew and she abandoned herself to the heady feeling
evoked by the brew of moonlight, song, and the admiration in the eye of her partner.

A few dances later, breathless and laughing, Isabel
left her last partner and decided to take a respite from
the crowd. She turned in the direction of the Silver
Rose—and stopped.

There at one of the tables Elish sometimes moved
outside in the evenings sat Jake.

With his bad leg propped up on one chair, he leaned
back in another, tilting it so only two legs touched the
ground. He studied the fan of cards he held with what
looked like grave intensity. In front of him a half-

empty whiskey bottle stood like a centurion over a haphazard pile of coins. Three other men, one Isabel recognized as a miner, the others strangers to her, sat around the table, eyeing Jake.

As she watched, a smile slowly transformed his face, making him look like a *bandido* in bed with a bag of stolen gold and a wicked woman. Laying down his cards, he spread out his hands in an expression of mock regret, then swept the pile of money across the table, adding it to his winnings.

One of the men rose, shaking his head, and when he did, Jake glanced up and, as if he'd planned it, looked directly at Isabel.

She stared back, trapped for a moment by the unexpected.

Jake stared a minute before recognizing her. She looked different with her hair a loose tangle and her dress like firelight poured on her skin, different enough to make him throw aside his first instinct to nod then let her go on her way. He didn't need the distraction, and Isabel Bradshaw had a way, with her weeds and her touch, of sidetracking him.

But with several shots of whiskey in him, the night and the uncertain light looked bewitching on her, prompting him to be reckless about inviting trouble.

"Well, Mrs. Bradshaw," he said, loudly enough to command her attention. "I certainly didn't expect to see you here."

"My thoughts exactly," she said, walking up to him. "When I said you were improving, I didn't mean you were up to what must be your usual routine of nightly carousing about town."

Jake awkwardly levered off his chair, stuffed his winnings into his pocket, and plucked his bottle off the table. "I'm used to doing as I please. It's been a long time since I had anyone following me around, telling me how to take care of myself."

"That I can believe. You said yourself you never stay in one place long enough to get close to anyone, so I suppose there's never anyone waiting for you, wondering what sort of scrape you've gotten yourself into this time."

His face changed, and for an instant so brief that Isabel wondered if she'd conjured it out of moonlight and the heat, she saw a glimpse of a pain that went much deeper than the wound in his leg. She hadn't expected her light words to touch him but in some way, without meaning to, she had hurt him.

The knowledge of it brought a rush of mixed sadness and concern, and Isabel stood still under his gaze, searching his face for some clue to the difference between the man she thought he was and the stranger she hardly knew at all.

They stared at each other and for a moment, she held her breath. Noise and color around her faded so she focused only on him and eyes that looked black and fathomless in the low light.

Jake smiled at her then, setting her free, and leaving her convinced she'd let her imagination run away with her common sense. "What's wrong? Run out of things to chastise me for?"

Isabel smiled back, responding to the light challenge of his words. "There's no danger of that. What are you doing here? You really shouldn't be putting too much weight on that leg yet."

"Don't worry, angel." He leaned closer, so she felt the whisper of his breath against her ear. She started and sensed his smile. "I'm not ready to ride out of town just yet. You're going to have me in your bed a little longer.''

"You're the most—"

"Yes, I am," Jake said with a grin, enjoying the way his words brought a flush to her cheeks and fire to her eyes. He reluctantly moved away from the beguiling brush of her hair and the scent of sun and wildflowers that belonged only to her.

"I'll confess, this isn't pleasure but business."

"Business? At a saloon? I can only imagine what business that might be."

"I don't think you can. The only place in town I have a chance of finding out about Grey is right here, where the more they drink the more they talk."

"Don't fret, ma'am, Jake's not gonna go gunnin' for anyone tonight 'cause he's too busy taking a week's pay off any man fool enough to sit across a table from him," one of the men behind them spoke up, reminding Isabel they weren't alone.

When she and Jake turned to look at him, he grinned, touching two fingers to his forehead in mock salute. "Tye Harper, at your service, ma'am. And here to warn you it's dangerous business playing with Jake. He plays to win and the Lord take pity on the soul of the man who'd get in his way. Anyone in all of Texas can tell you that."

"Can they now?"

Isabel looked at Jake but he smiled easily and sat back down in his chair, propping both feet up. "And they can also tell you Texans love a good story. Tye here knows how to stretch the blanket with the best of them."

Tye laughed, leaning back in his chair, poking the

end of a cigar in his mouth. "My stories are all true, my friend. Especially the ones about you."

"I'd like to hear some of those stories," Isabel said, glancing between the two men.

"Would you now?" Jake said. "I wonder why."

He looked at her with a slow burning intensity, holding her spellbound. If he had touched her, taken her into his arms, she wouldn't have felt the power of him more explicitly. For a moment, Isabel believed he could make love to her without doing more than looking into her eyes and making her feel his thoughts.

And she knew from the look in his eyes anything, everything he thought was wicked as sin.

"I knew you were different. You're taking these festivities entirely too seriously." Jake's deep voice slid into her brief reverie, startling her into awareness of her surroundings again. "Why aren't you dancing? Or does your dedication to your weeds and herbs keep you too busy to enjoy a night's entertainment?"

"Oh, no," she returned lightly, both amused and intrigued by his deliberate diversion. Unable to resist, she taunted, "I assure you, I find many ways to entertain myself."

Before he could reply, she turned with an engaging smile to Tye Harper. "They're getting ready to begin another song. Would you dance with me?"

Looking slightly stunned, Tye accepted her invitation and followed her to the edge of the couples waiting for the music to begin again. He glanced back at Jake then quickly turned to Isabel again, apparently not liking the look on Jake's face.

"Does he worry you?" Isabel asked, taking his hand and leading him just to the place she wanted.

"What? No—no, I wouldn't say that. It's just that

I've always gotten the feeling he has a hand on his gun even when he's not wearing it.''

Isabel smiled up at him, tempting him to forget Jake sat a few feet away from them. She wanted him to look only at her and she wanted Jake to see it.

With his voice and eyes, he suggested more than once she wasn't as feminine as other women because she defied convention to support her family and care for her house and business without depending on a husband.

So let him watch and then let him call her anything but all woman.

The music began again, a soft ballad that caressed like a velvet wind of the deepest night and had the bittersweet flavor of the longing. Isabel drew Tye into the dance, showing him the rhythm of a slow waltz with her hands and the sway of her body. He watched her with rapt attention and Isabel could see she had beguiled him, if only for the moment.

But it was for Jake that she danced.

Jake knew her intention from the moment she touched Tye's arm and enchanted him with her smile.

He watched Tye's hands on her and wanted to look away. But as she moved with the heartbeat of the music, her skirts twisting against her legs, he couldn't take his eyes from her.

She lifted her face to Tye, laughing at his attempt to keep her rhythm. Jake knew without a doubt, from the way she moved and smiled, that she felt him watching her. But she refused to turn and give him the satisfaction of knowing it mattered to her.

No longer his fairy creature with the gentle, healing hands, Jake saw her transform into an enchantress, fiery and elemental, weaving a spell of music and moonlight.

Her sensuous grace and that secret, knowing smile made Jake reconsider his sanity for ever thinking there was nothing provocative about her.

The music reached its peak and Isabel took a few steps from her partner so she moved nearer to Jake, close enough he could have reached out and brushed his fingers against her skin.

Her scent taunted him like a living touch, invoking a dizzying feeling in him that made him certain he'd drunk too much whiskey too fast.

Except even the best spirits never did what Isabel Bradshaw was doing to him, twisting his gut and starting a fire inside burning along his blood despite his determination to douse it quickly before it controlled him.

The ballad ended on a crying note and Isabel came to a sudden stop in front of him, her hands on her hips.

"You see, I do know how to entertain myself," she said, her voice breathless, her eyes triumphant. "Perhaps you'll remember that."

Jake searched for his voice. "Oh, I will."

Their gazes clashed and held.

Isabel caught her breath at the look in his eyes. Desire she saw clearly. And anger, too, at her or himself she didn't know. But the potent combination made her wonder who was the victor in the challenge she had flaunted before him.

He said nothing and his silence fired her own temper. She stiffened and started to leave him with a biting retort that would let Jake Coulter know without a doubt he couldn't intimidate her with that deadly expression of his.

Then Tye came up behind her with one of the cowboys from the cattle drive. They pressed closer, prac-

tically begging for a dance, and with some reluctance
on her part, the two of them at last drew Isabel back
into the center of the gaiety.

She glanced back once at Jake. He met her look for
a moment then deliberately turned back to the card table, picking up his whiskey bottle and downing a long
swallow.

Isabel looked away, trying to focus on Tye and his
good-natured banter. But no distraction could quite
quell the sudden, unexpected ache in her heart.

Jake, watching her again when she turned aside,
wished he could get up, ride straight out of Whispering
Creek, away from her, back to the lone and reckless
course he'd chosen. He didn't like the effect she had
on him. He didn't like being tempted by her gentleness
and her fire. It reminded him of the past when all he
wanted to do was to forget.

The past, though, had a way of catching up with him
when he least expected it.

And after tonight, he was going to have a damned
hard time ever forgetting Isabel Bradshaw.


Isabel thanked Tye and the cowboy for the reel as
they all walked over to a refreshment table Elish had
set up.

"I can't imagine living the way the Rangers do,"
she said before taking a swallow from a cool glass of
lemonade. She felt her face grow warm hearing the
coaxing tone she'd deliberately adopted, but she
couldn't resist the opportunity to learn a little more
about Jake. "I would hate never having a place to call
home for more than a few days."

Tye laughed. "They're a breed apart, I can tell you
that. They don't seem to belong anywhere but where

the wildest and the wickedest are, and even there, any
man with the sense God gave him would step aside
before he got within a hundred yards of one of 'em.''

"They sound...dangerous." *Like Jake.*

"That's a nice way of puttin' it, honey. There are
parts of Texas that are about the farthest from civilized
a man can get, and they've survived the worst that
frontier has to offer. It's made some of the Rangers
more outlaw than lawman sometimes. Still—'' Tye
glanced over his shoulder in the direction of the saloon.
"They're some of the best and Jake Coulter is better
than most. In any fight, he's the man I'd want beside
me because I sure wouldn't want him across from me.''

Isabel's gaze moved almost involuntarily behind Tye
to where Jake sat. He looked up and their eyes met.
Isabel shivered. What sort of man was he to command
both respect and fear?

She realized then that Anita, all rouge and low-cut
lace, stood next to Jake's chair, her hand caressing his
shoulder. Anita had no doubt been counting the hours
until she could again try to tempt the town's intriguing
visitor into her bed.

And a man like Jake would no doubt take advantage
of the offer as soon as he felt even half able.

*What does it matter?* Isabel asked herself. He meant
nothing to her, after all. It was foolish to stand and
watch Anita bend low to see Jake's hand, to see him
flash her a smile, his eyes move in obvious admiration
over her.

Another round went to Jake and he scooped up his
winnings and his bottle, and with a word to his com-
panions, got to his feet. Isabel watched as Anita draped
against him and steered him into the Silver Rose.
Abruptly, she turned away.

*You're acting like an idiot,* Isabel told herself firmly. *A man like that could never mean anything to you.* Determined to forget the crazy feelings he roused, Isabel headed into the crowd, promising herself she would not succumb to the temptation ever again.

Jake gave Anita a dismissing glance. "Thanks for the offer, but you'd better find yourself another cowboy tonight. I'm not up to your brand of entertainment right now."

He saw the flare of temper in her eyes and shrugged it off. The woman was trouble without a doubt. But the kind of trouble he'd had a lot of experience avoiding.

"I won't forget this, Jake Coulter, you can gamble your last dollar on that. I don't cotton to rejection from any man." With a nasty smile, Anita whirled away, giving him a deliberate glimpse of black stockings and red petticoats.

Regretting his impulse to follow her into the Silver Rose, Jake found an empty table. He settled into a chair, staring moodily out the saloon window. He'd done it to distance himself from Isabel and that bothered him more than anything else.

Watching her with Tye and what seemed like every other man in Whispering Creek had put him in a foul temper. Though why the devil he should give her a second thought, above getting help for his leg, confounded and irritated him.

Jake shoved aside the whiskey. He'd definitely had enough tonight. Any more and he'd probably do something stupid.

He forcibly reminded himself what a woman with

all the sweet traits of a good wife and all the hidden treasures of a lover could do to his life.

He'd learned that lesson the hard way. And he had no intention of repeating it.

Isabel found herself wandering through the crowd in the direction of the Silver Rose. Unable to stop herself, she glanced in the window, fully expecting to confirm her suspicions Jake would be spending the night with Anita.

Instead, she saw him sitting alone at a table, staring at the bottle in front of him as if he wanted it to disappear.

Surprise and relief flooded through her, followed quickly by curiosity. Surely Anita hadn't turned him down?

"If you want him so much, why don't you go get him?"

Isabel spun around to find Katlyn looking at her, brows raised, one hand on her hip.

"I don't want him!"

"Oh, is that why you've been staring at him all evening, because you don't want him? I'm not the only one who's noticed. A couple of people commented about how you could be so fascinated by a long rider. You—strong, practical Isabel."

Isabel blessed the darkness that hid the heat rising to her face. "He's not an outlaw and you know it. Besides, I'm only worried about his leg. All of my trouble will be for nothing if he does something to start the bleeding again."

"Ah, I see. Ever the healer, aren't you, sister? Maybe if you say it enough, you'll convince yourself it's true.'' Not giving Isabel time to reply, Katlyn spun around and headed back to the dancing.

Isabel sighed, not sure what she would have said in reply anyway. She started toward the street, intending to return to the sanctuary of her house.

A loud, slurred voice from behind stopped her.

''So—you the one they call the witch?'' A big, burly man ambled up to her, his spurs clanking against the porch floorboards. ''Tye Harper told me how you fixed up Coulter.''

Isabel nearly choked from the smell of whiskey and tobacco on his breath. From the corner of her eye she saw two more men—hands from the cattle drive by the look of them—stumbling up behind their friend. One of them finished off the last dregs from a bottle and tossed it aside to fix her with a leering grin.

Darting a quick look around, Isabel said firmly, ''I was just leaving.''

''Oh, no you ain't. I got a hurt that needs tendin' real bad. And I hear you're just the one to fix me up.''

Isabel, fervently wishing for her knife, took a hasty step back. Before she could sidestep the big man, all three had backed her against the wall. The big cowboy fumbled with his belt buckle.

Gathering her courage despite her quivering insides, Isabel fixed the offending man with what she hoped was a cold, intimidating glare. ''The only thing I'll fix for you is a night in the jail. Now let me pass.''

Raucous laughter answered her attempt to force her way past the men. ''What's your hurry, honey?'' one of the men taunted.

''Yeah, it ain't nice to turn away a man in need. I thought you was supposed to be a healer.''

''And it looks like you're all alone,'' the first man

said. "I don't think any of them cowboys you been dancin' with is comin' for you."

"She doesn't need them, she's got me."

The three men jerked around clumsily at the sound of the baritone voice simmering with threat.

"And just who the hell—"

"Jake…" Isabel whirled to find him standing in the doorway. Relief trembled through her.

He met her eyes with cool assurance. "I was just seeing the lady home." Not waiting for her answer, he stepped across the porch to take her arm.

"Now just a minute." The big cowboy took a step forward.

In a flash Jake's six-shooter was in his palm, aimed right at the man's heart. "One more step and it'll be your last."

Isabel caught her breath at the quick change in Jake. His eyes and voice were ice, every muscle tensed.

"See here," the man sputtered, backing up. His two friends stumbled over themselves in their hurry to get down the stairs and away from Jake. "All I wanted was some doctorin'."

"Get it somewhere else," Jake told him in that voice that made her shiver. Soft, dark, dangerous, like velvet sheathing a steel blade.

Before Isabel could react, Jake moved closer to her, so close the slightest motion from either of them and his skin would kiss hers. The scent of him, whiskey and leather and musk, surrounded her like incense.

The cowboy hesitated, then, apparently not liking the look of Jake, waved a shaking hand. "Ah, hell with it." With a great clumsy effort, he turned and shoved through the saloon doors.

Jake watched him until the doors slapped closed on

him. Then without a word, he holstered his gun and wrapped an arm over Isabel's shoulders, guiding her to the quiet darkness of the narrow space between the saloon and the next-door building.

He stopped her there, raising his hand to slowly trace a line down her cheek to her lips.

"Are you all right?" he asked. The fierce urge to protect her that had overwhelmed him when he heard the cowboy threaten her still raced through his veins like liquid fire.

Isabel's mouth moved over the word *yes,* but she couldn't find the breath to give it sound. Instead she nodded weakly.

His swift change from hard to tender left her reeling, as did his quick defense of her. Not once had Douglas ever come to her aid for any reason, much less over a drunken cowboy's advances. For as long as she could remember, she had fought her own battles.

But tonight...tonight, Jake made himself her protector. Without question, without hesitation. And now he stood ready to give her comfort, to shelter her from trouble.

She gazed up at him. How easy it would be to surrender to the temptation. How much she wanted to.

Jake shifted so he held her trapped in the shadows between both his arms, her back pressed to the wall. The intense warmth in his eyes seared her from skin to soul.

"I never wanted this," he said hoarsely. "But after seeing you dance for me... You were daring me to want you, weren't you?" He leaned closer, his mouth brushing her temple. He felt her tremble and slid his caress lower to her cheek. "Are you afraid, angel?"

"No." The word released on a quivering breath. "Never."

"You should be. You should be careful with your challenges. You leave me no choice but to answer them."

Not giving her time to even think of a reply, Jake pulled her against him and covered her mouth with his.

The instant he touched her Jake knew he should have stuck with the women he paid for. He'd come to Whispering Creek to find trouble and here it was.

Except it wasn't the kind he could fight with a gun, a fast horse and a smile.

He half expected her to push him away, but instead she met him on his own terms, fire to fire. He deepened his kiss, the feel of her against him through the light cotton of her dress a thin resistance between them.

She murmured his name like a plea, reaching to draw him even closer, and Jake was lost.

Isabel wanted to tell him she had no power or desire to resist him, either, tonight. Without hesitation, she abandoned herself to his kiss, the danger she instinctively felt when she first touched him only intensifying her longing for him.

She thought she'd convinced her heart to defy it. But in this moment she realized just how wrong she was.

Nothing in her life had prepared her to resist Jake Coulter. He tasted like whiskey and sin, and fit against her hard, a match for her softness. The combination of that and the urgent pressure of his hands and mouth made her feel reckless.

In all the months she'd been married to Douglas, she'd never experienced more than a stirring of desire. How could she have guessed one kiss from Jake would feel like being swept into a storm, leaving her greedy for every sensation, needing even more?

Since Douglas, she had tried to avoid trouble, but now she invited it into her arms, wanted it to last forever.

Except nothing about Jake was forever.

A sharp pain tore at her heart. How could she bear this again, needing so much then losing everything?

Abruptly she broke away, leaving them to stare at each other, breathless in the heated silence.

"Isabel—" Jake began.

"No." She hurriedly put her fingers to his mouth, stopping his words. "Don't say you're sorry. Please."

"I wasn't going to. Not for that." He stepped away from her, raking a hand through his hair. He drew in a ragged breath. "I never meant...I only wanted to protect you." He gave a short bitter laugh. "It should have been from me."

"Don't. I wanted this," she admitted, so quietly she wasn't certain he could hear her until his head jerked up. The heated look he gave her nearly crumbled her will to keep her distance.

"I want you," he said roughly. "You're making me crazy and I don't know how to stop it."

"It has to stop. It's wrong. *I* was wrong, now and before. I won't let it happen again. I can't." The last words ended on a broken sound. She backed away from him, her hands clenched at her side as if she fought to keep from reaching out. "But I'm the one who's sorry, Jake. More than you'll ever know."

Her anguished words hit hard, stopping him from going after her. She was right. They couldn't give in to this need, these feelings. Isabel deserved more than a few nights' pleasure and he could never promise her anything beyond that.

*But you're wrong about one thing,* angel, he told her silently. *No one's sorrier about that than I am.*

## Chapter Six

A sharp crack, then a long, rolling grumble of thunder drew Jake's attention from the maps he'd spread over his bed. Rain rattled the windowpane and the sky looked as dark as twilight, though it was barely three in the afternoon. He rubbed at the bridge of his nose, deciding that neither the sudden summer storm nor his determination to track Jerico Grey's trail on the maps Cal Reed had provided him were distraction enough from the source of his trouble today.

He'd hardly slept last night after his unexpected encounter with Isabel. The scent of her, the feel of her in his arms, her surprising abandoned response to his kiss, had haunted him, stirring up feelings he didn't want or need.

Finding her in trouble, he'd reacted without thinking. Except he knew he hadn't been driven solely by his instincts as a lawman, but because of a sharp, sudden need to protect her. Not any woman in trouble. Her.

"Damn you," he muttered, not sure whom he intended the curse for, Isabel or himself. Ignoring the ache in his leg, he shoved the maps aside and got up from the bed to stare out the window at the driving storm.

He didn't want to feel protective of Isabel or anyone, ever again. He didn't want to be tempted to linger any longer than it took to get his job done.

Yet for the first time in more years than he cared to remember, he felt a strange reluctance to get on with the job. Her home full of strays, including even the children and her sister, was a sanctuary from the harsh world outside; for him it offered a reprieve from running. Isabel brought love and warmth and security to all who crossed her threshold.

And that notion scared the hell out of him.

Jake started to turn back to his maps and force himself to focus on his job instead of feelings he couldn't resolve, when a loud crash and a piercing shriek had him reaching a hand toward his gun belt even as he started for the door.

At the sound of someone pelting across the floor below, a door being slammed open and then, "Oh, not again! This blasted roof!" he left the guns and went to investigate.

"I'll bet the whole roof was ripped off this time!" he heard Nate say before he saw the two boys dashing up the stairway.

"Hi, Mr. Coulter," Nate said, "come and see what's happened to Nana's and Aunt Katlyn's room this time. I'll bet there's water everywhere!"

"We'll probably have the biggest flood ever with all this rain," Matt added gleefully.

"I don't think your mother is going to be as happy about this as you are," Jake predicted, as he limped after the two boys downstairs and into the bedroom at the back of the house.

Indeed, he found Isabel glaring up at a large hole in the ceiling, ignoring the rain pelting her face. "I'm sure

I fixed this part of the roof when I made repairs in the spring.'' She flung up a hand, shaking it at the gaping hole. ''What happened to the wretched patch?''

''This is the third time in three months! It nearly fell on me this time!'' Katlyn scurried around the room, trying to move clothing and bedding from one corner to another to escape the rain. ''What are we going to do? Everything is—it's—wet! I'm wet!'' she snapped, swiping a splatter of water from her cheek.

Isabel, soaked and indignant, looked at her a moment as if she hadn't understood Katlyn's outburst, and Jake couldn't help it. He started to laugh and Matt and Nate, after a glance at the two women, began giggling, too.

After shooting a scowl at all three offending males, Isabel glanced back at the hole in her roof. ''I'm glad you three find this so entertaining,'' she grumbled. ''My house is falling down around me and all you can do is stand around laughing. Katlyn, here—'' she grabbed up several dresses and a quilt and pushed them into Matt's and Nate's hands ''—take these to the kitchen and spread them over the chairs to dry. And ask Nana to—''

''I am here. How could I not be? It sounded as if the whole roof was falling around our ears.'' Esme suddenly appeared in the doorway. ''*Ay,* but this house will be the death of us yet. There are two leaks in the boys' room, but this—''

Esme tsked over the hole, studied Isabel, Jake and the boys in turn, seemed satisfied by what she saw, then went to scoop up an armful of bedding. Pushing it into Katlyn's arms, she turned the younger woman toward the door. ''Come and help me spread this to dry. I already have the boys' blankets by the fire. You are no good to your sister in times like these. Matthew, Nathan, come, before you are soaked.''

Jake stepped aside to let Esme guide Katlyn and the boys to the stairs and then looked at Isabel with a grin. ''Well, I can't say it hasn't been an exciting stay, Mrs. Bradshaw. You don't charge extra for this, do you?''

''I fixed it! I did! It should have been fine, but this damned storm…'' She kicked at the splintered wood and warped square of tin the wind and rain had brought down into the room.

''Such language,'' Jake murmured. He came up to her and took her arm, leading her away from the hole and the shower of warm rain. The rain had soaked her dress and the cotton clinging to her like a second skin reminded him too clearly how she had felt in his arms last night. He forcibly put the memory aside to concentrate on the problem at hand.

Isabel tried not to react to the feel of his hand wrapped around her arm, the warmth of him evident through the wet, cold material of her dress. ''I need to do something about this,'' she said, annoyed at the breathless sound of her voice, not sure if she meant the roof or him.

''Yes,'' Jake said softly, ''we do.''

They looked at each other. An unspoken need breathed between the silence, communicated by his touch, the quickened beat of her heart.

Jake later wondered if both of them would have damned the consequences and succumbed to it if a loud crack of thunder coming almost simultaneously with the sound of the boys pounding across the floor hadn't broken the tenuous bond between them.

''Mama, we put the clothes by the fire and—what's

wrong?'' Nate asked, looking from Isabel to Jake, sensing the tension between them, if not the cause.

"Nothing," Isabel said, "nothing. Just the roof, of course." She took a step from Jake to peer up at it again. "I'm going to have to do something with it now before the rest of it comes down tonight."

"We could nail up one of the quilts over the hole," Matt suggested. He scrunched up his nose as he stared at the gaping hole. "It would probably leak, though."

"Of course it would," Nate said, pushing at his arm. "We need something else, like, like...maybe a door."

"A door? That'll never work!"

"How would you know? You want to put a quilt up there!"

"Nate, Matt, enough." Isabel rubbed her temple, feeling a little overwhelmed. It hadn't been a particularly good day and now this. The roof was bad enough but she hated for Jake to see her standing around, looking helpless and indecisive.

"You know," Jake said, stepping up to look more closely at the hole. "It's almost evening. There's no chance of fixing the roof properly in this storm and in the dark. But if you have a scrap of tin and a few nails, I think I could get up there and get it closed up enough tonight to keep you from flooding."

Nate nodded eagerly. "We have some in the closet beside the kitchen. And I'm sure we have some tin in the shed. I can get it, Mama!"

"I know where the nails are. Big, long ones, right, Mr. Coulter?"

Jake nodded, suppressing a smile at Matt's serious expression. "You remembered what I told you when we were nailing up the dresser drawer."

"Every word," Matt said, beaming at the praise.

"Can we get them, Mama? And can we help Mr. Coulter fix the roof? Can we?"

Isabel hesitated, not sure she wanted to admit she couldn't take care of her own house by letting Jake resolve her problem, even temporarily. Before she could reply, though, Jake gave the boys one of those grins she found so infectious, earning him wide smiles in return.

"I'd be glad of the help," he told them. "Your mama's a good healer, but my leg still isn't the best yet. And I don't know where your tools are."

"We know! Mama—"

"Go ahead and get the tools," Isabel said, relenting at their eagerness. "But I'll fetch the tin. It's still storming and I don't want you drenched."

She hadn't finished the sentence before the boys were out of the room, racing out to fetch Jake what he needed. "You don't have to do this," she said, turning to Jake when they'd gone. "I can—"

Jake ran a hand through his hair, shoving a dark wave from his brow. "I know. I never doubted it. But everyone needs a hand now and then. Even people who are too proud or too stubborn to admit it. Besides," he said, smiling slowly. "I owe you one for not cutting off my leg."

"Proud? Stubborn?" She whirled away. "You don't owe me anything."

"Isabel…" Her name sounded like a sultry suggestion spoken in his rough-edged voice, causing Isabel to catch her breath a little.

Jake took her by her shoulders and turned her firmly back around to face him. "It wasn't an insult. It was a compliment. You couldn't survive, especially taking care of so many others, if you weren't proud and stubborn—and independent. Listen,'' he said, when she remained unyielding. ''I'm not offering to move into your bed. Just to patch up your ceiling.'' He cocked an eyebrow, a corner of his mouth curving in a half smile. ''Or maybe you doubt my skill.''

''I've only seen how fast your hand finds your gun. I've never seen you use a hammer. Building is a different sort of skill than gunfighting.''

Lord, the woman could spit venom when it suited her. But he knew enough about her now to realize she was angry with herself. He'd found one thing she *couldn't* do alone and it rankled her no end.

''You might be surprised at how handy I am,'' he said coolly.

''I don't see you as a carpenter, that's all,'' she said, her eyes straying to his mouth, thinking of the way it had felt against hers. ''Not after last night. I mean,'' she added hastily when his smile broadened, ''the way you handled those cowboys. It's obvious you're skilled at what you do. Even with only one good leg, you're pretty handy to have around in a fight.''

Jake recognized her light tone as her way of easing the tension between them and he responded in kind. ''I suppose I'll take that as a compliment. I hope you'll feel the same after you've seen me do battle with your roof.''

Isabel started to reply but Matt came bolting into the room, interrupting. ''Mama, Mr. Coulter—you have to come now! Nate went and got the tin by himself, but it's so big he got it stuck in the door of the shed!''

Isabel took one look at Matt, his wet hair and clothes plastered to him; mud spattered up his pants legs and smeared on his nose. Then she looked at Jake and the effort he was making to hold back a grin was her undoing.

She began to laugh, so hard her legs weakened and she plopped down in the middle of the flooded bedroom floor, ignoring the water and debris around her. She knew she both sounded and looked slightly hysterical, but the laughter felt good, a brief release from the tension and worries of the day.

Jake and Matt stared at her, then exchanged a baffled look.

"Mama?"

"Are you okay?" Jake asked.

"I—I'm fine," Isabel said, trying to catch her breath. "It's just…it's just been such a bad day and then this, and Nate and Matt and—oh, it just all seemed so ridiculous!"

Shaking his head, Jake went and put a hand on Matt's shoulder. "It's all right. Go on down and tell your brother we'll be there in a minute to get the tin out of the door."

When Matt nodded and scampered off, Jake turned to Isabel. "Can I get you one of those weed potions you're so fond of or is this your usual reaction to disaster?"

"Would you rather I cry on your shoulder and wail about how helpless and alone I am?" Isabel said tartly. She struggled to get to her feet, fighting with her wet skirts.

Jake grasped her at the waist and pulled her up, catching her off balance so she had to steady herself against his chest to regain her footing. He felt warm and solid under her palms and for a moment, a sweet longing surged through her, a yearning to rest against his strength, to find comfort in his embrace.

In the next moment, she realized just how impossible that wistful desire was. Not because of the storm and the collapsing roof and the boys yelling at them from the front door, but because there was nothing permanent about Jake Coulter. He might help her one day, but he'd be gone the next. And she'd learned too well already anything less than forever was nothing at all.

Holding her, Jake fought the urge to take her into his arms and make her forget everything but the fire that had kindled between them from the moment she'd touched him. Outside, the thunder rolled and the wind twisted and cried, but the storm she created in his blood roared in his ears and battered his heart, making a mockery of the wildness around them.

Isabel pulled away, making an ineffectual attempt to smooth her damp hair and skirts. She looked toward the door, wetting her lips with the tip of her tongue. "I should go and—"

"—get the tin out of your shed door, I know. I'll help."

Isabel hesitated before reluctantly nodding her agreement. Inside, she fought to regain control of the common sense that told her she had no business courting this particular kind of trouble. She'd been right when she first thought Jake dangerous. Only she had never guessed the danger would be to her heart.

Now all she had to do was find some way of protecting herself against it for the remainder of his stay in Whispering Creek but at this moment, she had no idea how.

Matt dried the last dessert spoon and handed it to Isabel to put in the drawer. He hesitated beside her, scuffing the toe of his boot on the floor.

"Mama?"

"Mmm?" Isabel, finishing putting the last of the dinner dishes away, glanced at him. "What is it, sweetheart?"

"Mama, I don't like storms and neither do the animals." He blurted it out like a guilty confession. "Trouble has been hiding under the desk in our room all day. Please, can you...and maybe you, Mr. Coulter, come to our room and say good-night?"

Jake and Nate stood across the kitchen with the tablecloth stretched between them, folding it. Jake glanced at Isabel before he answered. She chewed her lip for a moment, then smiled a little, giving her approval.

For some reason, that small gesture twisted something in his chest. He grinned back, unable to stop himself.

"I'd be glad to come," Jake said. "I might even be able to scrape up a bedtime story, if you'd like."

Nate's eyes grew wide. "Can you tell us one about outlaws and killers?"

Isabel immediately frowned. "Nate, I don't think—"

"Well, how about if I tell you one about *bandidos* instead? I'll tell you how my leg ended up under your mama's knife."

"Yeah!" both boys agreed enthusiastically.

"You can sit in the chair we use at our desk and prop your leg up on our chest," Matt offered. "Trouble might even come out to listen. He likes stories."

"You'll have that bird telling the stories before long," Jake said with a chuckle.

"Yours is the one I want to hear," Isabel murmured, as she untied the apron from behind her waist. "You boys go on up and get washed up for bed. I want to give Nana this drink. This weather makes her bones ache.'' She poured a hot cup of herbal tea into a pottery mug, the fragrant steam with its echoes of sage and honey scenting the air. ''This ought to soothe her.''

''Nana's getting older all the time, isn't she?'' Nate asked as he shoved the tablecloth under the dry sink.

''Everyone gets old, honey. But Nana is strong. She doesn't let anything stop her, and certainly not a few aching bones.''

Sending Nate and Matt off with the tea for Esme and promising to come to their room shortly, Isabel turned back to the kitchen to finish tidying up.

''It was nice of you to offer to tell them a story,'' she told Jake, not looking at him.

''You make it sound as if I don't know the meaning of the word,'' he said.

The smile in his voice made her shift to look at him. ''It's—I didn't mean…''

''Never mind. You know,'' he drawled, leaning against the wall to watch her, ''I wondered just who you were talking about before, your grandmother, or you.''

Isabel shook her head at him, her mouth twisting in exasperation. ''You never give up, do you? I admit, the Castillo women have never been any good at being dependent. We've never had much chance to be. I'm sorry to disappoint you.''

''I don't know about your mother, but your grandmother's formidable enough to scare any man into submission.''

His teasing tone made it impossible for Isabel to stay irritated with him. She laughed despite herself, tossing down her dishcloth and resting both hands behind her on the table. "My mama was nothing like Nana, but for all her gentleness, she had an iron will. Once she resolved to do something, nothing would stop her. If anyone tried to dissuade her, she'd just give them that implacable, serene smile and go on her way."

"Your father was a lucky man," Jake said, wanting to encourage her unexpected confidence. He liked hearing her talk about herself, her past, but only because he was curious about her, he told himself. She was different, intriguing. Just watching her made him wonder what secrets, what passions lay hidden inside.

At the mention of her father, her face clouded over. "My father's luck depended on the turn of the dice or the cards he drew. He couldn't stay in one place longer than his so-called luck lasted, not even long enough to see me born. I didn't even know about Katlyn until she found me after her mother told her about me."

Isabel's father, then her husband… Small wonder she was so fierce about being self-reliant, Jake thought.

*And a good reason why I should keep my distance. The last thing she needs is another man in her life who can't be counted on.*

"I guess it's about time I started that story," he said briskly to break the air of intimacy her confession had spawned. He straightened, grimacing when pain stabbed his leg.

Isabel moved to his side. "All that climbing and crawling around on my roof in a thunderstorm certainly hasn't done your leg any good," she said, brushing her fingers against his shoulder. "You should have let me take care of it." He worried her and that unsettled her. Because her worry was less as a healer for a patient than as a woman for a man she cared about.

"Save your fussing for someone who needs it," Jake

said. The words came out more brusquely than he intended, but he needed the protection they gave him against the insidious warmth stirred by her touch. ''I'll survive.''

His tone stung. ''If you do, it'll be despite yourself.''

He flashed her a cocky grin. ''It usually is.''

# Chapter Seven

"And when I crossed into the New Mexico territory I thought I'd lost them," Jake was saying as Isabel slipped into the boys' room a little later.

They sat upright in their beds mesmerized by Jake's story. Trouble peeked out from beneath the desk, giving a little nervous cawk and ducking back when Isabel entered. When Jake looked up and paused, she took a seat at the end of Matt's bed, encouraging him with a smile and a wave of her hand. "Go on, please. It sounds like you're just getting to the good part."

Jake gave her a long, lazy look, a slow smile curling at the edges of his lips. For the first time since he'd come, he actually looked somewhat relaxed. Much of the tension that held his jaw in a hard line had eased. His eyes focused on the boys instead of canvassing here and there as they usually did. For the moment at least, he looked as if he didn't have to be aware of every movement around him.

He sat opposite Matt's bed, his arms raised, elbows bent and hands knotted comfortably behind his head. Stretching his long legs out in front of him, he rested his black boots on the boys' pine toy chest.

Isabel wondered if the teller or the audience was enjoying the story more.

"Anyhow, the day was hot for the season, and my horse hadn't had time to get used to the change in the weather," he said. He used his voice well, she thought, giving the tale just the right amount of drama and excitement to please the boys. "We both slowed down, certain we'd lost them. Boy, were we wrong."

"Did the *bandidos* sneak up on you?" Nate leaned toward Jake, resting his elbows on his knees.

"Well, truth be told, Rio and I got a little heavy-eyed in the afternoon sun. We'd been pounding ground for days with next to no sleep. We had to outride the gang, you see. Once we crossed the border and with the weather so hot, we both slowed up. I confess, I must have caught a few winks when we hit a straight stretch, and Rio probably did the same."

Isabel couldn't contain a giggle. "Somehow, I don't think this is the ear-sizzling tale they expected to hear."

Matt's and Nate's mouths had begun to gape in disbelief. "Rangers don't do that, do they?" Matt asked.

"All I can say is dead tired is dead tired, no matter who you are." Jake shifted his leg to another position. "So, there I am half asleep when something like a bolt of lightning wakes me."

"What was it?" Matt's eyes looked like they would pop out of his head. "The *bandidos?*"

"Well, in that split second, it sounded like a crack of thunder. But I knew differently when I saw my leg."

Isabel shook her head. "It's a wonder you're alive."

"Well, it's a good thing my trigger finger works even when my brain doesn't," Jake said, flashing her that grin that never failed to catch at her heart. "Many a night my hand's found my gun before my head knew I had company.''

Thunder boomed overhead and Matt gripped his quilt. ''How many of them were there?''

''Four. And all of them uglier than cross-eyed boars and twice as mean.'' Isabel bit her lip to keep from smiling and rolled her eyes, and Jake winked at her before continuing.

''They got lucky with the first shot, considering they'd all drunk too much tongue oil to see straight, let alone hit what they were aiming at. That was probably the only reason they didn't kill me. I had a second to turn Rio around and shoot back. Rio and I bolted out, me shouting and hollering and shooting two-fisted, Rio kicking up dust. We were making enough noise to scare the devil himself.''

''Wow!'' The story came to life in Nate's bright eyes. ''Now that's the way it oughta be!''

''It's insanity!'' Isabel blurted out. ''Are you a lawman or a madman?''

Jake shrugged. ''Takes a little of one to be the other.''

''So, did you get them all?'' Matt asked, gripping his blanket in both fists.

For the first time, Jake hesitated. Then, more seriously, he said, ''Only one.''

''You're supposed to kill the bad guys,'' Nate objected. ''That's your job.''

''No, it's not,'' Jake said before Isabel could ask Nate where in the world he'd gotten that idea. ''I don't like killing. But if it has to be done, it's better to be the one on the back side of the gun than looking down the barrel.''

''Is that the moral of your story?'' Isabel asked.

From the look in her eyes, Jake guessed she was none too pleased with his blunt honesty. "No, it's the truth. Life doesn't always give you the luxury of choosing."

Nate and Matt looked wide-eyed between their mother and Jake, sensing a change in the lighthearted feeling between them.

"It's a tough lesson." He turned to the boys. "But living here, if you don't learn it, you won't be telling stories like this one."

Anger surged in Isabel, flared briefly, then retreated. She wanted to contradict him, to tell Matt and Nate it wasn't so, to shelter her boys from the harshness of life as long as possible. And yet, something inside asked a more disconcerting question.

What would a father—a real father—say to his sons? Was Jake taking a deliberate risk with her to protect Matt and Nate? Was he telling them something he knew they had to hear, but would never learn from her?

"Listen." At last she found her voice, pleased she sounded calm and reassuring. "The rain's finally letting up. I think you both can sleep now. Say goodnight to Mr. Coulter."

"Can you teach us to shoot?" Nate seemed not to hear her. "You must be the best there is to take on four *bandidos*."

"Not quite," Jake said. He glanced at Isabel.

The set look on her face told him he'd overstepped his bounds. He'd pushed the limits with her for the sake of the boys, knowing he'd have hell to pay for it.

To her credit though, she had held her tongue, gently diverting the boys rather than wage battle with him in front of them.

"I won't be staying long enough for that, Nate.

When you're a little older, you talk to your mama about learning to defend yourself.''

"I'm old enough now! If I'm going to be a lawman, I have to practice a lot so I can get as good as you."

*And wouldn't your mama love that,* Jake thought to himself, suppressing a smile. "There are plenty of respectable jobs where you might get lucky and never have to use a gun."

Jake stood and limped over to ruffle Nate's hair. For a moment, he stood looking at the little boy, thinking of his own son who hadn't lived long enough to admire a quick draw, a fast horse and a good story. "Go to work in a bank or a dry goods store and you'll have a lot less chance of ending up limping around like me."

"Naw." Nate scooted down under his quilt. "Who wants to hear stories about bankers?"

Isabel rose and doused the lantern. "Mr. Coulter certainly has given you boys a lot to think about tonight," she said quietly. She pulled the covers up and kissed them. "I hope your dreams don't keep you up more than the storm."

As Jake pulled the door closed behind Isabel, he paused outside. They stood inches apart, an awkward silence settling between them.

He'd upset her, but he wanted to have the chance to tell her why. He nearly told her, too, that talking to them reminded him of his youth, time he'd spent listening to his father's tales. That it made him think of what he would have told his own son if he'd had the chance.

"I managed to talk Elish out of one fine bottle of brandy," he said at last, breaking the silence, "if you'd like to share it with me."

"I don't—"

"Ah, I should have guessed you'd prefer your own concoctions," he said, trying to lighten the mood between them and not succeeding if the wariness in her eyes was any indication. Best to make his escape while he could.

"Sleep well then. It sounds like the storm is finally giving up." Abruptly he turned and headed toward the stairs.

"Wait."

Isabel's mind warred against her emotions, creating a disturbing conflict of needs. She needed to make clear her fear her boys would romanticize his way of life, a life she could never approve of. She wanted to tell him how it touched her to watch him take time to give the boys a little of himself.

She didn't want to like him. Yet tonight a part of her craved his closeness.

"I wanted..." Isabel stopped, not certain what she wanted to tell him. "I wanted to talk to you."

Jake turned with a rueful smile. "I thought as much."

"And well, after this day, a warm brandy sounds fine."

"I'll get it. Do you want an extra log for the fire?"

Isabel nodded. "I'll see to that."

"I should have known." Jake wondered if she ever let anyone help her without a fight. It surprised him she hadn't kicked up more of a fuss about him patching the roof.

"I—I have to look in on Katlyn anyway," Isabel said, uncomfortable with the look her gave her. She fumbled for some explanation that would sound reasonable. "She was upset about the roof."

Jake said nothing yet the expression in his eyes gave

her the feeling something she said reminded him of his past. What, she couldn't imagine.

Finally he stirred, smiling a little at her. "I'll meet you by the fire, then. I can find some glasses, at least, while you check on your sister."

She nodded, and hurriedly went to peek in on Katlyn who would have been horrified to hear the sound of her own snoring. The tea Isabel had given her earlier had done its job. Beside her, Nana slept soundly. She pulled an extra blanket over them both, then for some reason went to her own room instead of directly to join Jake.

Stealing a quick glance in the looking glass above her bureau, she saw a reflection that truly reminded her of a witch. Dozens of tendrils had escaped her braid, sticking out this way and that all around her head and down the middle of her back. A stubborn smudge of something dark marred one cheek.

Embarrassed that she'd gone through the entire day looking so frazzled, she pulled the ribbon from her braid and dragged a brush through her tangled masses. She then poured water into her basin and used it to quickly wash her face and neck.

Primping was hardly in her vocabulary, but tonight seemed special. He'd actually asked to spend time alone with her. And she had words to say to him alone. Part of her was still upset with him.

Part of her couldn't wait to have him to herself for a while.

She reined in her errant thoughts. The reason she'd agreed to sit with him was she didn't want her boys hero-worshiping a lawman who was only a step better—and certainly no less dangerous—than the outlaws he tracked.

But as the thoughts formed, Isabel dabbed a drop of rose water on her throat and wondered if the other ideas floating around in her mind about him weren't even more dangerous.

She had to stop this growing infatuation. Maybe one of Nana's potions will do the trick, she told herself wryly.

Right now, bats' tongues and boiled cactus root, buried at midnight under the full moon, seemed the only way she'd ever fully get Jake Coulter out of her system. And if she didn't get over this foolhardy attraction to him soon, she might be willing to give that remedy a try.

Isabel found Jake lounging on the long couch in front of a blazing fire, his leg propped on an embroidered footstool. His broad shoulders stretched the width of the couch. She couldn't help but notice he'd unbuttoned the top few buttons of his flannel shirt, revealing a glimpse of coppery skin and coffee-colored silken hairs.

"You certainly look comfortable," she said, trying not to stare.

When she walked in, he straightened and grazed her from head to toe. "And you look—different. More like you looked last night. Pretty."

"As opposed to my usual not-pretty."

"I didn't mean that," he said. "It's just that you look more…relaxed. Maybe it's your hair. It's nice to see it down. What I'm trying to tell you is that I like the way you look. You're a beautiful woman, Isabel. You ought to be told that."

She flushed, hiding her discomfort at the warmth his words evoked by moving briskly to a chair next to him.

"Just like my boys *ought* to be told they need to learn to kill?"

Jake sat up a little. "Changing the subject, are we? Although I had a feeling that was coming."

"I don't want them thinking that killing is the only resolution to a problem."

"Neither do I. That was the point. But maybe I didn't make it too well. I'm not used to talking to youngsters." He looked away, absently running his fingers over the edge of the glass in his hand. "From as far back as I can remember, my pa always said things straight, no matter how ugly. He said the sooner I learned the way of things, the longer I'd live. Something about talking to your boys tonight reminded me of that."

Taken back by the sincerity in his voice, Isabel felt her irritation subside. "If you were trying to warn them about the dangers of growing up here, I thank you. It's just, I've tried to raise them up to respect life, to protect and nourish it."

"You're a wise woman," Jake said, holding up his glass in salute to her. "Your boys are lucky to have you."

"I can't believe your mother never tried to instill the same things in you." She gave a little laugh to cover her awkwardness. "Most mothers feel compelled to do that."

"My ma died when I was just a boy. I don't even remember the sound of her voice." His gaze drifted to the hearth, settling on the blue tinted flames. "From now on I'll let you choose the bedtime stories."

Suddenly Isabel felt all twisted up inside. Jake Coulter, surrendering that easily? How was she supposed to react to that?

She struggled to read him, but his expression offered her no hint of his true thoughts. "They enjoyed your story. All I meant was, that would have been enough."

Jake rubbed at the moisture on his glass. "Of course," he said at last, his voice low and graveled, full of an intense emotion she couldn't explain.

The sound of it silenced any inclination on her part to continue their discussion. She'd fully intended to set him straight about what to say and not to say in front of her sons. But somehow all of her words no longer mattered.

He understood far better than she expected. She felt it, heard it in his voice and in the silent language of his body's retreat. Instead, her only urge now was to comfort him, to help him, in the same way he had offered his help to her, easily, without expecting any return.

"By the way," she began in what must have seemed to him a strangely light tone, "I meant to tell you...I like the way you look tonight, too."

After the words sank in, he lifted his eyes and glanced over to her. "If that's true, you'd better enjoy it while you can. I only shave when I'm in the company of civilized folks."

"I suppose that's not often and always temporary, considering what you do." The words slipped out before she could catch herself. She regretted them at once.

Jake didn't respond, instead pouring a generous splash of brandy into a small glass and handing it to her.

"To your speedy recovery," Isabel said and lifted her glass.

Jake started to reciprocate the toast then stopped,

twirling the glass in his hand. "Somehow the sound of that doesn't have the same appeal it would have the day I got here."

"What do you mean?"

He shifted against the cushions, straightened a little and stared into his glass. A heavy wave of dark hair fell loose over his brow and Isabel's fingers curled with the impulse to brush it back.

"Nothing," he muttered, taking a long draw on the brandy. "Only that mattress up there is beginning to feel a hell of a lot better than the rocks and sagebrush I usually bed down in."

"Ah," Isabel said softly. She took a sip of her own brandy and looked to the fire.

She sounded almost disappointed, Jake thought. Disappointed because she expected a different response from him, or because she wanted him out of her life and away from her family?

Looking at her, he saw nothing in her expression but a pensiveness that could mean anything. He meant to turn away but his eyes stubbornly stayed on her profile. The glow of the firelight warmed her skin and wove pure gold into the rippled silk of her hair. His hand clenched around the glass at the thought of touching her, running his hands over her, losing himself in her warmth.

Once, when he'd believed in forever, he'd dreamed of having a woman like her—beautiful, giving, passionate about living and loving. Now he knew *forever* was just a word. And he'd learned a hard lesson about the danger of dreaming.

Cursing under his breath, Jake forced himself to look away. If it weren't for his damned leg he wouldn't be here now, making himself crazy over something he could never have.

He'd considered leaving. But he had little choice of accommodations in Whispering Creek. And he half suspected Isabel meant more to Grey than she confessed. If Grey came back for her, Jake couldn't be better situated to both corner his prey and protect Isabel and her family at the same time.

Besides, much as he hated to admit it, he still needed Isabel's help with his leg. She was the only one who could heal him, in body if not in spirit.

Jake swirled the brandy in his glass, working to hide the frustration snapping at him. "You know," he said, to break the silence more than because he had anything to say, "this is one of the small things I miss about the last comfortable place I stayed."

"Where was that?"

"Home."

At first Isabel thought she'd misheard him. Not once had he ever used the word *home*. "You had a home?"

"You look surprised," he said, smiling a little.

"Do you blame me?"

Jake laughed wryly. "No."

"I just never imagined you—settled." Even now, the image of Jake choosing to stay in one place seemed impossible. "What happened?"

"Fire," he said shortly. "Took me two full years to build that house. It was a fine little hacienda. Built solid and tight. I finished it just in time."

"In time for what?"

"For the birth of my son."

Isabel sat stunned a moment, simply staring at him. Then, without thinking, she gulped down the rest of her brandy. It burned down her throat, more fiery than the hottest green *chile* she'd ever tasted. For a single instant, she wasn't sure which was worse, the ache in her throat or the pain she clearly felt in him. "You had a son?"

"A baby boy. He died in the fire."

"And his mother?" Isabel dared, her heart breaking for him.

"His mother, too. I wasn't there. I couldn't get to them in time." Jake tossed back the rest of his brandy. The muscle along his jaw tightened.

For a long moment, Isabel wasn't certain he'd continue. Then he said, so low she wasn't sure if he was talking to her or himself, "I didn't save them. In fact, days passed before I found them. If I'd been home, where I belonged, they'd still be alive. Instead, I was out trailing a gang of train robbers."

"I—I'm so sorry, Jake." Isabel couldn't stop herself from kneeling beside him and touching her hand to his arm. "I'm sure you thought you were doing the right thing at the time."

"I did. We were protecting the town from a gang that was on its way to San Antonio. Except I should have been home, protecting my own. So—" he looked at her, attempting a nonchalance he didn't feel "—now I have the trail to call home and no regrets."

"You're a liar," she said softly.

"Think so? Well, you're right about one thing. I don't have any business telling your sons how to grow up. I don't know that I would have been much good at it with my own boy." He paused, then added, "but I would have liked to try."

"Oh, Jake…"

Tears shimmered in her eyes and he touched his fingertip to her cheek as one slipped free. "Are you crying for me, angel? Don't. You'll only hurt yourself."

"Maybe. But I'm willing to take that risk."

Her tender words so moved Jake that for minutes he couldn't speak. They sat for a timeless silence, she leaning to rest her cheek against his thigh. He stroked his hand over her hair, finding solace in the simple caress.

"What are you thinking?" he asked at last.

"That at least you came home."

"What?"

"My husband would never have known if we had lived or died. Once he walked out that door, we never heard from him again. Not until the wire came telling us he was dead."

"The man must have been crazy, a fool or both." His hand slid to her chin, lifting her face to his.

The stroke of Jake's fingers against her skin left her breathless. Isabel's lips parted, seeing the fire now in his eyes and anticipating his kiss with a need equaling his.

He bent to her, his mouth just grazing hers before a furious pounding at the front door startled them apart.

They stared at each other before Isabel, grasping at her senses, broke free and scrambled to her feet. "I can't imagine who it can be."

"Whoever it is, I hope for their sake it's life or death," Jake said darkly, following her, limping, to the door. He moved beside her as she pulled it open.

"Cal?" Surprise vying with concern, she ushered him in. "You're drenched. What in the world are you doing out at this hour, in this storm?"

"Sorry to barge in on you, Belle," Cal said. He gave

a hoarse rasping cough then ignored Isabel's frown. "I need to talk to Jake."

Jake stepped in front of Isabel. "What's happened?"

"There's been a robbery at a mine near Taos. Looks like Grey's work. I've got a posse rounded up, but I'd like to have you along with us."

Isabel started to protest, but Jake didn't give her a chance.

"Just give me a minute to get my guns."

## Chapter Eight

"You can't—" Isabel found herself talking to Jake's retreating back as she turned from Cal. She hurried after him, stopping him with a hand on his arm as he started up the stairs. "Are you crazier than I think you are? It's only been a short time since I took a bullet out of your leg. You can't go riding off in this storm, chasing after Jerico and who knows how many others. You'll tear the wound right open."

"I haven't spent the last six months chasing Grey all over Texas and this territory to pass up a chance to find him now." Shaking off her hand, he started up the stairs, Isabel close on his heels.

"Cal said he has a posse formed. Let them do the job."

"It's not their job to do." Jake pushed inside his room, grabbing his gun belt and buckling it over his hips. He pulled on his duster, shoved on his hat and turned to leave, finding Isabel blocking the door. "I don't think you're big enough to stop me, and this time I'm not going to willingly swallow one of your sleeping potions."

"Jake..." Isabel wanted to say something to him,

anything to keep him from riding off on a fool's mission. She told herself it was because she worried about his leg. She feared it was because she cared about what happened to him.

"Don't say anything, it won't make any difference," he said softly. Coming up to her, he looked down at her a long moment, his gaze intense as if he wanted to memorize the look in hers.

Gently, he rubbed his knuckles against her cheek, his touch almost tentative. "Have some of those weeds ready for me when I get back. I think I'll need them."

Isabel didn't trust herself to speak and only nodded. Stepping aside, she let him move past her and down the stairs, following him down and out to the front porch. She watched as he pulled himself into the saddle in one lithe motion, waiting until the storm and darkness swallowed him before going back into the sanctuary of her house.

Knowing she watched him go, Jake pushed aside the feeling he was abandoning her for the sake of the job. This wasn't San Antonio and she wasn't Lily. The only thing Isabel Bradshaw meant to him was a temporary haven. If he could just convince himself of that, the rest would be easy.

The hour's ride to the Lucky Dog Mine was enough to put aside anything on his mind but the stinging slap of rain and wind and the knifing pain in his leg. Limping around Isabel's house, he'd almost forgotten the pain; riding at full gallop over uneven ground, it returned full force.

But he'd crawl on hands and knees if it meant finally catching up to Jerico Grey. By the time he, Cal and the five men making up the posse reached the mine, Jake wondered if he'd have to do just that.

They pulled up on a ridge overlooking the mining camp, and Cal nudged his horse up beside Jake's. "Dark enough to scare a bat and with this damned storm we wouldn't hear a stampede if it was nippin' at our heels. You think he's still around?"

"Probably not," Jake said, hearing the frustration in his voice even as he shouted to be heard above the storm. "But I wouldn't take that for granted. Last I saw him, Grey had three men riding with him. Riding in blind isn't my first choice."

Cal nodded in agreement. "I'll send the rest of 'em circling around to make sure we don't run into any surprises. Then we can check out the office."

Leaving Cal to organize the posse, Jake slid off his horse, steadying himself a moment as his injured leg threatened to buckle. Then, unholstering one of his Colts, he started down the ridge toward the office.

He edged his way down the muddy slope, working his way over the rain-slick ground to the rough wooden shack that served as the mining office. The darkness, broken only by slashes of lightning, made it nearly impossible to know if anyone was near the mine, let alone if anything was in his path.

Jake reached the door of the office and felt a hand on his shoulder. "Anything?" Cal asked, close to his ear.

"No, there's not much chance anyone is still here. But they may have left someone behind. Who told you about the robbery?"

"One of the two men the mine hired as security. Seems they got nervous about all the robberies close by. Man says three of 'em came in a few hours after the mine closed. He'd been checkin' the first shaft and was on his way back when he saw these three jump his partner. He didn't stick around but hightailed it to town.'' Cal spit at the ground. ''A real hero.''

''Let's see if we can find his friend.'' Jake eased open the door to the office, Cal, breathing hard, at his back. An empty silence greeted them.

Cal fumbled around until he found a lantern and coaxed a flame from it. When he held it aloft, Jake could see whoever had been here had left the office in a shambles. The safe lay on its side in a corner, its door blown off the hinges.

As Cal searched the room, Jake moved out the back door to check outside again for the missing guard. He nearly tripped over the man, sprawled out a few feet from the rear of the building. When Cal came up behind with the lantern, Jake could see the man had taken a bullet in the chest.

''Not much we can do here but get him back to Belle,'' Cal said, ''though I don't think she'll be able to do much for him.''

Jake nodded, feeling a tight knot of frustration inside. He helped Cal get the man up so they could carry him back to the horses, but his mind worried at the details of the robbery.

Cal would write it up as another of Grey's robberies, but Jake wasn't so sure. Grey's path was heading straight back to Whispering Creek, of that he was certain. Why, he wasn't sure, yet. But would Grey dare show up there tonight?

By the time he and Cal had rounded up the rest of the posse and gotten back to Isabel's house, soaked to the bone, his thigh aching like the devil, the only thing Jake was truly certain of was he was ready to fall off his horse. His leg felt like it was on fire and when he slid out of the saddle, it was even odds whether it would support his weight.

Isabel met him at the door, reaching out to take his arm before he'd made it across the porch. "I would say I told you so, but you look like you don't need a reminder. Come inside and I'll—"

"There's someone else who needs you more than I do," Jake said, gesturing to the wounded guard Cal and two men from the posse were carrying to Isabel's front door.

"Put him over by the fire," Isabel said, hurrying ahead to clear a place on the couch.

The commotion drew Esme and Katlyn from their beds, and as Isabel ran out back to pump fresh water, she saw Matt and Nate peeking around the kitchen corner.

"Mama?" Matt said. "What's wrong?"

"Jake and Sheriff Reed brought back someone who's hurt. It's all right, I'll take care of him. You go on back to bed."

"Yes, yes, come, *mis hijos*," Esme prodded, coming up behind Isabel. "You can best help by getting back into your beds."

Isabel left Esme to care for the boys, and sent Katlyn to the kitchen to make coffee for Cal and the rest of the posse. To her surprise, Jake stayed behind, standing near as she pulled aside the guard's vest and shirt to get a look at his wound.

"What can I do?" he asked.

"You don't need to—" She stopped at the look on his face and said instead, "Start handing me cloths from that pile. I need to get some of this blood and mud washed away so I can see how best to stop the bleeding."

For the next hour, Jake stayed by her side, watching as she worked feverishly over the guard, refusing to admit defeat even when he could see she was fast losing the battle to save the man's life.

She channeled all of herself into the fight—spirit, mind and body—giving Jake a new appreciation for her skill and dedication. At the same time, watching her became painful. He had to stop himself from pulling her away, telling her to surrender to the inevitable, knowing only she could make that decision.

Finally, Isabel gave a ragged sigh and closed her eyes. She laid a hand on the guard's shoulder and crossed herself, quietly murmuring a prayer before stepping back. Her shoulders slumped as she sank into a chair, putting a shaking hand to her temple.

That defeated air, so unlike her, moved Jake to go to her, bending on one knee beside her and taking her hand in both of his. "Isabel...you did everything you could."

"If I could have seen him sooner—"

"Nothing would have changed. You know that." He gently put his fingers to her chin, turning her to face him. "You know that. You can't save everyone."

"This from a man who's sworn to protect nearly everyone," she said, trying and failing a shaky smile. "I understand here." She touched her forehead. "It's here," she said as she touched her heart, "I have problems."

Not sure what he could say to comfort her, Jake put an arm around her shoulders and pulled her against his chest. She leaned against him for several minutes, her silent tears wetting his damp shirt, her body trembling with emotion and exhaustion.

She pulled back only when Cal appeared at the doorway, looking from where Jake and Isabel sat to the man on the couch. "I'll get some of these boys to take him to the jail. He can stay there until morning."

When Cal and the men from the posse had taken the guard and started for the jail, Isabel at last took a good look at Jake, seeing the lines of pain etched in his forehead and the return of his pronounced limp.

"Go on up and get those wet clothes off. I'll be there in a minute to look at that leg."

He only nodded, too tired and in pain to think of a suitable rejoinder. By the time he'd dragged himself up the stairs to his room, stripped off his damp clothes, washed away the mud and grime, and crawled into bed, Jake decided he could sleep for a few days with or without one of the disgusting-tasting elixirs she was sure to bring.

He moved enough only to open his eyes when Isabel came into the room, setting down the tray she carried by his bedside. "You can skip the lecture," he said when she started to speak.

"I wasn't going to say anything. Let me see how much of my work you've undone," she said, pulling back the edge of the quilt to bare his leg to her scrutiny. She gathered her courage to voice the question haunting her. "Was it Jerico?" she asked, averting her eyes from his scrutiny while she lifted away the old bandage.

"I don't know."

Isabel looked up in surprise. "But I thought Cal said—"

"I know what he said. But Grey's been lying low since he crossed the border. He's wanted in this territory for more than a dozen robberies. My guess is he's looking to come back to Whispering Creek, get his gold or whatever it is he's heading here for and move on up north. Once he gets what he wants here, it's only a few days' ride to the Colorado border. And far as I know, that's one place he isn't a wanted man. Yet.''

"But you'll follow him there if you have to."

Jake shrugged. "I'm planning on leading him in the opposite direction. He murdered an innocent man just outside San Antonio. Left an invalid widow to feed seven children. I won't rest until I see his neck in a noose for that."

"You've probably set yourself back weeks tonight," she murmured, hoping to distract Jake from talk of Jerico.

Jake winced as she pressed a soaked cloth to his thigh. She stroked her fingers over the ache, easing it a little with her soothing touch.

He tried to focus his thoughts back on Grey and away from her disturbing nearness. "He knows I and lawmen all over Taos County are looking for him. Why take the chance of getting caught by pulling another robbery so close to town?"

Isabel sighed. Obviously, there was no stopping this man once he got his mind set on a thing. "Greed?"

Jake shook his head. "Grey may love money, but he's not stupid. I'm beginning to wonder if the rumors about him stashing gold in the mountains are true."

"He left it here, all these years? I can't believe that."

"I trailed Grey from Texas straight back here. There's something here he wants. But it must be somewhere he can't easily get to. Or it's something besides the gold." He looked directly at her, his eyes challenging. "Someone, perhaps."

Isabel avoided his probing stare. She briefly considered his suggestion, then shook her head. "I can't imagine where or what—or who."

"I guess I'm not going to find the answer tonight," Jake said. He groaned at the pain in his leg, leaned back against the propped-up pillows and closed his eyes as Isabel finished rebandaging his leg and pulled the quilt back over him.

"I told you not to go," she said softly, touching his forehead.

"I told you I had to. That's why I'm here."

"Mmm...well, you won't be here much longer if you keep reopening this wound. Here—" She handed him a mug of tea brewed with willow and sage. "Get some rest. It's nearly dawn."

She started to move away. But Jake put the mug on the bedside table and reached out and took her hand, stopping her.

"Isabel..."

His hesitation surprised her. She could see the indecision on his face, as if he wasn't sure what he wanted to say—or not certain if he wanted to say anything at all.

She didn't know how to respond and didn't know if she wanted to now, in the waning hours of the night when despair reached its zenith and she most needed comfort. She didn't want his pity, and she didn't want to take solace from him, knowing it would be fleeting.

Jake recognized the conflict in her eyes. Reason told him he should let her go. He should turn away from her before his thoughts turned to the softness of her full lips, the memory of how they felt burning beneath his. He should say good-night.

Instead, he slid his hand from hers, up her arm, until his fingers tangled in her hair at her nape. He pulled her to him even as she moved forward to reach for him.

The moment her mouth met his and he tasted her on his tongue Jake knew he was setting them both up for more pain. After all the years of being alone, riding with ghosts and thieves at his back, a dangerous warmth began creeping into the emptiness in his heart. She threatened to turn his life on its head, yet feeling her pressed against him, the abandonment of her kiss, he wasn't sure if he cared.

Half lying across Jake's chest, Isabel felt an almost urgent need to lose herself in his strength. A wildness rushed through her blood, making her light-headed with wanting, needing. She couldn't think, couldn't remember why she shouldn't be here, in his bed, in his arms, wanting so much more than just his kiss.

Jake fought the urge to press her back against the bed and take the paradise she offered. The sharp ache of desire tightening his body was more painful than the pain in his leg.

But he sensed the desperation lacing the passion in her. She needed, she deserved more than a few hours of stolen pleasure. And he couldn't give that to her.

Isabel felt his withdrawal even before his mouth slid from hers and tried to push away the hurt it caused. She struggled up, hoping her trembling legs would carry her out his door.

Jake started out of the bed after her but she stopped him with a raised hand. "Don't. Just…let me go. I know what you're going to say."

"I can't promise you anything beyond tonight. That's not what you want."

"You don't know what I want, Jake Coulter. You don't know anything about me."

The door shut behind her, leaving him alone to face what he did know about her.

*But you're wrong about one thing, angel,* he told her silently. *I know you want more than memories of a few nights' loving.*

She needed everything. And tonight, he wanted to be the one to give it all to her.

Except he was the last man who could, though she was the first woman to stir doubt in him about the path he'd chosen. With Lily, he'd been sure of what he wanted. Isabel made him wonder if what he wanted was only a fraction of what real love could offer.

It was a crazy notion, not worth considering.

Yet the uneasy thought and his last image of her, tears shimmering in her eyes, her unbound hair a golden halo, stayed with him until after dawn broke, making him feel his aloneness as never before.


Bright morning sunlight beamed through the kitchen window and Nate, sitting across the kitchen table from Matt, glanced conspiratorially over his shoulder.

Finding Nana absorbed in frying bacon and keeping an eye on her baking biscuits, Nate leaned close to whisper to his brother.

"Mr. Coulter thinks Jerico Grey hid a bunch of gold somewhere around here. He said that's why Grey's coming back."

"Stolen treasure?!" Wide-eyed, Matt gulped down his milk. "Did he say how much?"

"I couldn't hear too much. He and Mama were talking low. It was real late. I had to sneak up the stairs to listen. It was your snorin' that woke me in the first place."

"I don't snore. Take it back!"

Esme turned to look at the boys, brandishing a wooden spoon. "Enough! Finish your breakfast or you will be late for lessons."

"Where's Mama?" Nate asked, snatching a biscuit from the fresh batch Esme laid on the table.

"Your mama is not yet awake."

"She's probably tired. She was up all night with Mr. Coulter trying to figure out where Jerico Grey stashed his gold!" Matt regretted what he'd said even before Nate slapped the heel of his palm to his forehead in exasperation.

"Tell everyone in town, why don't you?"

"Nana knows already, don't you, Nana?"

"All I know is both of you are filling up on dangerous nonsense instead of biscuits."

"What kind of dangerous nonsense?" Isabel wandered into the room sleepy-eyed, her mind clouded after her short, fitful rest.

"*Ay,* that devil you brought into our home has their minds running wild with notions of hidden treasure. They should be thinking of doing sums and reading books, not such wickedness."

Pouring a cup of coffee, Isabel took a seat near the boys. "Nate, Matt, is this true?"

Nate's chin went up defiantly. "I heard, Mama. Jerico Grey hid some gold or money here and he's coming back for it now."

"No one knows that for sure. Least of all boys who ought to be in bed, instead of listening to someone else's conversation." Isabel suddenly wondered what else Nate had overheard. "What else did you hear, Nate, exactly?"

"Nothin' much," Nate mumbled. He crumbled an edge of his biscuit between his fingers. "You were talking about the gold and Jerico Grey and then it got real quiet. I got tired of waiting so I went back to bed.''

Isabel felt her grandmother's eyes boring into her and her own face grow hot at Nate's innocent words. She tried to ignore both and put on a sufficiently stern facade. ''Well, whatever you heard, it was too much. If I catch you eavesdropping again, young man, I'll box your ears. Is that clear?''

Nate ducked his head. ''Yes, Mama.''

''Good. Now as to the story about hidden treasure, it's only a rumor. There is no gold hidden anywhere around here.''

''Mornin'.'' Jake's voice, heavy with lack of sleep, more a growl than anything human, cut short Isabel's attempt to quell the boys' excitement. He limped heavily into the kitchen, looking rumpled, the shadow of a beard darkening his jaw.

''You'll tell us the truth, won't you, Mr. Coulter?'' Matt piped up before Isabel could stop him.

''That's quite a first question for the day. Truth about what?''

''Matt—'' Isabel began warningly.

Esme shot Jake a glare cold enough to freeze fire and let him pour his own coffee. Jake nodded to her but decided against attempting any other greeting. He was too tired and too sore to do battle with the house's resident witch.

Matt got up to take his plate to the sink. ''About the treasure. Did Jerico Grey hide treasure here or not?''

Jake made his way to the table and eased himself onto the bench across from Isabel. They looked at each other with the weight of the night between them. Jake had never seen her so weary. Her cheeks had lost their glow, her eyes their sparkle. Because of him. He'd moved in and brought trouble with him.

He ought to leave, and yet…leave her now? He didn't want to imagine what might happen.

"Truth is, I don't know the truth, Matt," he finally said, banishing the ghosts in his mind. "There's a lot I'm still trying to figure out."

"Well, why else would he come back?" Nate asked point blank.

"You've been thinking about this, haven't you, son?"

"He's been doing some sneaking around closed doors," Isabel said shortly. "I thought I made it clear, this wasn't your business, Nate."

"But what else is there to think about, Mama? Nothing this exciting ever happens in this town."

"I will show you much excitement if you two do not take these lunch pails and leave for your lessons now. *¡Vayanse!* Go! *¡Pronto!*" Waving her wooden weapon, Esme shoved the pails in the boys' hands and shooed them out of the kitchen.

"Okay, okay!" Grumbling and casting Esme disgruntled looks, the boys shuffled out the door, waving to Isabel as they went.

As the door closed, Esme began clattering pans with unnecessary vigor. "Dirt, blood—we will be cleaning all day."

"That couldn't be helped, Nana. A man was dying. You wouldn't have had me turn him away for any reason, and you know it."

"I know only that *he*—" she looked pointedly at Jake "—has brought nothing but problems to this house. Only you refuse to see it, Granddaughter."

With that, Esme stalked from the kitchen, letting the door slam shut behind her.

Isabel turned to Jake and held out a hand. "She worries for me, too much sometimes."

"And I'm the devil come to corrupt her angel. I suppose this is her doing." Jake pulled a twisted bit of leather from his pocket and handed it to Isabel. "I found it outside my door this morning."

She looked at the three blue, yellow and black strips twined together and suddenly burst out laughing.

"Are you going to let me in on the joke?" Jake asked, beginning to suspect the little scrap had some nefarious meaning.

"Oh...I—I'm—it's..." Laughing so hard tears welled in her eyes, Isabel had to stop and catch her breath before she could continue. "I'm sorry," she managed to gasp at last, swiping at the wetness on her cheeks. "It's just, of all things she chose—that."

"Should I be impressed or worried?"

"Neither. It's just one of Nana's curses, a very old one."

"So what is this—" Jake prodded the leather with his fingertip "—supposed to do?"

"It's, um, a charm for making a man, well...let's just say, Nana intended to severely limit your nighttime activities."

"I don't see much charm in that," Jake muttered. "Is that the kind of trouble I'm supposed to have brought you?"

He posed the question casually enough, but the glint in his eyes told Isabel he was baiting her. She smiled sweetly. "It's rather late in the day for her to be worrying about my virtue, don't you think?"

"Oh, I wouldn't say that," he drawled. A slow smile

spread across his mouth. "You have a number of worthy virtues, angel."

Hectic color flooded her cheeks and Jake's smile broadened into a grin.

"Well, being a good housekeeper isn't one of them," she said, feeling ridiculously flustered by him and his provocative insinuations. "I have too much work to do this morning, and I have to confess, after last night, after losing him..." Her voice trailed off. She sat absently fidgeting with her spoon.

Jake reached across the table and quieted her small hand, enveloping it in his. "You gave him all you had to give and more. Nothing short of a miracle could have saved him."

Isabel raised her eyes to meet his. "You sound like you mean that."

"You know I do." Gently he turned her hand over in his palm and stroked it with his index finger. "I've never seen anyone give so much of herself, care so much she'll break her heart over a stranger. You're a special woman, Isabel."

The tenderness of his touch and his words sent a stream of warmth through her. Dark circles shadowed his eyes, yet there she saw sincerity and pain, caring and regret.

When he released her hand she smiled tentatively at him. "Why don't you go back upstairs and rest? You look awful."

"Thank you, ma'am. Allow me to say the same about you."

Isabel laughed. "That came out wrong. You know what I meant."

"What I know is that there's work to be done around here today. And I've always found hard work to be the

best cure for a heavy heart or a burdened mind. Since
we both have a little of each, what do you say we help
each other? I'll tackle your roof.'' Jake took a long
draught of his coffee before shoving away from the
table. ''Now, where did you say those nails are?''

''I didn't.'' Isabel stared at her mug, not trusting
herself to look at him.

''Look, if it makes you feel better, this is selfish.
Lying around up in that room all day is about the worst
torture I can imagine. Why can't you just accept my
help and be done with it?''

Slowly, Isabel looked up and met his questioning
gaze. ''Because I don't want to need you. For anything.''

Jake stood silent a moment. Yet how could he blame
her, considering her past? He felt an odd, painful mixture of respect for her proud independence and regret
she felt compelled to use it to build a wall against him.

He didn't want her to start depending on him. He
didn't dare let that happen. She'd only hate him the
day he walked out on her. But he did want to help.
Anyone would, he assured himself, considering the
care she had shown him.

''Think of it this way,'' he said, trying for an offhand
tone. ''If I weren't here, you'd be paying to get the
roof fixed.''

Isabel frowned, tapping her fingers against the table.

''Damn woman, you're stubborn.''

''Look who's talking.''

''Fine, how about you just think of it as a way to
pay you back for all of your doctoring? I'm sure other
folks pay you with goods and deeds. Isabel—'' he covered her hand with his again ''—there's no crime in
letting someone help you. Even me.''

Isabel tried to consider his offer reasonably, finding it difficult with his callused fingers creating a pleasurable friction against her skin.

She could ill afford to hire someone to repair the roof. And the truth was she'd only been up on a roof a few times in her life and it wasn't an experience she was eager to repeat.

"All right," she said at last. "I admit, I'll sleep better knowing my roof isn't going to fall in next time it rains."

"I hope getting those words out didn't hurt too much," Jake said. Moving with difficulty to his feet, he started toward the door, then looked back at her over his shoulder. "I know how you feel about asking for help. If it makes you feel any better," he said with a wink and a grin, "I'll let you thank me properly later."

# Chapter Nine

By early afternoon, Isabel had finished grinding the last of the Kinnikinnick leaves. Humming to herself, she sifted the coarse powder into a jar and sealed it tightly.

She was glad to have finished the tedious job before the boys returned home from school. Expecting them any minute, she hurried to tidy up the counter in her shop. She wiped off bits of leaves, seeds and roots that had spilled, polishing several jars and setting them back on her shelves, then swept the floor.

When the shop door opened she looked up with a smile, expecting Matt and Nate. Instead Katlyn plunged in, carrying an armful of books and papers which she dumped, as usual, in a heap right onto Isabel's clean counter.

"You're working, I guess that's a good sign." When Isabel looked confused she added, "I only meant Matt must be feeling better or I know you'd be sitting with him."

"Feeling better…? What are you talking about?"

"Matt, and his stomachache." It was Katlyn's turn to look bewildered. "Nate took him home a few hours

ago when Matt said his stomach was hurting. He
seemed truly to be in pain so I let Nate leave as well
to make sure he got here safely...." She trailed off,
biting her lower lip as she watched Isabel's expression
look increasingly worried.

Isabel fought a sudden irrational surge of panic, telling herself the boys had probably decided playing hide-
and-seek in the meadow was more exciting than working sums. "But they're not here," she said as calmly
as possible. "I haven't seen them since this morning."

"Then—I don't know where they might be. I hon-
estly thought Matt was ill," Katlyn said, holding out
her hand in a little pleading gesture.

"I've got to find them." Isabel threw aside her
broom and, without waiting for Katlyn, hurried into the
house to find Esme. She ran around the corner, heading
for the kitchen, and nearly cannoned into Jake as he
stepped down from the last stair.

"Whoa, there," he said, catching her lightly with
both hands on her shoulders. "Where's the devil on
your tail?"

"Matt and Nate are missing," she blurted out before
she could think not to.

Jake scowled. "Missing? Are you sure? Boys are apt
to run off and play the moment they're free from lessons, aren't they?"

"Katlyn said Matt told her he was ill today so he
and Nate could leave school early. They've gone somewhere, for some particular reason, I just don't know
where or why! They've never lied or sneaked off like
this. I'm worried."

"Take it easy," he said, smoothing a hand over her
hair in a soothing motion. "We'll find them." When
Isabel looked at him in surprise and started to protest,

Jake stopped her with his finger on her lips. "Don't tell me you don't want my expert help. Hey, I'm used to tracking murderers and thieves over frontier territory. How hard can it be to find two small boys who've got to be close to home?"

"I hope that's true, but—"

"What is all the noise here?" Esme demanded, pushing open the kitchen door. She held a large carving knife and eyed Jake's hand still on Isabel's shoulder before turning to her granddaughter. "What is wrong?"

Briefly, Isabel explained. Despite Esme's disapproval, she made no attempt to move away from Jake's touch. He felt steadying, a comfort that helped keep her rising sense of alarm at bay. By the time she'd finished, Katlyn had joined them.

"I looked in their room and called out back," Katlyn said, her brows drawn together in concern. "They're not here. Maybe one of the other boys would know. Matt and Nate are great friends with Tommy and Luke Parker. They might have told them something."

"The Parker ranch is almost a half hour's ride from here," Isabel said, although she admitted talking to the Parker boys might be the best course of action. Speculating where Matt and Nate had gone could lead them on several useless searches.

"Is there a cave near here?" Jake asked abruptly.

"A cave?" Isabel repeated, not understanding why he would want to know.

"A cave. Where an outlaw could hide stolen gold."

Realization started to dawn on Isabel. "Of course, that's all they talked about at breakfast. But where—?"

"Surely they would not be so foolish," Esme mut-

tered. She stopped herself. "Then again, they are boys.
A man might very well be so *loco* as to look for an
impossible treasure, and boys and men are not so very
different."

"Where?" Jake repeated, trying to ignore the old
woman's palpable disdain. He came close to Isabel,
gripping her arms. "You know this area. I don't think
they would go blindly searching for a cave. They had
to have something in mind."

"Yes..." Isabel thought a few moments before seiz-
ing on an idea. "There is a small cave, in the foothills
behind the community house where they take their lessons. But it's difficult to get to and how can we be
certain that's where they've gone?"

"We can't, but I'd say it's a good bet for a place to
start looking. Katlyn, you get word to Cal and he can
check at the Parker ranch while we go find that cave."

"I'm on my way," Katlyn said, grabbing her bonnet.
"When we find them, I'll turn them both over my knee
for weaseling out of my classroom like that!"

Jake saw fear and fury rising in equal measure in
Isabel's eyes. "I think you'll have to wait in line," he
said as Katlyn rushed past him.

"They're my boys. I'll go. You can't—" Isabel began, but her protest died at the warning in his eyes.

"Not without me. Can you ride or do we need a
wagon?"

Esme gave a snort of derision. "A wagon? Ha! She
will be your equal in the saddle, be assured, Señor
Coulter. We Castillo women do not raise our daughters
to be the fainting violets you are used to! I will wait
here in case they come home," she said to Isabel, then
waved both hands, sending them away. "Now, go!"

"Give me a minute to change," Isabel told Jake, not

giving herself time to think. "I'll meet you at the barn."

He nodded, and she hurried to her room to pull on a pair of leather pants and cotton shirt. The pants had belonged to Douglas, but he'd abandoned most of his clothing. Isabel had altered them to fit, finding them far more practical than petticoats and a skirt.

She'd long ago tossed convention aside. Women's clothes only got in her way when she had to ride hard, as often she did when reaching someone quickly meant the difference between life or death. She grabbed her battered wide-brimmed hat and ran out the back door to the barn.

Jake was there, holding the reins of their horses already saddled and ready. He'd strapped on his six-shooters, she noticed. They hung on his wide black belt, slung low across his hips, drawing level to his fingertips. She saw he'd also buckled a garter to his right leg with a menacing-looking long knife thrust in its scabbard.

He handed her her reins then threw a leg up over his horse, the dark denim of his pants molding a muscular thigh as his heavy black duster slipped to one side. He tugged at the rawhide rope that hung from his saddle then pulled his broad-brimmed hat low on his brow. The look of him and his sheer size in the saddle cut a menacing figure, enough to cause anyone who crossed his path to want to turn and ride the other way.

Yet right now, Isabel found his huge form reassuring rather than unnerving. She had to admit, if only to herself, right now she needed his strength, wanted his protection. She breathed a silent thanks for his clear determination, knowing nothing would stop him from bringing Matt and Nate home safely.

Isabel looked as if she'd take on Satan himself to find her boys, Jake thought as she easily lifted herself into the saddle. He tried not to let his eyes stray to the long legs and womanly curves embraced by the supple leather pants. "You look like you've done this before," he said gruffly, yanking his hat a little farther down his face.

"Not all the people who need healing live in town or end up in one of Elish's beds. If I have to get somewhere quickly, riding is easiest without a skirt." Wheeling her horse around she kicked it into gallop in the direction of the meadow.

Jake urged his horse after her, cursing the protesting pain in his leg. It took them nearly an hour to ride out of town, through the cedars and junipers that lined the old Pioneer Pass and up into the rocky foothills of the mountains. When they reached a level spot near a creek, Isabel slid off her horse. Jake followed suit and after letting the horses take their fill of the water, they tethered them to a stand of ponderosa pines.

Squirrels scurried boldly underfoot and scampered up and down tree trunks nearby. From a distance, a wolf howled long and low. Isabel shivered at the sound.

"We'll have to walk from here, up there," she said, pointing almost straight up above their heads. The vague outline of a rugged trail led up, then sloped downward into darkness.

"It's not an easy path," she added, with a meaningful look at his leg.

"It's a little late to be telling me that. And you should know by now, I never take the easy path," Jake said, with a little sardonic laugh. He grabbed a long stick to use as a support and looped a coil of rope over his shoulder and arm. He then grabbed the lantern he'd tied to the horse's saddle and held up a hand, inviting her to lead the way. "After you, ma'am."

They'd better be here, Jake thought, by the time they'd reached the spot where the path angled downward. The climb wouldn't have been easy with two good legs, but it was hell with only one. He just prayed his hunch and Isabel's guess paid off.

He easily read her inner struggle to hide her fears in the haunted look in her eyes and it touched a place in him he thought he'd buried with his wife and child. Her capacity for loving and giving seemed boundless. The sight of her hurting made him wish he could take the worry, the fear from her and heap it all upon himself.

Not that he didn't have his share of anxiety. The idea of the two boys wandering around in the mountains, with wolves and black bears picking up their scent, shot new energy into him.

And the fact a different kind of killer, Jerico Grey, might be hiding close by didn't set well with him at all.

"It's down this way," Isabel called over her shoulder, catching hold of an outcropping of red stone to keep from sliding down the shifting, rocky slope that led to the entrance of the cave. "Nate found it here. He's just like a mountain goat, and he made us all come up and take a good look at it. The climb didn't seem so bad then."

She was rambling and she knew it, but Isabel couldn't seem to stop herself. If anything had happened to the boys—

"Oh, no!"

Jake heard the fear in her voice before he saw the slide of rocks nearly blocking the entrance to a smallish cave. Pushing past Isabel, he picked his way over the rocky ground to test the area around the cave and peer inside at the inky darkness.

A soft rushing sound echoed inside and Jake frowned. "Sounds like there's water nearby."

"Mr. Coulter?" From inside the cave, the small voice came out of the darkness.

"Nate?" Jake pushed his head and a shoulder around the pile of rock. "Are you and Matt in there?"

"Y-yes. But Matt is stuck. And there's water in here. I-It's cold!"

"Are you hurt?" Jake called back to him.

"We're not hurt, but I won't leave Matt. He's afraid."

Jake heard the fear in Nate's voice that the boy bravely tried to hide. He decided both of them were probably terrified at the turn their little adventure had taken.

"Don't worry," he said, hoping he sounded confident and reassuring. "Your mama and I will have you out in no time."

"I'm small enough to fit through that opening," Isabel said, trying to get around Jake. Her heart throbbed, the need to reach her sons tearing at her insides like a wild thing.

"No," he said, blocking her path with his big body. "We don't know if those rocks will collapse or what's inside. We've got to get enough rocks away to see what we're facing."

"Mama?" Matt's frightened voice came to her from inside the cave. "Are you coming to get me? I can't move my foot."

"I have to do something now!"

"We will do something, but you won't help them

by making the situation worse. Isabel—'' Jake's hands gripped her shoulders, his eyes held hers. "I understand what you're feeling, but we're going to get them out. I promise you that."

Isabel looked at him searching his eyes for reassurance, desperately wanting to believe he could deliver his promise. Her need to trust him warred with her fear for her sons. He gazed back at her, his eyes calm, certain.

In the end, she took a deep breath and squared her shoulders. "You're right. Let's move some rocks."

Jake nodded his approval. He gave her a quick, hard kiss and then turned and started lifting away the rocks blocking the entrance.

They worked feverishly, side by side, for what seemed to Isabel like an eternity, taking care to do it slowly so the rocks didn't shift again.

At last, Jake flung one of the largest rocks aside and shoved his head and shoulders inside, holding the lantern aloft so the flickering light cast a pale light around the small cave. "Nate? Matt?"

"We're here!" Nate called from a far corner.

Jake could see the cave had a fairly level floor that branched out in two directions, one leading to a black tunnel, the other sloping down into a pool of water. On the other side of the pool, Nate and Matt huddled against a narrow ledge, Matt with his legs almost totally immersed in the black water.

"This'll be interesting," Jake muttered under his breath as he tried to figure out the best way of reaching the boys without both him and Isabel getting trapped. "Straight across that water looks like the easiest," he said over his shoulder to Isabel.

"You have no way of knowing how deep it is."

"No, but I don't trust either of us to try navigating that ledge safely. Unless you have a concoction that'll help me walk on water, I don't see a better way of getting to them."

Isabel chewed at her lower lip, looking around the cave, trying to think of any other way. Before she could admit defeat, Jake had tied one end of the rope to a protruding outcropping of rock, tugging at the length of it to make sure it would hold fast. Then unbuckling his gun belt, he left it lying at her feet. Next, he shed his duster and hat and looped the end of the rope around his waist.

"Jake—" Isabel began.

"No reason for both of us to go swimming."

"Be careful," she said softly, so only he could hear.

"I'll get them, don't worry."

Isabel briefly touched his face. "I know you will," she said, and the surety in her voice made Jake feel he could pull apart the mountain barehanded if he had to.

"Okay, guys," he called to Matt and Nate, "I'm coming to get you."

Moving slowly, he edged his way to the pool inch by cautious inch then eased down into the water, gritting his teeth at the sudden shock of cold. His feet fought for purchase on the slippery rock beneath.

"This wasn't a real good idea," he told Matt and Nate, as he eased toward them. He skidded sideways, nearly losing his balance, fighting against the rocky uneven floor of the pool. Water lapped at his chest, making the pool harder to walk through.

When he finally reached the other side, he got a solid foothold on the rocks near the edge and reached out to grasp Nate's shoulder and Matt's arm. "Are you all right?"

"Matt's stuck," Nate said, wiping a wet sleeve across his nose. "We walked around the edge, but Matt slipped and got his foot caught in the rocks. I tried but I couldn't get him loose. I didn't want to leave him, but I didn't think anybody would find us here."

"You're lucky your mama remembered this place. Coming here alone was a bad idea. You've scared your mama out of ten years of life."

"Is Mama mad at us?" Matt asked in a small voice. He clutched at Jake's arm like a lifeline and Jake could feel him trembling with cold and fear.

"Your mama just wants you safe. Now let's take a look at that foot and see if we can get you out of here."

"I want to go home," Matt said.

Jake chuckled. "Me, too, son. Now you hold still just a minute."

Running his hand down Matt's leg, Jake found the point where his foot was wedged between two rocks. After a few minutes, he managed to shift the rock enough to free him, lifting him up on the ledge to sit by Nate.

"Okay, partner, let me take a look...." Jake probed at Matt's ankle. It felt slightly swollen. Matt flinched when Jake gently turned it, but it didn't appear broken. "You'll do until your mama can get her hands on you. Now let's get out of here."

One at a time, Matt first, Jake held the boys high against his shoulder and carried them to Isabel. When they were all outside the cave, Jake slumped down against a flat rock, watching Isabel alternate between tightly hugging her sons and scolding them for taking such risks.

"We only wanted to find the stolen gold," Nate said for the fourth time.

"You're lucky we found you. Lord only knows what might have happened to you if we hadn't been able to find this place again." She bent over Matt's ankle, shaking her head. "Jake's right. I don't think it's broken, but it's badly wrenched."

"I'll carry Matt back down," Jake said, dragging himself upright.

Isabel cast an appraising eye over Jake. She knew his leg was in agony. After the ride to the mine and now this he'd be lucky if he didn't wind up flat on his back again. "Can you?"

Jake acknowledged her fussing with a wry grin. "Just barely."

"Mr. Coulter rescued us. He's a hero," Matt said through quivering lips.

"I think if you were in the market for a hero, you got a bad bargain," Jake said, trying not to take Matt's admiration to heart while at the same time feeling an odd mixture of warmth and regret.

Isabel smiled at Jake, her eyes bright with tears of relief and laughter. "I wouldn't say that. A little bedraggled maybe, but definitely our hero. After all, who else could fix the roof and rescue my sons all in one day?"

Without giving herself time to think, Isabel put her arms around him and hugged him close, not caring they were both wet and dirty, or that the boys watched in wide-eyed interest. They were safe. That was all that mattered.

For a moment, Jake held her tightly, breathing in the scent of her, letting himself accept her gratitude and share in her joy in finding her boys safe. Then, aware of their audience, he gently loosed his hold and brushed the tendrils of hair from her forehead before releasing her.

"Come on, Matt," he said gruffly, scooping up the little boy to hold him firmly in his arms. "Let's get down this mountain."

The trek down was slow going and by the time they'd reached the bottom, the afternoon had lengthened into twilight. Cold, wet cloth clung to their skin, and both boys shivered uncontrollably in the rapidly cooling evening air. They found the horses and mounted. Matt rode cuddled in Isabel's embrace, and Nate with Jake, leaning back against his chest, Jake supporting him with one arm.

Later that night, after Matt and Nate were stripped of their damp clothing and tucked into bed, Isabel discovered the house quiet and empty of the search party Katlyn and Cal had assembled. Jake sat at the kitchen table with a cup of coffee, still in his damp, rumpled clothes.

He looked up when she came in. "Everything okay?"

She nodded as she took a seat across from him. "Thanks to you." Isabel's smile wavered as she said softly, "Thank you, for everything. Rescuing my sons—" All of the day's dread, the fear of what might have happened if Jake hadn't been there, welled in her heart and her voice caught a moment. "You have no idea how much that means to me."

Jake lowered his eyes to stare at the coffee cup in his hands. "I think I do," he said quietly.

His words, laced with a memory of pain that sounded as recent as yesterday, pricked at Isabel's heart. She knew he was thinking of his own son and his wife. Reaching over the table, she touched his hand, wishing she could take away the hurt.

He took her hand in his, idly rubbing his fingers over hers. "I don't think Matt and Nate will be running off to explore another cave any time too soon," he said, his gaze fixed on the patterns he made on her skin.

Isabel tried to keep her voice light, finding it difficult when everything in her focused on him. The risk to his leg he'd taken today for her and her boys, the tenderness she heard in his voice, his disturbingly gentle touch, all spoke of a very different man than the rough-riding Texas Ranger.

She had begun to know this other side of him. The part of him that he had tried to cast away, who once loved and gave himself to a wife and child, who now might be fighting somewhere deep inside him to stay alive.

"I hope it scared them out of trying anything so stupid ever again," she said softly. "But knowing my sons' penchant for adventure, I doubt it."

Jake looked up at her. "You're probably right," he said, laughing a little. "It never stopped me. I remember when I was about Matt's age, I decided I was too old for my pony and figured it would be more exciting to ride my pa's biggest stallion bareback, like I'd seen the Apaches do. I wanted to be one of the Indian braves, to have the freedom to ride without a saddle, as fast as the wind."

"And did you?"

"For about ten minutes. It was the wildest ride of my life. After Pa caught up with me, I couldn't sit for a week."

"And was that the end of your bareback riding?"

Jake laughed. "Of course not. A few days later, I

started practicing riding my pony bareback. Got to where I could ride as well with or without a saddle. I kept it a secret from my pa for several months. When he found me doing it one day, he was so dumbfounded he just shook his head and walked away. Sometimes, when a boy's got a mind to do a thing, there's no stopping him.''

"You haven't changed much," Isabel said, smiling at the vision of a young Jake hell-bent on mastering bareback riding, no matter what the risk.

"Oh, and I suppose you never did anything to drive your mama to distraction."

"Well…there was one time I tried to ride standing up on the back of my pony." She laughed outright at Jake's mock expression of shock. "I wanted to be a trick rider like the ones who came through town one summer. I hated it when Mama insisted I ride in the cart like a proper lady. I liked riding fast and furious, feeling the wind in my hair and the sun on my back."

"I've seen your wild side, when you dance, when you ride," Jake murmured. His fingers now stroked against her wrist, where her pulse quickened. "A wild angel. That's what you are. That, and my angel of mercy."

He looked at her fully then, his eyes almost black in the flickering lamplight. He made no attempt to hide his hunger and need for her and the naked intensity of it made her tremble.

It also frightened her. They had shared too much for her to pretend he meant nothing to her. Yet she didn't dare acknowledge he meant anything to her, knowing one day soon he would leave.

Abruptly, she pushed away from the table, not trusting herself to stay so close to him without wanting to be closer still. "I should get you something for your leg. After today—"

"Isabel, stop." Jake levered himself out of his chair and moved to block her path. He easily read the conflicting emotion in her eyes even if he hadn't recognized her sudden rush to talk as a sign she wanted to hide her feelings from him.

Very gently, he put his arms around her and drew her close until her cheek pressed against his chest. She resisted for the time it took to draw a breath then let him support her as she leaned into him. For a long time he just held her, stroking her back, feeling the tension in her ebb away.

Then she pulled back a little to look up at him and Jake couldn't resist. He wanted to hold her, be held by her, hear her heart in his ears, feel her breath on his skin, lose himself in the giving warmth of her.

Before Isabel could speak, Jake leaned close and kissed her. The caress of his lips upon hers, tender, with an underlying possessive strength, warmed the coldness fear had put in her heart. No man had ever made her feel so alive and so needy.

She had thought, with Douglas, she could learn to do without more than occasional affection and a night now and then of what passed for intimacy with him. But with Jake, she realized how much she had missed. She now longed to know the meaning of the fierce elemental need he evoked in her—to know how much more a man and woman could share.

His tongue tasted her lower lip and she opened to him, sparking the fire that had been between them from the beginning. Jake pulled her fully against him, urgency replacing tenderness.

How simple it had been—a glance, a word or two,

a touch, and he had lost himself to her. Her hands slid over his shoulders, inviting him closer, and he fought to keep control of his reason, reason that told him he had no right to this feeling.

He gentled his touch, slowly, until at last they drew apart. She looked up at him and the delicate blush on her skin, her lips still parted by his kiss, the desire in her eyes nearly made Jake forget why he shouldn't take all she wanted to give. ''Isabel…''

''I suppose you've been thinking my behavior isn't very proper for a widow and mother,'' she said lightly, breaking free of his hold to turn from him.

His withdrawal confused and unsettled her, and above all else, she didn't want to hear him apologize, to know he didn't feel the same depth of emotion she did when they touched.

Jake stopped her, his fingertips on her face guiding her gaze back to his. ''You're tired and vulnerable. I don't want to take advantage of that.''

Pride surged up in her and with it anger. She glared at him. ''Is that what you think? That I wanted your comfort and your pity? Believe whatever you'd like, but if you think I'd let you take advantage of me, Jake Coulter, you're crazier than I thought! I know what I want—and what I don't want.''

''Pity? If that's what you think this is about, you're the crazy one, lady.'' Circling his arm around her waist he pulled her up hard against him. He wrapped her hair around his hand and kissed her with all the pent-up need and longing he had inside.

The intensity of their passion left Isabel feeling dizzy. She held to his shirtfront, wanting the hot pressure of his mouth on hers, the scent of him, the hard and rough feel of him against her hands and her skin.

As abruptly as he kissed her, he let her go, so quickly she swayed a little with the force of losing him.

"Dream about that tonight, sweet Isabel," he said roughly. "I know I will."

Isabel put a trembling hand to her lips as they stared at each other. Dream about him—oh, she would dream. Sweet heaven, from this moment she wondered if she would ever do anything else.

# Chapter Ten

Isabel turned from side to side, examining the fit of her new dress in the mirror. She'd indulged in the dress for Katlyn's engagement party, a picnic hosted by the Parkers at their ranch. The Parkers had practically adopted Daniel, and, when they learned of his engagement to Katlyn, insisted on organizing a celebration.

She and Nana had worked all week cutting and stitching the deep-blue cotton, Esme's skilled fingers putting the final tailoring into the cinched waist and bodice so that it hugged Isabel close. The off-the-shoulder scooped neck and short puffed sleeves gave the dress the Spanish flavor Isabel had wanted.

Would Jake notice, she wondered as she pulled a shawl, finely woven in shades of gold, from her drawer? He'd accepted the Parkers' invitation and agreed to escort her, the boys and Esme to the party. But she suspected that had more to do with his wanting to learn more about Jerico than a desire to attend a social with her.

*Dream of me,* he'd said. She had, though long ago she'd learned just how dangerous dreams could be.

Isabel sighed, thinking how difficult it was becoming

to imagine her house without him. All week, she'd kept busy compounding various remedies. While she worked in her shop, rode out to Etta Black's house to treat the old woman's broken ankle, or combed the meadow for a new supply of thistles, Jake had, without telling her his plan, enlisted the boys in helping him repair and repaint the broken shutters all around the house.

Jake would have made a wonderful father, she thought. When Matt pounded his thumb with the hammer, Jake comforted him and corrected him. When Nate nailed a whole set of shutters upside down, Jake had made a joke of it and showed him how to turn them around. She'd often come upon them laughing over some minor mishap or with their heads together, plotting their next chore.

Every time Isabel volunteered to help when she ventured outside to offer lemonade or water, the boys shooed her away, proud to be doing ''man's work'' with Jake. Until he'd come into their lives, they hadn't shown how much they'd missed having a father.

And watching Jake working, sweating, flexing, day after day, she hadn't realized how much she missed having a man.

A few evenings Jake had gone into town to see Cal or go to the Silver Rose to find out what news there was on Jerico's whereabouts. Once, at Cal's request, he'd ridden out to the foothills north of town, easily picking up the trail of an out-of-work miner who'd taken to thieving horses. Jake had made short work of delivering the man to the jail.

But he'd never missed supper and he was always up before dawn the next day, ready to go to work with the boys.

Isabel tried to appreciate his effort, take pleasure in his company, and not think about the day when she'd wake up and find him gone.

Satisfied she'd done all she could do to look her best, Isabel headed to the front room to meet the others. She was surprised to find Jake, alone, waiting at the foot of the stairs. He looked up as she neared, the warm approval in his eyes giving her a rush of purely feminine self-satisfaction and making her glad she'd fussed over her dress and hair.

"Now I see what took you so long," he said, unable to take his eyes off her as she moved toward him.

The sight of her stepping gracefully closer, her hips swaying provocatively beneath a dress that hugged her every curve, heightened the fever in his blood. All week, he'd fought the attraction of her angel's smile and her innate sensuality. And he'd bet his last dollar she had no idea how she could make a man crazy with just a glance from those turquoise eyes. Her beauty came effortlessly.

Yet her seduction was more than simple beauty. He'd known plenty of lovely women. None of them, not even Lily, had twisted him up inside like Isabel.

But none of them had Isabel's well of strength, the compassion and caring that seemed to come as naturally as breathing to her. She made him feel she could equal him, in courage and sheer stubbornness to overcome whatever life threw at her.

But Isabel didn't want a protector, she wanted a partner. She didn't want just today, she wanted forever.

"You're staring," she said, laughter in her voice. "I didn't think I looked all that odd, but maybe the change from what you're used to seeing is too startling."

As she stepped close enough to stand only inches

from him, Jake struggled to find his voice. "That dress, I've never seen you wear it before. It's perfect. You look amazing."

When she gave him a radiant smile in return for his compliment, it was all Jake could do to hold himself back from pulling her against him and kissing her until they both forgot everything but each other.

"I think I'd better strap on my gun belt. I have a feeling I'm going to be fighting to keep every male in Whispering Creek away from you tonight."

"No need," Isabel said with a light laugh. "Most of them are already afraid I'll hex them or turn them into prairie rats."

"Maybe we should take along some of your grandmother's curses just in case. Besides, then she'd have fewer left for me."

Jake held out his hand to her. Isabel's voice caught in her throat as she laid her palm against his. A step from him, the scent of him made her heady as the incense from a midnight fire. Wind and leather and male, it was the essence of him—a little wild, definitely dangerous, and all man.

All the way down the hallway she, too, had been taking in everything about the way he looked—the perfect fit of black pants molding his muscular legs and narrow hips, hat sitting at just the right angle to emphasize the strong, defined lines of his cheeks and jaw. And now standing so close, she felt the power of his broad chest and shoulders outlined against the white cotton shirt.

Finally finding her voice, she met his eyes. The warmth there made her catch her breath. "You look mighty fine yourself, Jake Coulter. You'll have all the girls in town ready to cater to your every whim today."

Jake tucked her hand in the crook of his arm. He leaned close so his rough-edged voice caressed her ear. "They can do cartwheels across the meadow if they want to. The only woman I want at my side today is you."

"Be careful what you say," she said a little unsteadily. "I might begin to believe it. Besides, have you forgotten you're escorting a witch? You never know what magic I might cast."

"You cast your spell on me from the minute you threatened to cut out my heart with your knife." Jake tossed her a rakish grin when she shook her head in mock exasperation. Then he suddenly sobered, stopping her turn toward the front door by taking both of her hands in his. "You're most of the reason I'm dragging myself out to this party. You've managed to tempt me into forgetting everything but you today."

Isabel's pulse quickened at his words, but she didn't want to give them any deeper meaning than his admiration for a pretty woman. Yet her traitorous heart rebelled and threatened to believe she might mean something more to him.

Something about him was different today—or maybe it was only hopeful thinking on her part. She didn't know and she wished she didn't care as much as she did.

To cover her confusion, she smiled and teased him with a coy tilt of her head. "Only most of the reason? Should I be disappointed?"

"The boys are the other reason."

Her impudence immediately fell away. "Jake—"

Jake silenced her with his kiss. For a moment, his mouth moved against hers, warm and urgent, and Isabel felt herself leaning into him, inviting him closer.

He responded by pulling back. Only his quickened breath and the glint in his eyes told her the brief caress hadn't left him unmoved.

"We'd better go," Jake said, rubbing her fingers between his, reluctant to break the contact. Her perfume, something sweet and spicy, taunted him, a constant reminder of her nearness. "Your grandmother had the boys put the basket in the cart already and you can bet by now they're as restless as two broncos in a pen."

"Yes, well…" Feeling dazed, Isabel glanced over her shoulder. "Katlyn—"

"Daniel came earlier and picked her up in the Parkers' buggy. There's just you and me, angel."

Settling her hand on his arm, Isabel tried to gather her wits. "Thank you for volunteering to drive the cart for us."

"The offer's only good so long as you agree to sit on the bench next to me."

"I may have to do battle with Matt and Nate for that honor."

"Well, you may not appreciate my solution, but I already took care of that."

Isabel looked up at him. "Should I even ask?"

"I promised to teach them a card trick today so they could show it off to the Parker boys and the other kids there."

"You're determined to corrupt them despite me, I see."

As they stepped outside and toward the waiting cart, Jake lowered his voice to a husky whisper. "Because of you, angel. Because of you."

By the time Jake rounded the last bend through the open slatted gate that led up the dusty drive to the

Triple Star Ranch, the cook was already raising a racket with the dinner gong. A slight breeze rustled the leaves in the cottonwoods and the branches of the Ponderosa pines. It cooled the afternoon heat and scented the air with the blended essence of the whispering meadow and the mountains; soft, earthy, and warm meeting crisp, heady and cool.

Jake stopped the cart near several others and helped Isabel down, his hands spanning almost the whole of her waist. He offered Esme a hand, but she waved him away.

"No, no. I am not so old, yet. You go fetch the basket." Jake returned Isabel's grin as he backed away and hefted out the large wicker basket from the back of the cart.

"Come on, Nana," Matt tugged at her hand. "The chuck wagon's set up over there. And I'm hungry!"

Nate ran along beside Matt, who half dragged Esme toward the crowd gathered around the wagon and fire pit where two sides of beef and huge slabs of goat slowly roasted over the open flames.

Isabel and Jake lagged behind. Though she had looked forward to talking with friends all week, Isabel suddenly found herself wishing she could steal away and spend the evening alone with Jake. But Carol Beth Parker had already spied them and was headed their way to put a quick end to that daydream.

"Here comes our hostess," Isabel said, nudging Jake's arm. "It's too late to change your mind now."

"Pity," he returned, his gaze sweeping over her.

She tried to look suitably stern, a difficult task with her heart running wild. "Try to at least pretend you're civilized."

"You're asking a lot." He flashed her a disarming

grin, then glanced at a plump woman in bright-pink calico advancing on them. "So that's Mrs. Parker."

"Yes, it is and she wants to be the first woman in town to get a good look at you."

"Well, of course I do," Carol Beth said, smiling broadly at Isabel's embarrassment at being overheard. She transferred her twinkling gaze to Jake. "Mr. Coulter, I must say, you do live up to all those stories I've been hearing about you. A Texas Ranger, stolen gold and the return of that varmint Jerico Grey, why it sounds just like one of those dime novels my boys are so fond of."

Jake flicked a glance at Isabel. She flushed, wishing she'd told him about her boys giving him away before the party. The look he gave her was devoid of expression, but she knew him well enough to know he was far from pleased at being thrust into the center of attention.

Still, when he turned back to Carol Beth, he betrayed nothing of what he was feeling. He gave Carol Beth his most irresistible smile. Isabel noticed her friend's plump cheeks grow pink as he focused his full attention on her. "It was nice to be invited, ma'am. It's certainly a pleasure to meet you at last. And I hope you'll call me Jake."

"Well, now." Carol Beth preened a little. "I can see why you've turned Isabel's head. Charming and dangerous, that's a deadly combination for any gal."

Before Isabel could say anything, Carol Beth enveloped her in an enthusiastic hug. "Why, honey, don't you look pretty? That's got to be the finest dress I've seen in a month of Sundays. No one can stitch like you Castillo women."

Putting her hands on Isabel's shoulders, she turned

Isabel all the way around. "I never could put a decent seam in a pair of pants. But you, girl, have all kinds of healing skill in your hands." She winked at Jake. "I'm sure Jake knows all about that."

"Carol Beth—!" Isabel began.

Jake only laughed. "I've discovered a good many things about Isabel in the past few weeks."

"Most of them you probably would have been happy not to know," Isabel muttered, then put on a smile for Carol Beth.

"Well, come on, Digger's takin' the goat off the fire and Manuel has those hot chili beans in the kettle that you like so much, Isabel."

Isabel motioned to the basket draped over Jake's arm. "And we brought a peach cobbler and an apple pie. Oh, and some of those pumpkin sweetmeats your boys love."

Daniel and Katlyn walked by hand in hand then, Katlyn chattering as she led him toward the circle of guests gathered around picnic tables near the chuck wagon.

"They certainly seem happy," Isabel said, deciding her fears about Katlyn's marriage being rushed were probably unfounded. As long as Katlyn truly knew the man and the life-style she was marrying, it pleased Isabel to know her sister would soon be wed and settled in Whispering Creek.

"So that's the lucky groom." Jake studied the couple for a moment, noting Katlyn instantly became the center of attention, while Daniel hung back, standing stiffly at the outside of the gathering. "He looks a little green in the gills if you ask me."

Isabel smiled sweetly. "Then I'm not asking you."

"I'd say Jake's right on the money. Young Daniel's

already drownin' and he ain't even put his big toe in the water yet!'' Carol Beth laughed heartily, slapping Jake playfully on the back before turning to some guests just arriving. "You all go on and eat up now."

Jake hoisted up the basket and began to walk toward the table.

"Jake, wait." Isabel put her hand on his arm. "I'm sorry Carol Beth found out about you being a Ranger. The boys let it slip when we ran into her at the mercantile. Carol Beth's a good friend, but she's the worst gossip, so everyone in town probably knows and—"

"Isabel." Putting his fingers against her lips, Jake stopped her rambling apology. "It's not your fault. I can't say I'm happy about it, but it's too late to get riled about it now."

"People will be asking you about Jerico and the gold."

"It doesn't mean I have to answer. And I'm better than fair at keeping secrets."

Tugging at his hat in salute to her, he started off toward the food tables with her basket. Almost immediately, a group of ladies from the quilting circle pounced on Isabel, asking after her and her family, although she knew what they really wanted was to learn everything they could about Jake and his reasons for being in town.

She inwardly sighed, outwardly smiled, and resolved to say as little as possible about gold, Jerico and most especially about Jake.

"You know, I'm sure Grey's got that gold stashed up in the old Black Angel mine. I heard tell he and his gang holed up there after they robbed the Lucky Dog and that they're just waitin' for the next big payroll to come in from that mine near Lone Tree before they head down to Mexico.''

For what seemed like the fiftieth time in the last two hours, Jake listened to yet another theory about Jerico Grey's plans and whereabouts, this time from an old man who'd cornered him near the food tables while he was making good his escape from the quilting circle ladies.

It seemed everyone at the damned party knew—or thought they knew—something about Grey and was determined to share it with him. While he'd found some of the more outlandish stories entertaining, he hadn't managed to learn anything useful and his patience with the whole affair was quickly becoming nonexistent.

Worse, he'd seen almost nothing of Isabel since they'd arrived. She, though, seemed not to notice. Several times, he'd sought her out, only to see her across a room or standing in a patch of shade outside, talking and laughing with one group of people or another.

He nodded in what he hoped was an appropriate response to the old man's meandering story, while his mind focused on finding a way to leave the party without attracting too much attention.

''Now, Harvey, you're gonna talk Jake's ear off.'' Digger Parker came up behind the old man, slapping a hand on his shoulder.

''I think it's too late for that,'' Carol Beth said, joining her husband. She grinned at Jake. ''Everyone just finds you fascinating, I'm afraid.''

''I don't think it's me. I think it's Grey and his gold. They've all got their own ideas about why he's come back to the territory.''

''Why, it's because of Isabel Bradshaw, of course,''

a thin reedy voice piped up. A plump, carrot-haired woman, flanked by two of the quilting ladies, came up beside Carol Beth. "Everyone knows Jerico and Isabel were sweethearts. She'd probably have run off with him if he hadn't had the law chasing him."

"Louise Simmons, you don't know any such thing," Carol Beth protested. "Isabel was just a girl with a fancy for a wild boy who made pretty speeches to her. Even then, she had too much sense to take up with the likes of Jerico."

"Isabel hasn't shown much sense in the men she's taken up with," Louise said with a sharp sidelong look at Jake. "First Jerico, then when he's hiding in the hills, she up and marries his good friend, though anyone could see Douglas Bradshaw was never going to amount to anything."

"Do you remember how angry Jerico was when he found out she married Douglas?" one of the ladies said. "Why, I heard it took Elish Dodd nearly a week to clean up the mess and pry the bullets out of the walls after Jerico came back into town to see that Miss Devine and wound up going on a rampage there one night."

"You see, it just goes to show how much Jerico loved her," Louise persisted.

"I think you've been samplin' more than your share of Digger's special punch." Carol Beth ignored the woman's affronted gasp. She looked directly at Jake. "If Jerico's come back, I'd bet our ranch it's because he's stashed something he's stolen here and he wants it back, not because of Isabel."

"Too bad Douglas went and got himself killed," Harvey spoke up. "He and Jerico spent a lot of time together."

"The only person who knows anything is Jerico Grey and he ain't talkin'," Digger said. "Now, I don't know about you ladies, and you, Harvey, but I've got a thirst for some of that punch." Winking at his wife, Digger managed to lead the group away from Carol Beth and Jake.

Carol Beth immediately turned on Jake. "Now don't you be payin' Louise Simmons any mind. She's a worse gossip than I am, except she invents the truth as she goes along."

Jake silently questioned how much had been truth, and if he'd been right all along about Isabel's tie to Grey. But Carol Beth seemed so intent on convincing him, he only nodded and forced a smile. "Thank you for the warning."

"As if you took any of it to heart. Well, all men got a little bit of the fool in them, but you're a bigger fool than most if you think Isabel ever loved Jerico."

With that, Carol Beth abruptly changed the subject, leaving Jake alone with a tangle of truth and lies he was beginning to think he'd never get straight.

"You next, Mama! You next!" Matt skipped around Isabel, tugging at her hand to draw her into the circle of children and youths. Two of the older boys sat at the edge of the circle, guitars in their laps.

They had started a game of *escogiendo la novia,* choosing a sweetheart. It was a game Esme had taught her when she was Matt's age, a tradition passed down for generations in the Castillo family, and even now, she loved it. She'd shared it with her boys and now most of the children in Whispering Creek had learned it, as well.

"Come on, Mama," Nate insisted. "You're better at this than anyone."

"Oh, just once," Isabel said, laughing as she allowed herself to be drawn into the circle and took her place in the center.

"You can't look," Matt reminded her. "Even a little."

"I won't, I promise. You can't choose a sweetheart by looking."

Closing her eyes, she waited for the music to begin. A duet of guitars started and Isabel let herself be wooed by the music's strong rhythm, her body moving with its flying, joyful notes.

Her senses her guide, she danced without seeing, in and out and around the bodies of the unbroken circle, not touching anyone in keeping with the rules of the game. Many of the party guests gathered to watch, and several joined in at the children's urging, widening the circle.

Others on the outside murmured their admiration, because no one but Isabel could blindly move so gracefully without so much as brushing any one of the other players. At the slightest contact before the music was over, the sweetheart was chosen, and the game ended.

Isabel always made her own choice.

Sunlight sparked against her closed eyes and she felt the rush of warm wind on her face, the flare of her skirts on her legs. Everyone making the circle laughed and called to her as she danced.

For a giddy moment, Isabel pretended when she unseeingly stretched out her hand and chose her sweetheart, he would truly be the dream she cherished, the man she could give herself to, not one of her young partners in play.

Laughing with the sheer pleasure of the game and at her own absurd fancy, she spun around in perfect time with the guitar song and came to a sudden stop with the music.

"I choose—" She quickly reached out and laid her palm against a fast-beating heart. "You!"

Isabel opened her eyes. Jake looked back.

The circle of players and onlookers clapped and cheered, delighted with the dramatic ending of the game. Stunned, Isabel could only stare at Jake.

"Mama wins again!" Matt shouted. He hopped out of his place in the circle to skip around Isabel. "She wins the prize!"

"You have to kiss her," one of the girls from the circle called out. "That's the rule."

"Only on the hand, and only if you want to," Nate said, scrunching up his face. "Girls always want you to kiss their hands, though. Who knows why."

"Girls are a strange breed sometimes," Jake agreed, trying not to smile.

Taking Isabel's hand that still rested against his chest, he brought it to his lips.

He intended only the briefest of caresses, just enough to satisfy the rules of the game.

But from the instant he touched her, his good intentions vanished as if they'd never been. All he could think of was the way she danced, like making love with the music, and how much he wanted to hold her.

For a moment, time was suspended and they stood transfixed, Jake's mouth lingering on her skin, Isabel looking at him, her free hand half lifted as if to touch him in return.

Then the laughter and good-natured calls from the gathering around them intruded, making Isabel suddenly and acutely aware she had been standing in a very public place, for an immeasurable length of time, letting Jake touch her in a way that was sure to give the gossips fodder for weeks to come.

She quickly stepped back from him and dropped her gaze. He released her hand yet made no attempt to put any distance between them. Blessedly, the guests began moving away, becoming interested in another game started by the children and Digger's announcement the dancing would soon start.

"An interesting game," Jake said, clearing his throat a little.

"Yes, well, the children like it." Isabel tried to think of something else to say but every word sounded more inane than the one before. "The dancing has started. I should—"

"Yes, you should." With a slow hand, Jake reached out and trailed his fingers down her hair. "There isn't another woman who dances like you. Just watching you could make a man go blind trying to satisfy his eyes."

His touch lightly plucked at her nerves, sending a shivering sensation rippling through her. "If I danced now, would it satisfy you?"

"No," he said bluntly.

She smiled and no magic could have been more powerful. The secret, pleased look in her eyes made Jake doubt the wisdom of his confession. "Are you going to join me?"

"Not in this dance."

"Then maybe another."

"I don't think you want the answer to that," Jake said. This time he did step away, putting space between him and her tempting nearness. ''Enjoy the music. I'm going to talk to Cal for a few minutes.''

*And then I'm leaving,* he told himself, *before I do something really uncivilized and give the gossips more than stolen gold and an outlaw to talk about.*

## Chapter Eleven

It was nearly sunset when Jake decided he'd had enough.

He'd talked to Cal and made another trip to the chuck wagon with Matt and Nate at the boys' insistence. Finally, after nearly convincing himself to leave without her, he'd settled in on the grass and watched Isabel smile and laugh and dance with what seemed like every male in Whispering Creek.

And throughout it all, he'd had the distinct impression she'd done it just to rile him. Jake shook his head. He didn't understand her, and maybe it was better he didn't try. Maybe the conflict that kept creeping up between them would make it easier to walk away when the time came. Maybe it would make it easier to forget her, to exorcise her from his thoughts, his dreams.

And maybe after a lifetime or two he could convince himself of that.

After sitting so long, the stiffness in his leg made even getting to his feet an effort. He moved haltingly toward the house to retrieve his hat, thinking he might walk the mile or so back to town to ease some of the tightness in his muscles. Cal had already taken the boys and Esme back to the house, and Jake had no doubts Isabel could find someone to drive her cart back to town, if she didn't want to take the reins herself.

Seeing Daniel standing on the porch he walked out to say his goodbyes to the younger man. "You look like a man who's had enough fuss for one evening," Jake said, coming to stand by him.

Daniel shrugged. "I never was much for fuss. Kate wants it, though."

"When you love a woman and she's got her mind set on something, it's hard to say no."

Daniel gave a grunt of affirmation and Jake wondered how he'd managed to ever strike up a conversation with Katlyn McLain, let alone court her.

Letting a few minutes of silence creep between them, Jake asked about Daniel's plans for starting his cattle ranch. Hitting upon the one topic the young man showed enthusiasm for, he managed to draw Daniel out. Jake listened, remembering himself ten years past, full of dreams and confidence they would come true.

After a while, Katlyn called Daniel back inside. Jake offered his congratulations and goodbyes to them both before starting down the porch steps and over the yard to try to catch a ride with a family headed back toward town.

He'd barely gotten started when someone called his name. He turned back toward the house. Isabel stood on the porch, her shawl clasped around her like a shield, looking out at him.

"Did you decide to leave without me?" she asked, walking down the stairs to meet him. She resisted coming after him when she saw him start across the meadow alone, but his awkward gait roused an instinctive worry in her and overcame her anger.

"I didn't think you'd have any trouble getting an escort back. You seem to have plenty of admirers. Especially tonight."

"I have—! You've got a lot of nerve, Jake Coulter, talking to me about admirers!"

"And what is that supposed to mean?"

"You haven't lacked for admirers since you've come to Whispering Creek. Anita Devine seems only too ready to end your loneliness."

Jake stared at her a moment as if she'd taken leave of her senses, making Isabel feel foolish for ever opening her mouth. Then, to her surprise, he started to laugh. "What's the matter, angel, jealous?"

"Of you? How ridiculous. How you spend your time is none of my concern."

"You seem to be making it your concern. And you know why I've been to the Silver Rose a time or two. I need to know about Grey, and Elish's customers might have information I can use." He paused a moment, then said, "How about you?"

"Me? You think I know something about where Jerico is?"

"No, I think you know more about Grey than you've told me. Several people have told me you were close once. And Cal also said your husband and Grey knew each other, were friends even."

"We all grew up in the same town, of course they knew each other! This is crazy. We never have a conversation without you bringing up his name." Isabel shook her head and paced a few steps from him.

Jake regretted pushing her about a subject that clearly unsettled her. But some instinct drove him, something that told him she could unlock for him some crucial information about Grey. "Isabel—"

She turned back to face him, defiance in her stance. "No, you listen. I thought I loved Jerico once, when I was young and foolish. Then I learned what kind of man he was, how he burned with hatred, and it frightened me. He still frightens me. I never want him near my life again." Her voice shook a little. "That's all I can tell you. I can't give you what you want."

"You don't know what I want," Jake said roughly. He moved next to her and gently traced his fingers over her face before taking her hands in his, holding her tightly. "I promise you, I'll find him and then it will be over. He'll be gone from your life forever."

"And then you'll be gone, too," she said. "Won't you?"

Isabel saw the conflict of emotion cross his face and regretted backing him into a corner. She wasn't certain why she had done it, except suddenly she wanted to force some admission from him, to hear the blunt truth so she could convince herself she had no business letting this man anywhere near her heart.

"I'm sorry," she said softly. "I shouldn't have—"

"I shouldn't have, either. Let's call it a draw. Do you want me to take you back to the house?"

After a long moment's silence, Isabel spoke softly, "I don't want to go home. Not yet." She glanced to her left, where the meadow stretched out to the mountains. "I think I'll go for a walk."

"Now?"

She laughed. "Why not? It'll certainly be more peaceful."

"I could use a little peace myself," Jake said, smiling.

"Then come with me."

She started walking. Without thinking, Jake went

with her. A warm grass-and-sage-scented breeze disturbed the stillness as they walked through the whispering meadow. Edged at the horizon with scarlet and bitter orange, purple softness blended into the deepest clear blue, hinting at the canopy of starlight waiting for fullest night to shine.

Isabel led Jake to the top of the meadow's gentle knoll. Standing beside him at the peak of it, she looked out over the vista of meadow, mountains and forest spread to the horizon. Next to her, Jake looked more pensive than inspired by the view. The light wind molded his shirt to his chest and shoulders and ruffled his hair. He seemed to Isabel at that moment more a part of the wilderness than ever before.

She hugged her arms around herself and looked up at the twilight sky. "I've always loved this time of day. When substance and spirit become one, my mama used to say."

Jake leaned back against one of the cottonwoods, looking at her. "I'm on the trail so much, I forget there's a lot about the frontier to appreciate."

"And I can't imagine being anywhere else."

"It means a lot to you, doesn't it? Having a place to belong?"

"Maybe it's more having a place that belongs to me, a home. Something no one can take away from me." She struggled for the words, for feelings she'd long kept silent. "After my daddy left and then Douglas, I learned to make my own life and it's enough."

Her voice faltered on the last words, twisting Jake's heart. In the dim light, he could see tears shimmering in her eyes.

She made a visible effort to regain control over her emotions, drawing a breath and rubbing her hand over her hair, her skirt. "Haven't you ever felt that way about a place?"

"I felt that way once, about San Antonio." He avoided looking at her, instead focusing on the half moon.

"Yet you've chosen to call nowhere home now."

"I keep moving so I don't remember."

"Is that why you joined the Rangers?"

"No, I've been with them ever since I could handle a gun. I like being a lawman, it satisfies a need in me for balance, for justice. I just never should have tried to have everything."

Isabel felt the pain in him as if it were a heart wound. She laid her hand on his arm, feeling the tenseness there. "What happened to your family was an accident," she said quietly. "Spending the rest of your life blaming yourself only hurts you and keeps you from putting the past to rest."

He said nothing. Isabel let the silence stay between them. She wanted only to reach him, to offer the healing he needed. But she didn't know how.

"I never imagined I'd ever find anyone like you," he said softly, almost thoughtfully, and something in his warm, rough voice made Isabel feel hot inside. Glad the deepening darkness hid her flushed cheeks, she said lightly, "I'm not sure whether I should be flattered or not."

"You're so—alive. So willing to embrace everything and everyone, to care even when it might hurt."

"I'm a healer," she said. "That's what healing is about. This—"

She reached out and took his hand. Cradling it in hers, she rubbed her fingertips over his palm in a light circular motion, looking into his eyes with unflinching directness. "—this is healing. More than herbs, or medicine, or skill with a knife. It's the giving of strength and hope and—love."

Her last word came on a soft rush of breath and Jake caught it with his own. They stood poised in twilight's embrace, his hand in hers, her touch tremoring through him, kindling a slow heat. One motion, one word from her and it would become a wildfire in his blood.

The hunger her simple touch loosed in him nearly drove Jake to lay her down in the meadow grass with only moonlight and heat between them. She was taking him apart, making him burn inside, making him feel so intensely he couldn't think, want so much it hurt.

Isabel gradually became aware of how near she stood to him. The realization came like a gentle change—the warm pressure of his hand still held in hers, the scent of him, the awareness of his size and strength. She tried to breathe easily, to achieve some measure of calm.

But the way he looked at her, his eyes darkening like storm clouds, quickened her heart and coursed a restless ache of longing through her veins.

"I...maybe it's impossible to explain," she said, quickly drawing her hand away from temptation.

She couldn't surrender to this, no matter how much she wanted to. A step too far with him and she would compromise everything she had built, threaten her hard-won independence and security.

"We're so different in what we do, what we want."

The tremble in her voice betrayed her every word and he knew it.

"Are we?" Jake gave up the fight to keep any distance between them and reached out and pulled her into his arms. "I don't think we're that different. I think inside, we're the same, we want exactly the same thing. This.''

He kissed her deeply, thrusting inside to taste the sweet fire of her. She hesitated for a breath of time and then, with a little moan, leaned into him, pushing Jake over the edge of restraint.

Soft to hard, she fit against his body as if she'd been made for him alone, completing him. She held nothing back, giving as she took, not afraid to step with him into the fire, and her abandonment was his undoing.

Isabel welcomed the urgency of his kiss. She pushed her fingers into the hair at his nape, wanting him closer. With his body, hard and needy, branded on hers, she forgot fear.

There was only Jake and the way he filled the emptiness inside her and made her crave a fulfillment she never knew she needed. It evoked a longing to touch him that overwhelmed every reason she had not to.

He dragged his mouth from hers and she arched her neck to give him access to the curve of her throat. She clutched his shoulders as he set her skin afire with lips and tongue and teeth.

She gave a little mewl of pleasure and Jake gritted his teeth against the painful tightening of his body. He couldn't remember ever wanting a woman like this. Loving his wife had been tender and soft. But one sweep of Isabel's fingers over his chest and he burned. Hard, hot and fast.

Drawing her down with him, he knelt with her in the long grass and wildflowers, as he'd fantasized about doing from the moment she'd walked into the meadow. She touched her lips with his. He held her with his kiss while his fingers found the row of tiny buttons that ran down the back of her dress.

His hands shook as he forced them apart then pulled the material off her shoulders and down her arms. Laying her back in the grass, he untied the ribbons of her shift. The fragile material came apart in his hands, baring her to him.

"Jake..." she whispered, trembling as he brushed his fingertips from her shoulder to the hollow of her throat.

"You're beautiful," he said hoarsely, emotion catching in his throat. "I don't deserve this."

"This, more...everything." With a boldness born of the wild need he roused in her, she took his hand and guided it to the curve of her breast.

He traced his fingers around her softness, lightly rubbing at its sensitive nub until it hardened between his fingertips.

Desire, so fierce it took her breath, arrowed through her, low and sharp.

She cried out when his mouth replaced his hand, tasting, suckling, until she ached for a completion only he could give.

Needing to touch him in return, she unfastened his shirt buttons and spread her hands over his skin, the sensation like smooth, supple leather over steel. She felt his hand slide up her leg, pushing up her skirts, and mindlessly she reached for him, to draw him closer, against her, into her.

Jake wanted nothing more than to lose himself in her. Touching her was like an infusion of midnight fire and morning sunlight, both seduction and sweet promise.

But her willingness to give him everything without any promise of tomorrow made him determined to protect her from a choice made in passion. Instead of taking what she offered so freely, he abruptly gathered her against him and held her tightly, breathing the scent of wildflowers and sunlight that was hers alone, feeling the pulse of her heart against his.

When she shifted, reaching to touch him, he pulled back, sitting up beside her.

"Jake?" Her hand brushed his shoulder. He felt her move to kneel beside him. "I—I didn't...was it so wrong?"

"Wrong?" Jake turned to take her face in his hands. He kissed her gently, breaking away before desire could tempt him to more. "I've never felt anything more right in my life."

Isabel pulled the ends of her shift together feeling suddenly exposed by the intent look he gave her. His loving had left her dazed, his withdrawal now confused her. "Then why—?"

Jake got to his feet, looking down at her, his face tight with the effort it took to repress all he was feeling. "I can't give you what you need, what you deserve. I won't take from you and then walk away. I can't, not with you."

He strode a few paces away, his breathing ragged. Isabel sat alone in the night's shadows, glad for the shelter of darkness.

She still shuddered inside with the echoes of the pleasure he had given her. Nothing in her marriage or before had prepared her for the feelings Jake gave her and the remembrance of them left her shaken.

Yet she also felt strangely unsatisfied, as if she had been allowed only a taste of a promised feast before it was snatched away.

Or walked away.

*I won't take from you and then walk away.*

He all but promised her he would leave. And for her heart's sake, Isabel knew she should believe him.

## Chapter Twelve

For the third time, Isabel stabbed her finger with the needle, a droplet of blood staining the shirt she'd been attempting to mend. She flung it aside, giving up the work as hopeless tonight.

She wanted to blame everything on Jake. Since the night of the engagement party, he had kept his distance, making certain they were never alone even for a few minutes. In three days, he hadn't spoken more than a handful of words to her and Isabel wasn't sure whether to be thankful or upset.

She knew in her heart the real cause of her unsettled mood. She was afraid. Afraid she had gone too far in revealing her deepest desires, her needs, her longing. She had opened herself to him and left herself vulnerable to another heartache. Only this time, the measure of devastation would be incomparable to the hurt Douglas had inflicted. And for that, she had no one to blame but herself.

Sighing, Isabel retrieved the shirt and carefully folded it to put back in her sewing basket. She was about to give up for the night and take her dreams to bed when she remembered the goat.

Matt had brought it home two days ago, a pitiful, scrawny thing, barely old enough to be separated from its mother. Matt faithfully fed and cuddled the little creature but Isabel wanted to check a nasty cut on its foreleg.

Dousing the lamp in the parlor, she went into the kitchen to find her lantern. She took it with her, holding it high to light the path to the barn in the midnight darkness.

The night was unusually still. Crickets sang sporadically, and an owl hooted nearby. Isabel could hear her own footsteps crunching on the rocky path and echoing in the night.

When she reached the barn door and lifted the bar on the door a soft fluttering arrested her hand.

"Watch out! Watch out!"

"Trouble," Isabel breathed, pressing her hand to her chest. "You scared me out of ten years of living. What's the matter? Didn't you get enough dinner?" she asked as the raven followed her into the barn.

The raven bobbed his head as if in reply and Isabel laughed, throwing him a handful of corn from the feed sack. "There, greedy. Enjoy your midnight snack."

She went on to the small corner of the farthest stall where Matt had put his goat. Setting her lantern on the edge of the stall gate behind her, she bent to look at the almost pathetic little goat.

"Well, you'll survive, I hope," she told the little animal after a few minutes. "You wait here for a minute and I'll get something for that leg."

Leaving her lantern near the animal, who cried out in a voice that sounded eerily like an abandoned child, she moved to the tack room to get the salve for the goat's injured foreleg. She reached up to pull it off the shelf—and the lantern light suddenly went out, plunging the barn into darkness.

Trouble screeched and for several moments she listened to the wild flapping of his wings as he flew about the barn. Then the sound disappeared, giving way to silence.

Isabel tensed, her hand arrested in the motion of reaching for the salve. The goat might have toppled the lantern off the gate but if he did, she'd heard nothing. Even now, the dead quiet seemed absolute, save for the quickened sound of her own breath.

Then came a soft rustle like a footstep grazing the straw. The goat bleated and Trouble let out a sharp *cawk.*

The sudden sounds, coming together, jerked Isabel out of her momentary shock. She had one thought—to get out of the barn. Except she had to leave the tack room for the open space of the barn to get to the door.

Isabel didn't relish the thought of waiting for trouble to come to her. Gathering her courage, she listened for a moment for any sound that might tell her if someone else waited for her then sprinted for the door.

She reached to yank it open when large hands biting into her upper arms jerked her backward. Isabel gave a cry of surprise and pain.

Twisting, she tried to loosen her attacker's hold on her. He threw an arm around her, binding her arms to her sides, and clamped his hand over her mouth.

"Shut up," a muffled voice ground in her ear.

Pressed against a hard body twice her size, Isabel struggled to keep her footing as he dragged her backward toward the far end of the barn.

He breathed heavily in her ear with the effort to control her. From either side came the sounds of horses

and the milk cow restlessly bumping the wooden walls
of their stalls. Trouble let out a loud screeching cry.
The goat wailed like a starving baby.

Isabel fought against a rising panic. She couldn't
fight him on equal terms of strength and size. But, Lord
help her, she wouldn't surrender, either.

Swallowing the fear that threatened to choke her, she
forced herself to go limp in his arms. He kept moving
but his hold shifted a fraction to accommodate her sag-
ging body.

It was enough for Isabel to react. With all the
strength she could muster, she wrenched sideways, using her weight and his surprise to break his grip.

She stumbled, falling against one of the stall doors.
The impact caught her ribs and she sucked in a breath
at the sharp pain. Ignoring it, Isabel scrambled to regain
her footing and raced for the door, feeling her way in
the dark.

Yanking it open she ran out into the night, up the
path to the kitchen. She slammed the kitchen door behind her and leaned both hands against it, breathing
hard.

"Are you holding it up, or is it the other way
around?"

Isabel spun around so fast she nearly lost her balance. She caught her hand to her ribs, panting.

Jake stood near the big black stove, mug in hand,
his expression quickly changing from a faintly amused
smile to concern.

"What's wrong?" he snapped out. Leaving his mug
on the table he came toward her. He took her by her
shoulders, gripping hard. "Isabel? Are you hurt? What
happened?"

"N-no. I'm all right," she said more firmly. She

drew a deep breath and glanced back over her shoulder. "You startled me."

"Something happened. You're pale as milk." He ran his fingers frantically over her face to assure himself she was still flesh and blood and not a spirit. "What is it?"

"There was someone in the barn." Suddenly her knees felt wobbly. She took one faltering step toward a chair before Jake caught her and scooped her up in his arms.

He carried her to the living area and gently set her down on the big couch in front of the fireplace. "Stay here."

"Jake, no." She put a hand on his arm and he started away from her and out the door. "I don't know if he has a gun. Besides he's probably halfway to the mountains by now."

She knew trying to stop him from going to check the barn would be futile, but at the moment, all she wanted was his arms around her, chasing away the taste and touch of fear.

Jake took her hand from his arm and quickly touched his fingertips to her cheek in a brief caress. "I'll be right back."

In a few long strides, he was out the door without a backward glance. Isabel stayed on the couch for a few moments, trying to regain her equilibrium. Finally, she pushed to her feet and went through the hall to the kitchen. She hesitated for an instant, then grabbed up one of her kitchen knives and followed him.

At the barn, she paused outside the door, straining to hear anything inside. But in the long minutes she stayed there, she only once heard Trouble croak out,

"Watch out!" and a rustle of wings, followed by a string of muttered curses from Jake.

When Jake finally came out again, flinging the barn door open to let Trouble wing his way outside, his expression turned black when he saw her standing there.

"You are a damned stubborn woman, you know that?"

Isabel squared her shoulders and faced him undaunted. "Did you find anything?" she asked, ignoring the gathering storm on his face.

If anything, he looked even more grim. "Since it's obvious you're too hell-bent on this to do what's best for you, put that knife down and come in and have a look at this."

He'd relit the lantern and held it high as he led her to a corner of the farthest stall.

Isabel stared in surprise as the yellow flame illuminated the area. Someone had been digging in her barn. There was a good-size trench along the back wall, deep enough to accommodate a small chest, and dirt and straw lay piled up in the middle of the stall along with an abandoned shovel.

"But why?" she said, indicating the hole. "It doesn't make any sense."

"Someone thought it did. Are you sure there's nothing here? Maybe something your husband left behind?"

"Douglas wouldn't have left anything valuable behind. He loved women and whiskey too much. He spent everything he had and then some."

"Maybe he intended to come back."

"Here?" Isabel looked unconvinced. "Douglas left Whispering Creek faster than a cat with its tail afire.

He swore the only way he'd come back was in a pine box. Even if he did bury something of value in the barn, who else would know where to look? I can't imagine he'd tell anyone. Sharing wasn't Douglas's strong point.''

Jake appeared to think over her words. He was silent so long, Isabel prompted, ''You don't believe me?''

''I don't believe someone just decided to wander into your barn in the middle of the night and dig a hole. Do you?''

''I don't know what to think.'' Isabel sat down heavily on the milking stool next to one of the stalls. The goat started bleating again and she automatically got up and went to it, kneeling in the straw to hold it close and soothe it with long, petting strokes. ''I never got your salve, did I, little one?''

Leaving the goat for a moment, she went to the tack room and fetched the salve, returning to gently smooth it over the wound on the goat's foreleg. All the while, she murmured quietly to the small animal in a low, rhythmic cadence.

Jake, leaning against the wall outside the stall, watched her. The dim lamp cast her in gold and shadow, and for a suspended time, in the hushed stillness, she seemed to truly be an angel he'd chanced upon.

He'd thought briefly of chasing after the intruder, but the idea of leaving Isabel vulnerable quelled that notion at once. He'd have to take a different approach. Tonight he couldn't take a chance and leave her alone.

She sat back on her heels, giving the goat a final stroke, and the small motion dragged Jake back to reality.

Looking away from her, he forced his mind back to

the trouble at hand. He asked the first question that came to him, one that had been worrying at him since he discovered the digging in the barn. "Are you certain Douglas is dead?"

Isabel's head jerked up. "Am I certain...? Of course I am!"

"Did you ever see him after you heard he'd died?"

"This is ridiculous," she said, getting to her feet and closing the goat's stall door behind her. I *am* a widow and I don't know of any hidden treasure in my barn that might attract a thief with a shovel. If I did, I'd dig it up myself and pay for a new roof."

Jake watched her for a few moments before he blew out a long breath, some of the tenseness leaving him. "I'm sorry. I shouldn't have brought him up."

Isabel made to turn away but Jake reached out and caught her hand, stopping her. She let him draw her close. The whole night had been so upsetting, she simply wanted to feel the comfort of his touch.

The attack in the barn left her shaky inside, a feeling she didn't like. She felt vulnerable, afraid she would say something she would later regret.

"You deserved much, much more than he gave you."

"He gave me the boys. I couldn't have hoped for more than they've been to me."

He still held her hand but Isabel couldn't read the expression on his face. In the shadows he looked as unreachable as he had the first day she'd seen him.

"You were lucky to have found love with your wife. I envy you that," she said softly. When he said nothing, she screwed up her courage to ask, "What was she like?"

He didn't say anything for so long she thought he

might not answer. When he did, his voice was low and strained. "Small, dark, pretty. She loved beautiful things and she had a way of making the plainest things lovely. She was used to gentleness, a softness in her life. At times, I was almost afraid to touch her, she seemed so delicate. She needed someone to shelter her."

*Not like me,* Isabel thought. She would never inspire that feeling in him.

It surprised her how much that knowledge hurt.

Certainly she didn't want or need a man who treated her like fragile porcelain. She could and did take care of herself.

Yet she couldn't help but recall how good it had felt the times he had taken her in his arms to offer support and she had leaned on his strength.

"You must have loved her very much," she said, almost to herself, forgetting for a moment he was near, her hand in his.

"I did love Lily," Jake said quietly. He gripped her hand to turn her eyes to his. "But, like you, I also had illusions when I married. I convinced myself she would adapt to life on the frontier because she told me she shared my dreams. Maybe she wanted to, but she wasn't strong enough. I lost everything because I didn't want to see that. I don't want to risk that kind of loss ever again. Do you?"

Isabel looked at him, trying to give voice to the whirl of feelings, desires, needs inside her. She felt so much but didn't know how to describe it with words.

Finally, feeling she was standing on the edge of something much too deep, not knowing the danger of taking the next step ahead, she nodded.

"Maybe I'm a fool," she said slowly, "but yes. Yes I do."

Without giving him time to answer, she tugged her hand free of his, turned and ran out of the barn, leaving Jake in the shadows.

"You weren't planning on going into town, were you?"

Isabel looked up from her half-eaten flapjacks, startled by Jake's unexpected question. She hadn't seen him since she'd left him in the barn last night and it was the first sentence he'd spoken to her this morning. He'd come down to breakfast looking like he'd spent a sleepless night, his hair ruffled, a dark shadow of beard on his jaw. He was still buttoning his shirt sleeves as he strolled toward the coffeepot simmering on the stove.

Still feeling the embarrassment of baring her soul to him the night before, of speaking words she'd struggled to keep her own heart from hearing, she blushed and looked away.

Isabel's reaction caused Katlyn to eye Jake warily. "I'm not going in. Daniel and I have several chores to do together today. If you need something, you're on your own," she added before excusing herself for the Parker ranch.

Esme gave him a long appraising look before shoving a plate in front of him. Without a word of greeting she walked out of the kitchen toward Isabel's shop.

Isabel stole a glance his way, irritated that seeing him looking like he'd just rolled out of bed roused a strong, sudden desire to touch all and more of what the gape in his shirt exposed. At the same time, she remembered how good it had felt to be held in the tender protection of his embrace. Isabel realized Jake was waiting for her answer.

"No," she said, putting down her fork. "I have other plans."

"We're going gathering," Matt piped up.

"Nana said this is the season mallow will be growing thick as bees on honey around the lake," Nate said around his last bite of flapjacks. "And she wants some of those funny leaves she uses for love charms." He wrinkled his nose over the last words.

Isabel hid her smile. "We're going to have to find our own mallow and funny leaves this morning," she said. "Nana's not feeling up to a trek to the lake today."

Nate frowned a little. "It won't be the same going gathering without her. She knows where to find everything."

Jake took his coffee and his plate and sat down at the table a fair distance from Isabel. She was avoiding looking at him this morning.

"You can come with us today!" Matt chirped, syrup dripping down his chin. "We always take a picnic and then go swimming in the lake."

"Now that does sound tempting," Jake drawled, unable to keep his gaze from sweeping Isabel. He grazed over her so slowly she blushed. Immediately she looked away and he rued himself for letting the ache in his body get the best of him. Damned if she didn't drive him to the brink of madness though.

"Mr. Coulter?" Nate was reaching over the table tugging at his sleeve.

He caught Isabel staring at him, a million questions in the turquoise depths of her eyes. "I'm sorry. What did you say?"

Ten-year-old exasperation in his tone, Nate repeated, "I *said* it's lots of fun. And the woods are pretty this time of year."

Matt looked between his mother and Jake, his nose screwed up. "And what's more important than a picnic on a Saturday?"

Isabel smiled at him, ruffling his ebony hair. "Chores for one thing. You need to go and check on the animals. And I think today we can take that squirrel back to the woods."

In a flurry of excitement, both boys jumped up and hurried out the kitchen door, letting it slam in their wake.

Suddenly alone with Jake, all of Isabel's earlier discomfort returned. She shoved away from the table to busy herself gathering up the dishes.

He finished his coffee in one long draught and pushed away from the table. "I'm going to the jail to talk to Cal about what happened last night."

Isabel sighed, knowing from the resolve on his face she had no chance of dissuading him. "Be my guest, although I don't know what Cal is going to have to say about someone digging in my barn." Her back to him, she poured water from a pail into the sink and started washing plates.

She didn't hear him come up behind her.

Ever so gently, he eased his arms around her. She let out a little gasp, stiffened—then relaxed, dropping the dishes back into the water and leaning against his chest. He touched her bruised side with a gentle brush of his fingers.

"How are you feeling this morning?"

Isabel shrugged against him. "I'll survive." She didn't mention the purple marks on her upper arms and shoulders knowing it would only inflame his temper. And she didn't mention her bruised pride.

She was glad to feel the hard muscle of his chest supporting her as he rocked her slowly in his arms. The rhythmic motion eased the tension from her. She relished the sensation of simply being held. By him.

Jake knew she probably bore bruises she wouldn't reveal. But he decided not to press her. She looked so distraught this morning, the violet shadows under her eyes betraying her sleepless night. He wanted nothing more than to take her into his arms and keep her safe.

"Stay close to the house until I get back," he said. "I won't be long with Cal then I'll come with you on your gathering picnic. I don't want you and the boys out in the woods alone."

His words broke the soothing spell and Isabel turned out of his arms to face him. "I don't need a guard, if that's your reason for going along," she said stiffly. She avoided looking at him and began drying a plate.

"Isabel..." Instead of sparking his ire as her stubborn independence usually did, today, Jake knew he had to handle her with care. Gently, he took the plates out of her hands and set them down, gathering her hands in his. "You're courageous enough to take on the devil and—"

"And tough, sturdy and faithful. You make me sound like a dog. I'm well aware I'm not delicate and pretty and in need of protecting, so you don't have to pretend otherwise!"

Jake stared at her as if she'd suddenly sprouted wings and Isabel felt her face grow hot. Whatever had possessed her to say such foolish things? She sounded like a petulant child.

She opened her mouth to recant them when he

started to laugh, a rich, deep sound that filled the room. Isabel didn't know whether to be angry with him or laugh herself at her ridiculous outburst.

"You ought to take a good look in the mirror, woman."

Ignoring her shock of surprise, he took her shoulders, pulled her close and kissed her hard and so thoroughly Isabel felt her blood catch fire. Breathless when his mouth finally released hers, she could only gape at him.

"Isabel Bradshaw, you're strong, beautiful and passionate. Don't ever believe otherwise."

Letting her free, Jake grabbed his hat and shoved it on. "Don't leave without me. I'm looking forward to watching you bend over and pick your weeds."

He flashed her a wicked grin, leaving Isabel with her mouth gaping at his audacity. Picking up a napkin, she balled it up and flung it his direction.

Jake caught it easily. "You know," he said, flipping it back, "I think I'm going to enjoy this little adventure today."

## Chapter Thirteen

"Here!" Matt jumped up, causing the cart to lurch sideways a bit on the rough path. "You have to stop here! There's the yerba you need to make that yucky stuff Nana drinks."

"Good, Matt. You remembered." Isabel smiled at him and pointed to a spot a little distance from them. "Over there, under that old cottonwood, is a good place to spread the quilt." She turned to Jake. "There's a beautiful lake just beyond that piñon grove where we swim."

"Nate, give me a hand with the mares," Jake said, climbing down.

"Comin'." Nate shoved a small wooden cage out from under the cart bench over toward Matt and hopped down. "Here, you can let the squirrel go. I'm helping Mr. Coulter."

"Come here, girl," Matt said, lifting the cage to his lap and peering inside. The little red-furred creature eyed him back, nose twitching. "You don't really belong to me. But I wish you did."

"That's right, sweetheart." Isabel leaned over the seat and laid a hand on Matt's shoulder. "Your little wounded friends are only ours for a time, until they're well.''

Matt's bottom lip began to tremble and he chewed at it. ''She might have gone blind if we set her free sooner, right?''

''Mmm,'' Isabel murmured as she let Jake help her down from the cart. ''But the minute they're well again and they don't need you, they're itching to be set free.'' She turned her smile to Jake. ''Isn't that so?''

The jab struck home, but Jake didn't so much as flinch. ''We both know taking risks usually winds up causing pain.''

Isabel met his dark gaze with challenge. ''It's also true that if there's no risk, there can be no discovery.''

Isabel and Jake stood close, tension flowering in the short space between them. Neither noticed Nate had already released the mares from the cart, taken their reins and was waiting impatiently for Jake to help him lead the animals to the meadow.

Crinkling up his nose, Nate stepped almost between them and looked up at one, then the other. ''C'mon, Mr. Coulter,'' he said, jerking on Jake's shirtsleeve, ''Maya and Luna are about to take off.''

Jake turned and followed Nate, leaving Isabel to ponder his words. Jake had made it abundantly clear he was through taking risks. At least with his heart.

She walked to the back of the cart and grabbed the basket. ''Matt, help me spread the quilt, then you may go swimming.''

''Yes, Mama.'' Matt unfolded a quilt and began to spread it out, but mischief got the better of him and he couldn't resist the urge to plunge into it and roll himself up.

Isabel laughed, glad he was still very much a little

boy. She bent and rolled him round and round until he finally squirmed loose, breathless from the giggles.

After Isabel finally managed to organize the quilt and the basket, the boys ran ahead to take a swim. Jake reclined on the old quilt next to her, toying with a long blade of grass.

"Do you swim?" she asked, trying not to stare at the impressive figure of a man he made lying beside her.

"Well, I can get across a river if it's not too wide, but I'm not fond of jumping in if I don't have to. How about you?"

"I can dive off a cliff if it's not too high."

"That I'd like to see."

"Is that a challenge?"

Jake raised himself up on his elbows. "It is. But considering those bruises of yours, I take it back."

"Ah, too late for that. If I succeed, then I demand a reward."

"A reward is it? Well, angel, what can I offer you?"

His eyes made several suggestions, all of them wicked temptation.

Isabel colored but refused to let him unsettle her. "You have to come swimming with us."

"You've got a deal, lady," Jake said with that grin that never failed to tug at her heart.

"You'll regret this wager. Jerico and the other kids and I used to—" Isabel abruptly broke her sentence.

Why had his name of all names slipped from her lips? It's because that's usually what's on Jake's mind, she thought, dreading his reaction.

Jake felt the now familiar tightening in his gut he recognized as his response when he heard Isabel and Grey linked together. "You were involved with him a long time, weren't you?"

"If I didn't know you better, I'd say you were jealous."

"I am," he said without thinking.

He had taken both of them off guard with his unexpected words, but Jake refused to take them back and pretend they had some other meaning.

"I hate the idea of his hands on you, of him holding you, touching—" He broke off before the vision and the anger it evoked grew any stronger.

"I thought you kept asking about him because you believed I knew about the gold, that I was protecting him because I had loved him once," Isabel said wonderingly. She felt shaky inside, as if a reality she'd long accepted suddenly crumbled, showing her a completely different truth. "I never thought it mattered to you—like that."

"I told myself it didn't. But it does." Jake didn't touch her, but Isabel felt the power of his expression as sure as any caress. "It matters with him, with anyone. I didn't want it to, but I can't stop it."

"There is no one else. I never truly loved any man, not Jerico, not Douglas." *Until now.* They both heard the words but Isabel left them unspoken, afraid to give her feelings for Jake any name. "It's been a long time since I even had the feeling I could love someone, trust someone."

Her words went straight to his heart. Jake wanted to believe them. He wanted to forget them. They scared the hell out of him, that and this possessiveness for her he couldn't control.

*But if you asked me to surrender it all, angel,* he told her silently, *if you asked me now, I don't think I could say no.*

In the intent way he watched her, the tense stillness

of his body, Isabel sensed he waited for a response from her. Except she didn't know what he wanted to hear, only that it was important to him in some way.

Groping blindly for the right reply, she chose to try and comfort. "We weren't lovers. Most of the time I knew Jerico we played, as children. Didn't you have children you played with?"

*"Play?"* Jake shrugged off the word. It was obviously not what he expected or hoped from her, but some of the rigidness eased, leaving behind that familiar masked expression that told her nothing of his true feelings.

"That somehow strikes me as odd. My pa raised me to put in a day's work and to always watch my back. I don't recollect *play* being a word I heard much. Shooting targets was the closest I ever got to playing, I guess. But I did that alone."

Though there was no obvious emotion in his voice, Isabel sensed an underlying current in him, a longing perhaps for the childhood he'd missed. "No wonder you know how to get so much work out of my boys," she said lightly, not wanting to press him. "You've taught them so much. I want you to know how much that means to me."

"Believe me," he said, "they've done more for me."

Isabel's heart constricted. She ached for him and instinctively she moved to sit in front of him, taking his face in her hands. "Wounds won't heal unless we let them."

Jake reached up and covered one of her hands with his, his gaze probing hers. "Maybe you should try your own remedy."

Her hands slid away. "That's different. Douglas didn't break my heart."

"You keep telling yourself that. But he did break your heart. I see that in you every day." He took her hands in his warm callused ones. "You might not have loved him passionately, but you were in love with the dream you thought he would give you. A home, a family, a future."

She stiffened and tried to draw back but Jake held her fast. "Perhaps *you* should become a healer of hearts and souls," she said, pulling free and getting to her feet to move away from him.

Jake caught her and drew her back down. He lifted her chin with one finger, forcing her to meet his gaze. "There's nothing wrong with wanting that dream."

The words slipped out before he realized what he was saying. The last thing he wanted now was to talk about his lost dreams. Talking about them still left his insides shredded. He wanted only to bury the past somewhere no one would ever reach again.

Gently, before giving her a chance to respond, to read more into what he'd said than he meant for her to hear, more than he himself wanted to face, he bent and kissed her.

When he finally drew back, Isabel didn't know whether to cling to him and demand more, or run as far and as fast as she could, away from the riot of confusing feelings he roused in her.

"Why did you do that? Just now, that way?" she asked, not sure if she really wanted to hear his answer.

"Because I had to," he said.

"You had to kiss me?"

"Yes. Do you wish I hadn't? Do you wish I'd never kissed you, held you..." Gently, as if he couldn't help himself, he swanned his fingers over her cheek. "...touched you?"

Isabel's gaze fell. She sighed, not certain how to answer.

Except her heart knew there was only one answer. "No."

Jake relaxed a little, absently smoothing his hands over her arms. A hint of a smile teased his lips. "That's a relief."

Isabel made a face at him and tossed a handy pine-cone his direction. "Come on," she said, standing up, "I'll race you to the lake." Hiking her skirt up to her knees, Isabel smiled triumphantly and started running, her golden hair flying behind her as she disappeared into the dense woods.

"Isabel!"

Only her laughter answered him.

Jake shoved himself to his feet and, without hesitation, sprinted after her. His slight limp slowed him up, but wasn't disabling any more. And the exhilaration of the chase felt good. Especially when he knew his quarry this time was a wild angel who could enchant him with a smile and a touch.

When he caught up with the sound of laughter and splashing, the boys had already stripped down to their drawers and were diving and romping in the water like two young otters. At first he didn't see Isabel.

"Mr. Coulter!" Matt hollered. "Look, Mama's going to dive!"

Jake's eyes followed Matt's gesture to a jagged red-rock cliff above the lake. Atop the very edge stood Isabel, the soft white cotton of her thin shift fluttering around her bare thighs.

She grinned and waved down to him.

Jake's heart skipped a beat. "She wouldn't dare."

She stood on her toes at the edge of the precipice, graceful, ethereal, wild and angelic at the same time. Her hair shimmered in the sunlight, a thousand shades of gold, lifting in the breeze to encircle her head like a halo. At the same time the outline of her body beneath her shift reminded him to the point of utter torture how much all woman she was.

"Watch!" Nate shouted, jolting Jake from his daze. "Mama's good at jumping off cliffs."

"That I can believe," Jake said under his breath.

Stretching her body from her fingertips to her toes, Isabel stepped to the very edge of the cliff. Sucking in a deep breath, she launched off the ledge in a graceful dive.

Below the boys cheered wildly, whooping and hollering, splashing and paddling toward where she would land.

Jake held his breath until he saw her smiling face surface in the center of the pool.

"Well, I'll be damned."

She waved to him, heady with triumph. "You lose! Come on in, the water is delightful."

"I want an encore!" he shouted.

Isabel swam toward where he stood out of the boys' earshot. "And I want to see you shed that shirt and those pants."

"Do you?" The slow, lazy smile he gave her nearly stole her breath. "Has anyone ever told you you're shameless, ma'am?"

"Well sir, if I am, then you ought to feel right at home."

"You know something, angel," he said slowly, as if just coming to a realization himself. "I believe I do."

* * *

Jake stepped to the edge of the lake, bracing his feet. He sensed the mischief maker in her might tempt her to tug him in.

Instead she swiped her hand through the water, landing a huge splash smack in his face.

"You'll pay dearly for that one," he vowed, wiping the water away with the back of his hand. In a single fluid movement he pulled off his shirt and tossed it aside.

"Is that supposed to scare me?"

"It should."

"I don't scare that easily." Isabel stood in waist-deep water, boldly watching his every move. Her eyes fixed on the bronze ripples of muscle flexing as he raised and lowered his arms, but she tried to hide her admiration and appear unmoved.

Jake bent to yank off his boots, then bold as brass, staring straight at her, unbuttoned his pants and shrugged them down over his hips. Two could play this game.

"Nothing here you haven't seen before," he said easily, as if he undressed in front of her every day. "Is there?"

Isabel swallowed hard, her skin beneath the wet shift tingling at the sight of his powerful thighs and calves outlined with precision through his snug long johns. When her eyes drifted over his midsection, she tried to avert them from the rigid form of him barely hidden by the thin cotton knit. But her battle with propriety was lost before it had begun.

Jake smiled dangerously. "Seen enough?"

Isabel's bravado melted. She held up a palm in a motion of surrender. "I never meant—I mean—that's how we swim," she fumbled around the words, feeling foolish. "In our underclothes."

"I swim buff naked."

"You wouldn't—the boys..."

She glanced over her shoulder. Thankfully, the tall reeds at the water's edge sheltered them from the boys' view. They played on the other side of the lake, blissfully oblivious to the scene, engrossed in swimming, dunking, chasing underwater.

"It's a tempting thought," Jake said, then laughed at her mixed expression of alarm and a flicker of interest she couldn't quite hide. "I promise, this is as far as I go. But I will remember this place. It has interesting possibilities."

With that he dived in, and, for a moment, disappeared under the water. Then, before Isabel knew what hit her, he sprung up out of nowhere and had her in his arms. "How are your ribs now?" he murmured close to her ear.

"Much better."

"Good," he said.

Isabel leaned against him and the feel of his powerful body pressed to her, his hands stroking her skin unleashed an aching need in her. Isabel was glad the depths of the lake cloaked them because he held her so close, she couldn't tell where she stopped and he began.

She nearly forgot herself when Jake hooked a leg around hers. "I think you're asking for it," he said, just before he pulled her under.

Isabel came up flinging water his direction and they laughed like children, splashing and teasing each other in abandon.

In those few moments Jake enjoyed a freedom he'd

never known. He thought he'd been unfettered living his life on the trail, without the complications of attachments.

Isabel backed against him and desire surged over tenderness. Her laughter ended in a little throaty sound of pleasure when he pulled her up hard against him.

Jake held her there a long moment until both of them were breathless. Isabel trembled, and he felt it all down his length.

"Game's over," Jake rasped.

"I—I know," Isabel said as much to convince herself as to convince him. Dragging herself from him she waded a little away, far enough to put a cooling distance between them.

Jake stared hard at her, then dived under the surface and swam nearly to the opposite shore, challenging his body with another form of exertion until he could look at her without the overpowering urge to make love to her here and now.

Finally, he started stroking slowly back to the shore, where she waited on the grassy lakeside.

All at once the boys raced toward them, splashing and shouting, each clamoring to be the first to reach the shore.

"I won! I won!" Nate yelled, crashing into Jake.

A few lengths behind Matt swam up, huffing and puffing by the time he caught up with the group. "I'm starving."

"Me, too." Nate climbed out after Matt and then both boys went to fetch their dry clothes.

Isabel brushed her wet hair from her face. "How about you?" she asked Jake.

"Ravenous. All this exercise has given me an appetite."

A liquid warmth spread through her. Isabel knew it showed in her face. "I hope what I have to offer can satisfy you."

Flashing him a smile, she rose gracefully to her feet, heading toward the tree where she'd hung her dress. Isabel disappeared into the woods to redress, leaving him staring after her.

Jake took a couple more dives beneath the water to cool his blood. But though the water engulfed his body, it did nothing to quench the fire she had started in his heart.

"Matt, while I set out our supper, I need you to go gather a basket of antelope horns," Isabel was saying as Jake approached. She met him with an all too innocent smile. "Have a nice swim?"

Jake answered her with a frown.

Still smiling, Isabel turned back to Matt. "And Nate, a little ways back beside the path to the lake there were some mallow plants and a little tansy. Run and pick me a handful of each, please. When you get back, you can fill your plates."

"Yes, Mama," both boys said, greedily eyeing the food she was unwrapping. Together they trotted off to do their chores.

Jake smoothed a damp ebony wave from his brow and sat down on the quilt. Isabel handed him the *burritos,* apple tarts and beans to set out. "Even though you know you're tempting fate, this has been a fine day."

"I haven't the faintest idea what you're talking about," Isabel teased. "But I am glad you're enjoying yourself."

"You manage to make everything special."

She stopped serving and looked at him. "Your being here has made it extraspecial. I'm glad you came."

"So am I. I could get used to being with you, like this," he said softly.

Isabel set down the plates she was holding and looked straight at him. "Are you trying to tell me something?"

"Not really. Only that it can't be forever."

"Ah, I should have known." She knew this day had been too good to be true.

"I know what you're thinking," she said, sighing. "You're having a wonderful time, but—"

"I can't get my mind off finding someone digging around in your barn." Tension bit into his jaw, tightening it again into a flint-hard line. "This has been real nice, Isabel, but I won't feel easy about leaving you alone until I know who did it."

Rubbing at her temple, Isabel thought she might be needing some of that antelope horn. "Don't tell me. You want to go back and dig up whatever you think is in there yourself, don't you?"

Jake nodded. "If I find whatever that intruder was looking for, then I'd bet my last dollar I'll have the bait I need to catch myself one thieving, murdering son of a bitch."


Isabel stood in the barn doorway, watching Jake as he moved around inside, plotting out a course of action for his afternoon digging expedition. She felt uneasy about his determination to find something buried here, but couldn't define the cause of it.

Jake was right to insist on searching the barn, she knew. If there was something of value hidden here, she didn't want to endanger her family by letting it lie and risking another encounter with whoever decided to come back and retrieve it.

On the other hand, if Jake did find something, wasn't he inviting the person who wanted it to take it from him? Although as soon as the thought formed, Isabel knew he had planned that from the beginning.

"Having second thoughts?" Jake spoke close to her ear.

Isabel looked up to find him standing at her side. The smile tugging his mouth and the amusement in his eyes told her she'd been oblivious to him for several minutes. She shook her head, forcing a small smile in return.

"Not really," she said. "I just want to have it over with."

Studying her, Jake knew she evaded confessing her true uneasiness. She wanted it over with, but he would swear she was fearful about what he would find. Jake had an idea he kept to himself to avoid upsetting her further. If he was right, she'd find out soon enough.

For now, he intended to protect her as long as he could.

"It shouldn't take long," he said. "The barn's not that big and I don't think whatever's here is buried too deeply. The person who put it here probably didn't have much time to do a thorough job of it."

"You still think it was Douglas, don't you?"

"I'm not sure what to think," Jake hedged. "Let's just see what we find, then we'll figure out who put it here."

Isabel was spared having to answer him by the sound of voices nearing the barn. She and Jake expected Cal. Even though Cal wasn't well, he wanted to be involved in the search.

She recognized his voice talking with the boys as he neared and after greeting him, she left the men to their digging. Matt and Nate sprinted past her into the barn as she started for the kitchen door, calling to her over their shoulders, and Isabel smiled a little at their enthusiasm to join the treasure hunt.

Isabel walked into the kitchen, finding Katlyn and Esme hard at work. "If there is gold to find, those boys will find it," Esme said, as she punched down a loaf of bread dough.

Katlyn covered the bowl with a cloth. "Well, whatever's going on is the most exciting thing that's happened in Whispering Creek since I've been here!"

"Madness, that is what." Esme began shoving lumps of dough into the bread pans, then put the pans of dough, covered by a towel, on the warm stove to rise.

"Jake thinks Douglas hid something there," Isabel said.

"Bah! That man, he never had enough to fill his pockets, let alone anything worth burying."

Isabel shrugged. "I've decided Jake is as stubborn as they come. Once he gets an idea, nothing changes his mind." She moved next to her sister. "Katlyn, let me help you with that."

Taking one of two heavy pans from Katlyn, she helped carry it to the stove. Talking about Jake forced her toward admitting feelings she wasn't ready to acknowledge.

"I can finish," Katlyn said. "I need to learn, soon enough I'll be on my own. Besides—" she flashed a grin at Esme "—Esme says with another year or so of practice, I'll be able to make biscuits Daniel can eat without taking a pickax to them."

They all laughed and, for the next half an hour, worked preparing the evening meal.

An hour later, Nate and Matt burst into the room, their faces lit up with excitement.

"Mama! You have to come and see!" Matt danced excitedly in front of her. "Jake found the treasure!"

"It's big! It looks like two whole bagfuls," Nate added.

Isabel's stomach clenched. What had Jake found?

The boys rushed out ahead of her and she followed them outside and to the barn. Inside, Cal stood at the tack room door, Matt and Nate hovering behind him, craning to get a look.

Isabel stepped between them to where Jake knelt on the floor in a corner of the room. A pile of pried-up boards and dirt attested to his search. He turned to look at her as she moved next to him.

"What is it?" Isabel asked. "What have you found?"

Jake got to his feet, bringing two battered leather saddlebags with him. The bags were obviously heavy, bulging with their contents.

"Everyone believed Grey hid the stolen gold from all over Taos County somewhere up in the Sangre de Cristos. But I think it's been much closer than that all along."

Setting the bags on the ground, he flipped open the tops.

Isabel caught her breath and stared. She blinked and looked again, hardly able to believe the evidence of her eyes.

On her tack room floor was a king's ransom in gold.

# Chapter Fourteen

Isabel stared at the gold lying at her feet unable to believe her eyes. "There must be a fortune there. But how...?"

"It had to be Douglas—" Cal said, a raspy cough forcing him to break off. He mumbled an apology, stuffing his kerchief back into his pocket. "This has to be the gold from the Golden Horseshoe robbery, the last one Grey pulled before the Taos County marshall got too close and scared him out of the territory. But Grey'd never have left this much gold behind. Especially not in your barn."

"I know Jake is convinced Douglas had something to do with the robbery, but Cal, you knew Douglas. You can't think he robbed that mine," Isabel said.

"Belle, honey, you're right, I did know Douglas," Cal said, rubbing a hand over his hair, "and I think you'll do better to trust Jake than the memory of a man who spent more time warmin' one of the chairs in Elish's saloon than with his family."

Isabel glanced at Matt and Nate, craning around Cal to see inside and get a good look at the gold. Her caring for Douglas had long died, but she didn't want them hearing the worst about him, not now.

"Boys, why don't you go inside and tell Nana what Jake found. It's about time for supper, and you can help her get it on the table."

"But Mama, we want to hear about the gold," Matt protested.

Nate added his objections at being sent away but Isabel stood firm. "We'll be in soon. Go along now."

When they'd gone, reluctantly, shuffling their feet to drag out the walk from the barn, Jake straightened, dusting off his hands on his thighs.

He looked at Isabel, trying to judge her reaction to his find and the obvious conclusion her husband had partnered Grey in robbing the Golden Horseshoe. Finally, he asked, "Why can't you believe Douglas could have been involved?"

"He might have stolen something if it didn't involve risking his neck. He didn't have the nerve to pull off a robbery like that." She felt uncomfortable defending Douglas, even mildly. But calling Douglas a robber didn't make sense.

"But he did know Grey. And he did work at that mine. Maybe he knew something about the robbery and where Grey had stashed the gold and cash, and double-crossed him."

"It makes sense, Belle," Cal added. "Douglas did leave in a hurry. Carryin' this much gold would've slowed him down but it looks like he took the cash from the payroll and headed for San Francisco. He probably figured on coming back when Jerico took off south with the law on his tail."

Isabel rubbed at her temple. "If that's true, then who

was in my barn last night? It can't have been Douglas.''

"Grey must have figured out Douglas didn't have the gold when he left town," Jake said. "That meant Douglas had to leave it somewhere, and home would be the logical place to look. Apparently Douglas didn't have time to do much else with it."

"Then Jerico is going to know you have his gold." Isabel felt suddenly cold. "He's going to come for it."

"That's what I'm counting on."

The flint-hard look on his face told Isabel he'd counted on Jerico's greed from the beginning. He intended to set himself up as a target for Jerico no matter what the risk.

"So you're just going to sit in your room and wait for him to come to you? What a wonderful plan."

"No. I'm going to sit in a room at the Silver Rose."

"You can't be serious!"

Cal put a hand on her shoulder. "Now Belle—"

"No." Isabel shook off his hand to step directly up to Jake. "You're crazier than I thought. Every thief and gunslinger who comes through Whispering Creek stays at the Silver Rose, you know that. Once they find out you're holed up, sitting on a fortune in stolen gold, they'll come out of the woods like starving wolves after you to get it. Are you planning on staying awake with your back to the wall and guns drawn for however long it takes Jerico to find you?"

"Do you want me to stay here and wait for him to show up on your doorstep?"

"Damn you, Jake, I want you alive!"

A brittle silence followed her hot words. Her gaze clashed with Jake's. They stared at each other, oblivious to Cal.

Isabel found herself trembling, both with fear for him and anger at him for deliberately choosing to put himself in the way of danger. That it was his job, that he'd probably done it countless times before didn't matter. This was here, now, and the thought of losing him made her feel shaken inside.

Reason told her he was right to leave. He cared about her family and wanted to protect them and leaving was the best way.

Her heart, though, refused to listen.

Jake fought the urge to close the distance between them, sweep her into his arms and hold her against him until she felt safe again, until he felt right in leaving her to finish the job he'd come to Whispering Creek to do.

As much as he wanted Grey brought to justice, walking away from Isabel right now felt like leaving a sanctuary of the heart, turning his back on heaven.

Cal gave a hoarse, raspy cough, turning Isabel's attention to him and giving Jake the space he needed to check his emotions.

"Look, Belle," Cal said, his voice gravelly. For the first time since she'd come into the barn, Isabel noticed he looked chalky, his face drawn in deep lines. "Jake's right to move out. He'd be putting you and the boys in danger staying here when he knows Jerico isn't about to let this gold go."

"You can't think going to the Silver Rose is a good idea!"

Cal scratched at his chin. "No...but I think I have an idea where he could go."

Jake and Isabel both looked at him expectantly.

"My jail," he said. "It's not the best of accommodations, but between the two of us, I think we could keep away the vultures long enough to catch us a snake.''

Jake looked doubtful. "I appreciate the offer, but I can't ask you to risk your neck along with mine.''

"I'm not looking for an invitation. I may be an old geezer, but I can shoot straight and I've got the one place in town most of the varmints avoid like bad whiskey.'' Cal grinned. "And you can use the safe to lock your gold in. Most of the cells are empty right now save for Charlie Potter, who should be just about done sleepin' off his latest swim in the bottle. Can you think of a better place?'' he prompted when Jake still hesitated.

"I can't,'' Jake admitted. "I don't seem to have too many options right now.''

"Cal,'' Isabel began, "maybe you should let me have a look at you before you decide to lock yourself in the jail with Jake for heaven knows how long. I could—''

"Belle, that tender heart of yours frets too much. Don't you be worryin' about me. It's settled. Now...I think I'll wander down into town and have myself some dinner and then buy a drink at the Silver Rose. I think it might do us some good if an old man talked a little too freely about the stolen treasure we dug up in Belle's barn and are keeping at the jail.''

On his way out the door, he glanced back over his shoulder at Isabel. "Don't be too hard on the man, Belle. He's pretty handy to have around. I wouldn't want him leaving too soon.''

"So you're going through with this insane plan,'' Isabel said to Jake when Cal was gone.

"Do you have a better one?''

"I…" She wanted to say, *I want you to stay. If you leave, you won't be back.*

She had known all along he wasn't the kind to stay put in one place longer than his job lasted. But she hadn't expected his actual leaving to hurt so much.

"I can't stay," Jake said softly.

He moved toward her so close only a hand's breadth separated them. She could feel the heat of his body as palatable as a caress, a temptation to forget everything but the texture and scent and touch of him.

"You know I can't. It's not safe for you or the boys. I don't want to see any of you hurt."

"I know that, but I don't want to see you killed. There's got to be another way. Cal means well but he's sick, surely you can see that. How much help will he be if there's trouble?"

"I can take care of myself. But I can't take care of you if I'm here. You're too much of a distraction. When you're around me, all I can think about is you."

"But you're leaving all the same."

Jake gently rubbed his knuckles against her cheek. "I'm not Douglas. You know why I have to go."

"Jerico will kill you," Isabel said so quietly it was almost a whisper. She closed her eyes against the vision.

"Have a little faith in me, angel."

She opened her eyes and Jake saw the fire back there again, the determination to fight him on his decision, to fight for his life. Knowing she cared enough to argue so passionately for him twisted his heart and his gut. He wanted her to care, deeply and irrevocably; he wanted to warn her not to give her heart when he couldn't give his in return.

Couldn't or wouldn't? An inner voice taunted him and made it hard to face her direct look.

He closed the space between them, pulling her against his chest. One arm wrapping her to him, he stroked his free hand down her back in a long, gentle motion. "Can you do that for me?" he murmured against her ear.

His breath kissed her skin and that barest of caresses coupled with the stroke of his hand on her spine felt nothing like comfort and everything like provocation to Isabel. He spread fire through her veins, making her long for more than just the warmth of him through the cotton of her dress.

The tremble of her body and the little sigh she made leaning into his embrace clouded Jake's mind, nearly changing his intent to tease her into a potent desire to cast off their clothing, tumble her into a bed of hay and make love to her. Slowly, as if they had forever and a night.

Except the stolen gold at their feet reminded him he had a job to do.

He couldn't stay.

He didn't want to leave.

Isabel felt the tension in him and knew he fought between duty and surrendering to the passion burning them both alive. She longed to succumb to it, to seduce him into forgetting Jerico Grey, Douglas and the gold, even for a night.

But Jake made the decision for them both. Gently, with a brush of his lips against her temple, he put her from him, stepping back.

She could only look at him, catching her lower lip between her teeth to keep the sudden tears at bay.

"I'll get my things and then take this over to the

jail," Jake said, his voice rough and low. "I don't want it in your house any longer than necessary."

Isabel only nodded, not trusting herself to speak. She stood aside as he picked up the bags of gold, hefting them outside the barn. Once he had them out of the barn he turned as if to say something to her.

But Isabel looked away, stopping him. She wasn't ready to hear him say goodbye; she wasn't sure she ever would be.

Matt and Nate sat in uncustomary silence on two stools at Isabel's work counter in her shop, rubbing dried oregano between their palms until it crumbled onto the paper spread below.

Behind the counter, her faded blue work apron tied about her waist, Isabel formed the papers into funnels one by one, draining the fragrant oregano into glass bottles, marking them, corking them and placing them neatly on the shelves behind her.

Usually the work was a time for chatter and conversation. Tonight, no one spoke. The only sound was the clicking of knitting needles as Esme sat in the corner near the iron wood stove, rocking and humming to herself, crafting thin strands of gray wool into a sock for Matt. The faint smell of green *chile* stew wafted in from the kitchen. Neither Isabel nor the boys had any appetite at dinnertime, so she'd left it to simmer.

The familiar creak of the bottom step from the stairwell brought busy fingers to a standstill. Two sets of big eyes darted up to Isabel, questioning, needing answers, reassurance.

"He'll be safer at the jail. And so will we," she soothed. "This is for the best. He can't stay here anymore." Her own words sounded hollow to her ears.

She knew Matt and Nate drew no comfort from them, either.

Saddlebags draped over one shoulder, Jake strode into the shop. Immediately Isabel's eyes were drawn to the Colts slung on his hips. He hadn't worn his gun belt around the house or to the picnic and she hadn't missed the sight of it. Now the wide leather strap and loaded six-shooters were all she could see.

Dressed in black, guns at hand, the shadow of a beard darkening his jaw and his hat pulled low over his eyes, he reminded her forcibly of the dangerous outlaw she'd believed he was the first time she'd laid eyes on him. The cold, hard resolve on his face made him seem almost a stranger.

This was Jake. A hunter. A man without roots or ties to bind him. He would follow his prey first and always.

Jake swept the room with a hungry gaze, his heart in his throat. Damn, but he didn't want to leave this place. The boys. Even the familiar sight of Esme peacefully sewing in the corner somehow had become important to him, a part of his daily life.

And Isabel. Beautiful Isabel. Behind her counter, working as always, only this night instead of laughing eyes and a sweet smile he saw only fear that paled her skin, welling in the tears she struggled to hold back.

Esme got up when he came into the shop, leaving her knitting on the rocking chair. "I will go and see to the stew," she said, looking pointedly at Jake. "You, *señor,* will take some to the jail to eat. And do not think of telling me no."

Jake could hardly believe his ears. What had brought that on? "Thank you, ma'am" was all he could say.

Isabel only nodded, waiting until Esme tipped her head in recognition of Jake's reply, and left the shop before turning to the boys. "It's time to say goodbye to Mr. Coulter," she said, her words breaking despite her effort to appear strong.

Matt was the first to jump down off of his stool and run to throw his arms around Jake's waist. "You'll be back. You get him and then you'll be back, right?"

Wide, innocent eyes stared up at Jake, leaving him almost speechless. He dropped his saddlebags and returned Matt's embrace, crouching down to look him in the eye. "We'll see each other again soon, I promise."

Nate sat stiffly with his back to Jake until Isabel insisted once more he say goodbye. "Go on and shake Mr. Coulter's hand and wish him luck."

Reluctantly, Nate slid off his stool and walked slowly over to Jake. He extended a hand from a distance. "Good luck. I know you'll catch him. You always catch 'em. And then you'll be after the next one, right?"

"It's my job, Nate."

"Well, I'll never have a job that keeps taking me away from everyone I care about!" Nate jerked his hand back. "You're not any better than Mr. Bradshaw or my pa, up and leaving us when we need you here!"

With a strangled sob, Nate turned and ran from the room.

"Nate!" Isabel yanked her apron off and darted out around the counter.

Jake stopped her, with a hand on her shoulder. "Don't. There's nothing either of us can say that will make it better."

"Maybe not," Isabel said. "But I can at least tell him I understand how he feels."

She said the words without censure. But Jake felt the cut of them just the same, more keenly because of

Nate's distress. They'd all gotten too close for this goodbye to be easy.

Isabel turned to her younger son. "Matt, go on and tell your brother I want to talk to him before he goes to sleep."

Ducking his head, Matt let his arms drop away from Jake. "Yes, Mama," he mumbled. "Bye, Mr. Coulter. Thanks for teaching us about fixing things and playing with us."

After one more hug around Jake's neck, Matt scampered through the foyer and up the stairs, leaving Isabel to face Jake alone.

Her heart throbbed in her chest, words tumbled through her mind at lightning pace, but all she could do was stand there dumbly staring, waiting, hoping he would change his mind.

As though he read her thoughts, Jake took her face gently in his hands. "This is the only way to stop Grey."

Isabel nodded, unable to find her voice.

"When it's over, when I find Grey, we'll talk— about us."

"Us?"

He leaned closer and kissed her with such aching tenderness Isabel felt new tears burn against her eyes. "Us." She looked up at him. He bent and pulled her up hard against him, plundering her mouth with a possessive passion she returned with a desperate desire to burn the feel of him into her memory. Long moments they clung together, their unspoken need for each other revealing itself in one long, insatiable kiss.

Finally, breathless, Jake released her gently. Smoothing her mussed hair from her face with one hand, he whispered, "I'm only minutes away. I can be here in no time if you need me."

Isabel laughed weakly. "Why does just up the street seem so far, and why do minutes seem so long?"

"I think we both know the answer to that."

Jake picked up his saddlebags and straightened his gun belt. "Now is all that matters. That's why I have to go."

The slender figure slipped out the back door of the Silver Rose into the black night, her dark, hooded cape concealing her identity to any passersby. She glanced furtively from side to side then darted down the back alley behind the saloon.

At the end of the alley a buggy and driver awaited. Safely hidden inside, Anita Devine tossed her hood from her head and settled in for the long ride up the mountain road.

The buggy rattled and rocked up the mountain's edge until, after what seemed to her an eternity, it pulled to a jerking halt in front of an abandoned mine shaft. Near the mine's entrance a yellow glow shone dimly through the window of a small shack.

As the driver helped her from the buggy, Anita ordered, "Wait outside the door with your ear to it and your gun drawn."

Anita smoothed her skirts and sauntered toward the cabin. Before she reached the door, it swung open and a shadowed figure of a man appeared, waving her inside.

The steel-cold hatred that burned in Jerico Grey's eyes intimidated most people who had the misfortune of crossing his path. But not her. Not as long as she had the information he wanted.

# Chapter Fifteen

Jake paced the length of the jail, trying to focus his mind on the job at hand to keep from going crazy. It took him exactly three strides, five if he slowed his walk to a crawl to vary the pattern.

After two days holed up in the small jail with Cal he was ready to pack the gold on a mule, haul it out to the middle of the meadow, and fire off a few shots to let Grey know exactly where he was.

He and Cal had locked the bags loaded with the gold in the jail safe, barred the door, and loaded the rifles and Jake's Colts. Then it came down to waiting. To pass the time, they'd played endless hands of cards, and Jake had listened to Cal tell numerous stories about his early days as a lawman, and his courtship of Isabel's mother after her father had run off.

The latter story interested him the most, because it gave him new insight into Isabel's childhood and her determination now to provide a stable, secure home for her boys.

Jake also recognized a sadness, an emptiness in Cal's eyes that echoed his own loss. He knew too well what drove Cal to avoid ever giving his heart again, the resolve not to risk making himself vulnerable to another heart wound from which he might not recover.

"You know all that pacin' is makin' me nervous," Cal said from his seat at the room's single desk. He coughed, a deep, raspy effort that made him fight for breath and wheeze a little to regain it.

"Are you all right?" Jake asked, not for the first time that afternoon. Cal looked pale. His hand trembled as he reached for the glass of water on his desk. Jake saw he was sweating as if to fight off a sharp pain.

"This damn cough picked a bad time to act up on me," Cal rasped, trying to clear his throat with a drink. "I knew I should have listened to Belle's mother all those years ago and given up on tobacco. She always said it would put me in an early grave."

A spate of coughing shook him again, bending him over nearly double. Jake went over to him and waited until it was over before helping Cal sit back in his chair again. Cal put a shaking hand to his mouth, wiping away a trickle of blood.

Jake gave him one look and made up his mind. "I'm sending for Isabel."

"There's nothing she can do," Cal said. He leaned back and closed his eyes, breathing heavily. "I've known that for a long time and so has she."

"The only thing I know is you've got no business being here in your condition." He glanced out the front office window. "There's Digger's palomino. He must be over at the general store, I'll signal him and have him go and get Isabel."

Cal looked as if he wanted to refuse. Jake didn't give him the chance. He walked outside to stand under the shadow of the overhang, his hands hovering near his Colts. If Grey was out there somewhere watching the jail, he'd strike now. Jake scoured the buildings across from the jail, waiting for Digger. At last the burly old rancher came outside, carrying an armload of parcels. Jake shifted into the late afternoon sun, waving an arm to catch his attention.

Digger came over immediately and, after hearing about Cal's condition, went off to fetch Isabel back to the jail.

Half an hour later, an agitated pounding sounded at the door. Jake glanced out the window to see Isabel standing there, basket in hand, before unbarring the door and letting her inside.

"Digger told me I should see Cal," she said, drawing off her shawl. She glanced around the office. "Where is he?"

"Lying down in the back room," Jake said, jerking a thumb toward the rear of the jail. "He's taken a turn for the worse. He shouldn't be here. I thought maybe you could give him one of your weed potions to knock him out and get him to your place."

"Mmm...I'll see," Isabel murmured, busying herself with taking a bottle, cup and small leather bag from her basket. "I asked Digger to fetch Daniel to help get Cal back to my house. He can stay in your—in the room you were in. Although he's not going to be too happy about us hauling him back there."

Jake watched as she poured out a glass of water, added a spoon of sugar and vinegar, and mixed in a generous pinch of a green-gray powder from the bag.

"What is it?"

"This?" She stirred it a little. "It's gold weed. It'll help the cough and the pain, maybe let him get a little sleep."

"Cal said you know how bad he is."

Isabel nodded, a spasm of sorrow crossing her face. She sighed and picked up the cup. "If you mean I know he's dying, yes I do. But Cal doesn't want to talk about it so I don't. I just do what I can to make it easier for him."

She started toward the back. Jake stopped her with his hands on her shoulders. "I wish I could make it easier for you."

"I know," she said softly, a sheen of unshed tears glistening in her eyes. "But loving people, caring about them, is never easy. And I don't think I'd want it to be. It makes the rewards so much greater."

Reaching up, she kissed him, her mouth moving gently on his for a brief caress before she pulled away and slipped around him.

Jake stood alone a moment, tasting her sweetness. Then he followed her to the tiny back room where Cal lay near the safe that held the stolen gold. He found her kneeling by Cal, helping him to drink the elixir she'd made.

"Belle, I sure wish you'd find a way to make this fine medicine of yours taste a mite better," Cal was saying with a grimace.

"I'll let you in on a secret," Jake said, going down on one knee beside Isabel. "She does it on purpose to give you incentive to stay out of bed and on your feet to avoid drinking any more than you have to."

Cal attempted a short laugh that ended in a racking cough.

Isabel pushed him back down on the cell bed. "Digger and Daniel will be here soon, and they're going to take you back to my house. Don't argue with me, Cal," she warned, holding up her hand to stall any of his objections.

"I'll take care of things here," Jake told Cal as Isabel left the room to make Cal some tea.

"And Belle?"

"She'd be the one getting the bad bargain. But I'm going to do my damnedest to make sure none of this touches her any more than it already has. She deserves that much at the very least."

"She deserves a helluva lot more than that, but I think you already know that. But you're just like me. You've gotten too comfortable with being alone." Cal closed his eyes, his voice slurring a little. "Easier that way, I know. Except it twists you inside, and you don't realize what you've missed out on until it's too late."

*You're just like me. You've gotten too comfortable with being alone.*

The words echoed in Jake's head as he pulled the thin blanket back up over Cal's chest and quietly left the cell. Was that what he'd become? Warped by guilt and grief, alone by choice, segregating himself from warmth and caring because it was easier than risking the loss of it? And if so, what choice did he have now? He had to see this through. And that meant leaving Whispering Creek to take Grey back to Texas to stand trial. It was the only way to guarantee Grey would never touch Isabel's life again.

Hanging like a curved sliver of ice against the cold black sky, the moon shone high overhead by the time Isabel felt comfortable leaving Cal to go back to the jail with Jake's dinner. *He'll be famished by this hour,* she thought, untying the covered basket from her saddle. She tethered her mare to the hitching post and knocked on the door to the sheriff's office. Glancing quickly out the front window, Jake let her inside.

"You shouldn't have come back," he said gruffly.

Isabel stiffened. "Well, maybe I shouldn't have, but I was only thinking of your stomach."

Jake's expression softened slightly. "I only meant that it's not safe here for you."

"And it is for you?" Without waiting for his invitation, she swept past him and placed the basket on Cal's desk.

"Whether it's safe or not has nothing to do with it."

Jake's stomach grumbled at the smell of food, forcing a reluctant smile from Isabel.

"I knew you were hungry. Tell me these tamales and cinnamon tarts don't smell tempting."

Jake walked over to the desk and looked under the cloth covering the source of the spicy aromas. Isabel reached for the basket, but Jake laid a hand on her arm, stopping her.

Questions with no answers written in his dark, searching gaze, he drew her close. "Thank you," he murmured against her temple.

"For what?" She barely uttered the words before he caught her completely off guard and pulled her against him with an urgency that bordered on desperation.

"For coming back. Angel, my angel, Lord, how I've missed you."

"Oh, Jake. You're always on my mind."

"But my mind ought to be on this job and nothing else." He swept her forehead with a kiss. "For the first time in my life, though, the truth is the man I want means nothing compared to the woman I want." He backed away slightly and looked down into her eyes. "Does that make any sense to you?"

Isabel smoothed her hands up his cheeks and brushed away the heavy dark wave that stubbornly fell over his handsome brow. "Oh, yes, it makes perfect sense." She let his words sink into her like warm sweet-scented oil, soothing and stimulating her, body and soul. "I'm just very surprised to hear you say it."

"Not half as surprised as I am," he said, so near his breath fanned her cheek. "Isabel, dammit, I need you. All of you." He captured her face between his big, callused palms.

Hot emotions came like a wild racing wind, rushing at her all at once, and Isabel let herself become swept up in them. "And I want you. This, us, your touch, oh Jake, you have no idea…"

When he pressed his lips to the pulse point on her throat, he felt her blood rush faster in answer to his caress. His lips sought hers, the tenderness of their kiss lasting an eternity. In a moment between heartbeats, between breaths, between time, it was magic.

"Jake," she whispered breathlessly, winding her arms around his neck, his words, honest and knowing, melting her from within.

She had been kissed before, even by him. Yet tonight, the warm persuasion of his mouth, the taste of him, the intimate pleasure he made her feel when he slid one large hand over her throat and shoulder to bring her closer to him, made her believe this was her first kiss.

Held in the arms of his angel, Jake could almost believe in second chances. All these years of being alone, of turning his back on caring, a stubborn part of him had held on to the hope he could do something to deserve love again.

"I've waited, longed for this," Isabel whispered.

The ache in her voice echoed in Jake and he bent to plunder more deeply the sweetness of her mouth.

Her soft yielding was nearly his undoing. All at once he became acutely aware of the barrier of cotton embracing her breasts, the bare legs hidden beneath her airy skirt, the promise of her skin scented with stream water and mountain flowers.

She quivered with a quicksilver awareness of his lips, the tender caress of his tongue. The feel of his hands on her skin, strong and firm, made her forget all the reasons they shouldn't give in to this wondrous feeling.

Desire, primitive and powerful, welled in her, overwhelming every reason not to surrender. She pressed hard against him, soft flesh to rippling muscle.

Jake wound his hands in her hair, pulling her to him, yet he couldn't bring her close enough. He reached out to shove the food basket aside behind her. "As delicious as that smells, it won't satisfy my appetite. But this time, angel, I will be satisfied." Gently, he slid his palm down the small of her back to lower her to lie beneath him on the desk. "And so will you."

Isabel held to him, matching him breath for breath, motion for motion, her touch strong and certain.

She felt warm and supple in his arms, ready for him to discover all the pleasures she so wanted to receive, to give him.

He pinned her hands back against the desk, looking his fill of her face, her breasts, desire lighting his eyes. "You're so beautiful. I never imagined holding an angel in my arms, but here you are. And you're mine. All mine."

"Yes," she whispered, almost beyond words. "Oh, yes…"

Jake released her hands and tugged gently at the ties of her simple cotton blouse. Slowly, as though in homage, he peeled the blouse from her shoulders. Her breath came in soft pants, her pulse pounding in expectation of his touch.

Slipping her arms free of her shift, Jake released her breasts to his waiting hands. Isabel moaned softly as he brushed the pads of his thumbs over the tips, teasing them into taut points.

Jake took his time, lingering over each caress, drawing out each sensation, making a banquet of the feelings. The taste of her went to his head like liquid lightning.

Silk and fire in his hands, she pushed him to the edge of sweet madness, drove every thought from his head but the need to possess her completely.

Isabel writhed beneath him, crying out softly. He pulled back just enough to look into her eyes, to see the truth of her need there.

"Are you sure?" he asked, his voice hoarse with the effort to form words. "Do you want this, angel?"

"You. I want you. Oh, how I want you. Jake..."

Jake needed no more encouragement. He lifted her against him and carried her to the soft pallet in the back room between the cells and the front office. The light of a single lantern turned low filled the tiny room with an amber glow.

Jake's scent, the aroma of leather, tobacco and soap, filled the small space, feeding Isabel's desire until she thought she would die for wanting him.

No gentle wooing of the senses now, the naked intimacy of their feelings ripped away any pretense either of them had about being unmoved. Isabel heard the pound of blood in her ears, a primeval chant accompanied by the frenzied singing of her senses.

Jake heard it, too, as a savage pulse, threatening his

reason, his fortresses built against caring. Still, he forced himself to move slowly, savoring every sensation as though it were his first and last.

With a deliberation that made her want to cry out to release the coiling tension inside her, he slid his hand over her skirts, teasing her skin through the fabric with the promise of his touch.

Isabel matched his tormenting caresses, sliding her hand over his chest and lower in brazen provocation.

Jake caught her hand at his waist. Bringing it to his mouth, he lightly kissed each fingertip. He watched the delicate color flush her cheeks and her lips part with breathless anticipation. Isabel moved to unbutton his shirt and bare his broad chest to her butterfly kisses.

Her touch robbed him of any rational thought, any restraint. Shoving off his shirt and boots and pulling her fully into his embrace, he slowly slid his hand beneath her skirt, savoring every silken inch of her leg, her thigh, catching the tremble of her moist need in his hand, then holding her soft cry of pleasure with his mouth.

The intimacy of his kiss and his caress, the hard heat of his arousal pressed against her thigh, fed the wanting madness in her. It possessed her, became her, a thundering tenderness. Passion that felt like brilliant sunlight and velvet darkness, the bittersweet taste of forbidden paradise, an ache so deep it was an almost unbearable pleasure.

It consumed her and made her strong, so nothing remained of the hollow emptiness that haunted her when she was alone.

Jake felt the completeness of her response; not surrender, but an offer to share everything with him, all she was, all they were together, heart, body and soul.

He wanted to accept, to take all he could ask, all he could need.

He had dreamed of her like this, night after empty night. Only Isabel had ever made him feel this way. Only Isabel could make him whole.

Pushing her skirt away in one fluid motion he laid her bare beneath him. Isabel groped for the buttons of his pants. Together they jerked away the offending garment.

Isabel dug her fingers into his back, begging for his possession, bringing them together. The elemental rhythm of their loving, strong and wild, hurried and breathless, rushed them headlong into a blinding chaos of light and heat.

Pleasure burst inside her, spilling over in brilliant sensation, and she cried out softly. She clung to him, convulsed with a joy that transformed her. Sweeping her to the highest point of her soul and beyond, it held her in thrall to paradise for a moment of forever, before returning her to the arms of her lover in a fall of fire.

She took Jake with her into ecstasy, and in one wild moment, he believed the completeness of their joining would never end. Caught in the climax that shattered his aloneness, in that instant he dared to believe it would never return.

She was his healing angel, the woman of his heart.

How could he leave her?

His last thought gave way to exhausted sleep. Spent, they lay together for hours, clinging, wafting in and out of sleep, a gentle kiss here, a sweet caress there.

Isabel awoke before he did and lay watching him sleep. She relaxed with her face on his chest to feel the rise and fall of his breath. His scent lingered on her skin, his taste on her lips. She longed to curl up next to him and sleep the day away.

How could she stay?

Despite all his tenderness, his wild loving, did his sweet midnight words mean anything in the harsh morning light?

*More than I want to admit,* she thought. Much more.

"Jake," she whispered. She brushed her fingers over his roughened jaw then pressed a kiss there.

He came instantly awake, tensed, before his eyes focused on her. His smile came then, slow and satisfied. "You're here...with me."

For a moment, Isabel couldn't find her voice. She blinked back tears. "I have to go, it's nearly dawn."

Drawing a shaky breath, she sat up, searching for her discarded clothes. "I need to leave soon. That is, if no one has stolen poor Maya. I left her out in front, nearly all night it seems. I'm sure she's restless and I—"

Jake put his fingers to her lips, stopping the rambling words he knew were poor camouflage for her agitated feelings. "Isabel, I..."

He hesitated, not sure what he wanted, what he wanted to say.

"It's all right," she said softly. She leaned over him and kissed him tenderly, then quickly rose to begin pulling on her shift. "I didn't know it was so late. I guess we tired each other out," she teased, attempting a touch of humor to ease the turmoil in her heart.

"I've never slept better."

"Nor have I."

They looked at each other in silence for a suspended moment. Then Jake forced his gaze away to get up from the pallet, and pull on his pants and boots.

"I'll let you out," he said. As he did, his eyes moved toward the safe in the corner where the gold was locked. The sight shot a cold bullet of reality through him.

Isabel followed his gaze. "Time to get back to work?"

Jake avoided her question. Instead, he retrieved his shirt, shoving his arms into the sleeves without buttoning it, before strapping on his gun belt.

She hesitated, as if waiting for him to respond. After watching him a few moments, she walked ahead of him into the outer office. "Shall I leave your dinner?"

"That'd be nice."

An awkward silence, a sudden wordless sadness, fell between them.

Jake felt his heart twist.

"Be careful," she said. Stepping close, she reached up to kiss him one last time.

"Say hello to the boys and to Cal."

Raging emotions tied Isabel's insides in knots. The seconds it took him to unbolt the door seemed hours. Jake walked out in front of her, glancing in all directions.

Maya, seeing Isabel, whinnied in dismay. Thankful for the distraction, she went up to the mare and stroked her nose.

Before she could untie her horse, though, Jake reached out and wrapped an arm around her waist, pulling her into his arms. Burying his face in her hair, he held her close.

She trembled, fighting back tears, and Jake felt it inside. It nearly convinced him to take her back into the jail, keep her there by his side, and to hell with Grey, the gold and the rest of the world.

"Last night was real," he said, tightening his arms around her. "No matter what happens, last night was not a dream."

Isabel returned his embrace with equal fervor before gently pushing away. She smiled up at him, a bittersweet curve to her mouth.

"Yes, but we both also know dreams don't come true."

Jake had no reply.

# Chapter Sixteen

The faintest hints of light had started to paint the night sky with shades of blue and pink when Isabel slipped quietly into her garden.

A chill breeze skittered through the trees and grasses, but her last image of Jake made her oblivious to any sensation but the lingering warmth of his touch. She'd hated leaving his arms but she couldn't risk walking out of the jail in full daylight and having everyone know she spent the night there. Facing Nana and Katlyn would be hard enough.

Isabel didn't want to think about that now, or anything but the memories of being with Jake and their hours of loving. Sitting atop the stone wall that edged one of her herb beds, she looked out over the whispering meadow to the hazy shadows of the mountains, edged with the rose and orange of the nearing sunrise.

The cool breeze, scented with pine and wildflowers, caressed her face and threaded through her unbound hair. She closed her eyes, remembering Jake's touch and the way they had loved, sometimes wild, sometimes so tender it brought her to tears.

He cared for her, she knew that from the way he

touched her, the depth of his response when they loved. But caring wouldn't be enough to hold him here and even if it were, she wouldn't settle for anything less than the fullness love had to offer.

Because of that, it wouldn't do any good to sit and try to decide the future, so Isabel forced herself to her feet and quietly let herself into the kitchen. She was halfway across the room before she realized she wasn't alone.

"Katlyn!" She stopped in midstep, startled at the sight of her sister sitting at the kitchen table, bent over a mug. "What are you doing up at this hour? Is something wrong?"

"I might ask you the same thing, sister," Katlyn said, looking at Isabel with a suspicious sideways glance.

"What is it?" Isabel asked, noting the delicate violet shadows under her half sister's eyes, her body drooping. It startled Isabel because she was so used to Katlyn's restless energy, seeing her so listless raised Isabel's suspicions.

"Nothing is wrong, not really. I just—couldn't sleep. What about you? Was someone ill?" she paused, taking in Isabel's disheveled appearance. "Or just lonely?"

"No…" Isabel tried to think of an explanation that wasn't an outright lie but couldn't. "No, no one was ill."

She went and fetched herself a cup of the coffee Katlyn had brewed and sat down across from her. Studying her sister, she finally asked, "Did something happen between you and Daniel?"

Katlyn drew a finger around the rim of her cup, studying the dregs in the bottom. "No, nothing hap-

pened. I've just been…oh, I don't know!'' She threw
up a hand in a helpless gesture, her eyes appealing to
Isabel for understanding. ''I suppose its wedding
nerves. That's natural, isn't it?''

''It's certainly not unheard of,'' Isabel agreed. She
paused, choosing her words carefully. ''But if you're
certain this marriage to Daniel is right, that will pass
quickly enough.''

''Unfortunately, I find it too easy to have doubts,''
Katlyn said hesitatingly. She grimaced. ''I sound awful, don't I?''

''No,'' Isabel said. Smiling, she reached out to touch
Katlyn's hand. ''We all have doubts.''

''I can't imagine you ever doubting anything about
yourself, especially if it came to love.''

Isabel had to laugh. If only she knew the half of it!
''Sometimes I doubt the wisdom of loving at all,'' she
said more to herself than to Katlyn.

''You're thinking of Jake,'' Katlyn said when Isabel
flushed. She got to her feet. ''If I felt the way you do,
I wouldn't be nervous. I'd be good and riled. I'd tell
him it was about time he hung up his six-shooters and
put down roots. Here. With you.''

Katlyn flashed a smile, leaving Isabel speechless.
Was there anything the woman *wouldn't* say? And
yet…maybe her sister had a point.

Still, would it do any good to confront Jake with the
truth of her feelings? She might not have asked as
much out loud, but she'd asked him to stay with her
caring, her loving. With her heart.

And even after their hours together, she couldn't be
certain of his answer.

A little while later, feeling somewhat refreshed,
wearing a clean pale-pink skirt and ivory blouse, Isabel

poured out a fresh cup of coffee, laced with plenty of sugar, and carried it up the stairs with her to Cal.

A hoarse invitation to enter answered her light knock at Cal's door. Propped up against the pillows, Cal smiled when he saw the mug she held.

"I hope that's the kind of coffee that'll kick up in the middle and pack double," he rasped. "I'm feelin' the need this mornin'. Your fine elixir knocked me cold."

"I meant it to." She sat down in the rocker opposite the bed and looked at him, feeling tears prick at her eyes. There was so much she wanted to say to him but she couldn't find any words that didn't sound like meaningless comfort. "I wish there were something else I could do, Cal. You've been like a father to me, but..."

"Now, Belle, don't go cryin' over me just yet. I've got a little fight left. But there is somethin' you can do for me, and today." When she looked questioningly at him, Cal's smile broadened. "Get that man of yours over here."

"He's not— Jake won't leave the jail, not while he's got that gold there," Isabel said, not sure Cal was thinking clearly while at the same time trying to ignore his assumption she had some power to persuade Jake. "You know that."

"Digger and that oldest boy of his can keep an eye on Jake's treasure for a few hours. I'm sure Katlyn wouldn't mind having an excuse to ride out to the ranch to bring Daniel back here. You just fetch Jake for me."

"I'll tell him you want to see him, but—why?"

Cal grinned. "Belle, honey, this town needs a law-

man. And I ain't up to it right now. For the time bein'
I intend to pin my star on Jake Coulter's chest.''

Jake polished off the last of Isabel's dinner, and sat
with his boots propped up on the edge of Cal's desk
looking at the mug in front of him as if he could stare
the coffee he'd brewed into something drinkable. It was
nearly dusk, but the brew hadn't done its work in waking him from last night's dream. He was in trouble and
it had nothing to do with Jerico Grey.

It had everything to do with Isabel.

He'd never been much for rules, but since Lily, he'd
stuck to one he'd made for himself. To never let a
woman get near his heart.

But last night he hadn't just broken that rule, he'd
shattered it. Last night…in his mind, he relived every
detail of Isabel and their hours together. Just thinking
about her brought on a rush of desire so strong and hot
he had to close his eyes against it, his hand fisting
around the mug.

He loved her, and knowing it scared the hell out of
him.

Isabel, with her gentle, generous spirit, the wild and
tender way she loved, her courage and determination,
had upset his solitary life, made him question every
choice he'd made for the course of his life since he'd
left San Antonio.

But he didn't know if he could offer her all she deserved. Or if he could offer her anything after his job
in Whispering Creek was finished. Never before had
he run scared of anything, but he was afraid of loving
her.

And he was terrified of losing her.

A sharp rap on the door jerked him out of his brooding. Raking a hand through his hair and hastily buttoning up his shirt one-handed, he checked the Colts on his hips before glancing out the barred window.

Isabel stood on his front step like a dream repeated, and for a moment all he could do was stare. Then she knocked again, more insistently, prompting him to unlock the door and draw her inside.

They stood gazing at each other, she uncertainly, he intently, before Isabel attempted a smile.

"I'm sorry to come back," she began.

"I'm glad to see you. I—didn't think—didn't know if you'd come again." Unable to stop himself, Jake reached out and brushed his fingers over her hair, her cheek, then traced her lips, to assure himself she wasn't merely an image from his lingering dream. "Very glad."

He bent and touched his mouth to hers, intending to give her a brief caress, nothing more, something to dispel the awkwardness between them. Instead, she moved toward him at the same time and he found himself holding her tightly, kissing her with all the need and desire he felt inside.

Isabel felt an urgency in him, in the hard, insistent pressure of his mouth on hers. It was as if he wanted to brand her soul, to mark her as well and truly his. She felt an almost desperate need to touch him in return, to take from him and give something back so he would never be the same without it.

When they finally pulled apart, Jake was breathing heavily, as if he'd run a great distance. He took a few steps from her, trying to regain control, and Isabel allowed him the distance. She trembled inside with the force of her need for him. It made her vulnerable, a feeling she couldn't afford now.

"I needed to talk to you," she said at last, her voice not quite steady.

"Well..." Jake turned, raised a hand in her direction and let it fall. "We can try that."

"Cal asked me to come." She hurried over the words before she forgot why she had come. "He wants to see you, as soon as possible."

Briefly she outlined Cal's plan to have Digger share in the guard duties, and then paused, not quite sure how to tell him the final part, not sure of his reaction. But Digger would be here soon and she couldn't stand here just looking at him.

"Cal wants you to take over as sheriff." Jake said nothing, only stared at her, his storm-gray eyes unreadable. "Temporarily, until he can find someone to take on the job permanently. It's only for a little while...."

She trailed off, feeling a sick misery surround her heart. Jake probably suspected she had something to do with Cal's request. Looking away, she found herself unable to meet his eyes, to see the censure there.

"Isabel," he said softly, lifting her chin so their eyes met. A smile played with the corner of his mouth. "This isn't a surprise, I know Cal's had it in mind since we holed up in here. I don't think you had anything to do with it."

"How—of course I didn't! Just because we—well, I wouldn't try to force you to stay where you don't want to be!"

Jake laughed, pulling her into his arms. "I know exactly where I want to be, angel," he murmured, glancing toward the room where they'd made love hours ago. "But now's not the time."

He kissed her so thoroughly Isabel forgot to be annoyed he'd read her so easily.

They might have ended up back on the pallet where they'd shared their love if a pounding on the door, followed by Digger Parker's bass voice announcing his presence, hadn't pulled them apart. Jake cursed, and Isabel laughed at his irritation.

She gathered up her picnic basket and stepped outside while Jake and Digger exchanged a few words about the treasure in the jail, smiling when Jake joined her minutes later, hat and Colts in place.

"Well, Mrs. Bradshaw," Jake drawled, offering her his arm. "How about I take you home? I hate to keep Cal waiting in suspense."

Isabel took his proffered arm, welcoming the feel of him under her hand. "Oh, I don't think he's worrying about your answer," she said, a secret smile curving her mouth.

"He's that sure of himself, is he?"

"No." Isabel slowly let her eyes caress him. "He's that sure of us."

"You're back!" Matt ran to where Jake stood in the living room, hurling himself at Jake and throwing his arms around his neck. "I knew you'd come back, no matter what Nate said!"

Jake returned the exuberant embrace, surprised at the uprush of warm, sweet feeling that came with it. He'd missed this, not just the pure caring of a child, but the implicit trust, the certainty he would be there.

"But where are you gonna stay?" Matt said, releasing his stranglehold long enough to look at Jake. "Sheriff Cal has your room. He's sick and Mama's takin' care of him there."

"Well, partner, I'm not staying. I've just come to pay the sheriff a little visit." When Matt's face fell and his lower lip began to tremble, Jake gently cuffed him under the chin. "But as soon as I finish my job, I promise, I'll be back to see you."

"And we're going fishin', right?"

"You bet. I wouldn't forget that."

Nate's solemn face peeked around he corner of Isabel's shop.

Jake caught sight of him before he disappeared. "Nate, come on out here, son. Remember, I'm counting on you to dig up plenty of worms for our fishing trip."

Nate appeared around the corner, head hung, facing the floor. "Yeah? We'll I'm not gonna rush. Who knows how long you'll be chasin' Jerico Grey? He'll probably just grab his gold and run off. Then you'll be gone after him."

Jake strode over to Nate and bent down on one knee in front of him. "Whatever I have to do to finish up with Grey, you and your brother and I have a fishing date. Understand?"

Nate lifted his chin then, smiled first at Jake then at his brother.

Katlyn came down the stairs and laid a hand on Jake's arm. "Cal's expecting you. Daniel will help, too, at the jail."

"Are you riding back out there again?" Isabel asked.

"No. Daniel's coming into town. Cal wants to see him, too, so I'm going to sit out front and wait for him." She frowned a little, before putting her smile back. "Be careful, Jake. A lot of smiles around here seem to fade when you're not around."

"I'd say that includes yours, but I know better," Jake teased, lightly touching Katlyn's shoulder. "You just do whatever you need to do to bring that smile of yours back."

Katlyn nodded. "Funny. That's exactly what I've been thinking. Maybe you should take your own advice."

Cal struggled to sit up in bed as Jake entered his room.

"Don't. I'll come sit next to you." The room that had smelled so fresh, of Isabel's herbs, wildflowers and mountain breeze the day he'd awakened there, now seemed laden with the heaviness of hopelessness.

"Damned lungs have given out on me," Cal wheezed. "I'm weak as a field mouse. That's why I need you."

"I'd be happy to fill in for you, but only until you're back on your feet." He knew it was a lie, but Jake refused to accept his friend was dying until reality forced him to.

"I hoped you would. There's no one else I'd feel right about passing my star on to."

"Cal—"

"Oh, there's plenty who'd be willin' to take on the job," Cal said, waving aside Jake's protest. "But none of 'em are as good as you. It's in your blood, just like it's been for me."

Cal started to say more but a fit of coughing stopped him. He grabbed up a bowl off the bedside table, spitting blood into it before falling back against the pillows.

Jake handed him a cloth from the pile Isabel left.

"You need to rest. Let's make this right so you have one less thing to worry about."

"Over there on my dresser," Cal said hoarsely, pointing. "My star. Yours now. Get young Daniel up here to give us a witness."

Jake picked up the silver badge. After calling Daniel upstairs, he let Cal talk him through the formal oath, then helped Cal settle back again on the bed. Cal closed his eyes, his breathing labored.

"I won't let you down, my friend," Jake vowed quietly. "You can count on it."

Downstairs, Esme and Isabel had set out coffee and cakes for a bedtime snack. Jake walked in, feeling a little self-conscious about the responsibility his new badge placed on him.

For years now, he'd executed the law pretty much on his terms. The Texas Rangers in particular were given that privilege and that trust. He'd forgotten when he last had to answer to anyone for how he tracked down a man.

No one judged his methods, only his results.

Esme eyed the badge shining bright silver against Jake's worn leather vest. "Well, well, it is Señor Sheriff now, is it?"

"Nana, please," Isabel said, rubbing at her temple. "He's doing Cal a favor. He doesn't have to take the job."

"*Sí, sí*, it is an honorable thing you do, *señor*."

Inwardly, Jake groaned. Another round of debate with a lady who had a tongue like a bowie knife wasn't his first choice tonight. And he suspected Esme's sniping now had more to do with the way he and Isabel looked at each other than her suspicions about him taking over as sheriff.

"Why am I getting the impression you think otherwise?" he asked, helping himself to a warm vanilla cake from the tray. He might as well try to enjoy bantering with the prickly old woman. She had spunk and a mind of her own, traits he admired in her and in her granddaughter.

Esme sipped her coffee, her gnarled fingers clutching the mug awkwardly. "Maybe I think you are looking for a way to stay a little longer, eh? A way to have my granddaughter in your bed. Like she was last night."

"Nana—!"

"*Ay,* so it disturbs you to hear the truth. But you will know the truth when the new sheriff comes and Mr. Coulter has a perfect reason to leave you. Then you truly will have nothing, for he will have taken your heart."

Before Jake or Isabel could say anything, Matt and Nate ambled in, dressed in their flannel nightclothes.

Jake motioned them to him. "Just in time, fellas. I'm a little outnumbered here."

"Can we have a cake before bed?" Matt asked.

"You may each take one and eat it in your room. Nana was just coming to tell you a story." Isabel looked pointedly at her grandmother. "Weren't you?"

"Can you come too, Mr. Coulter?"

Jake took one look at Esme's set face and decided he'd better try his hand at making peace. "I'm sorry, Nate, but I've got to get back to the jail. Next time, I promise. Besides, I think your grandmother would like to tell you that story."

"Mr. Coulter's right," Isabel said. "Give us a hug and run on to bed."

After hugs and kisses, the boys tugged Esme up and walked with her to their room, leaving Isabel and Jake to exchange one long look of shared exasperation.

"I'm surprised she didn't poison my coffee tonight."

Isabel laughed. "Me, too."

He shared in her laughter. But when it trailed off, a melancholy silence fell between them.

"I need to get back to the jail," Jake said finally, getting to his feet.

"I need to say goodbye to you—alone." Isabel rose gracefully. She brushed her fingers over his jaw, her eyes the blue of a mountain twilight in the dim light, inviting him. "Katlyn and Daniel will be back inside at any moment. But there's no one in my room."

The fire he'd managed to keep banked most of the day roared up in him. Jake wanted to touch her in return, to hold her forever. But the briefest of touches now and Katlyn and Daniel would get an eyeful when they walked in the house.

"You know, if I come with you, I'm risking being turned into a lizard if Esme finds out," he said.

He couldn't keep his need for her from roughening his voice and Isabel heard it and smiled. She reached for his hand, drawing him to her. "Don't worry, my spells are more powerful than hers."

"I know," Jake said as he allowed her to lead him down the dimly lit hallway. "That's what I'm afraid of."

But when she came into his arms, the only magic on his mind was the kind they made together.

# *Chapter Seventeen*

For a long moment they stood staring at each other, desire a living, breathing thing in the silence. Jake felt the heat of it stronger than the desert sun at noon. It seared away every thought of leaving her for the vigil at the jail and left only a pure flame of need.

His head knew his work was with Digger and Daniel.

But his heart was with her.

Despite the long day, she looked fresh as springtime, her cheeks flushed pink as the ribbon she pulled from her hair. She shook her head slightly and her hair tumbled free. The fire behind them threaded the silken ripple with gold reflections.

Pine and sage scented warmth spread through the room, just enough to chase away the chill in the mountain night air.

He started to tell her how beautiful she looked. But Isabel laid her fingers on his mouth, stopping his words, as if she feared he would deny the feeling between them.

Instead, he followed her farther inside to where a large, soft bear rug lay on the floor in front of the fire.

Jake tossed another log into the blue-and-yellow flames, igniting them to a dance. When he turned back to Isabel, her turquoise eyes met his and he couldn't pull his gaze away.

Isabel let her touch become a caress as she traced the line of his jaw, soothing strain, taking pleasure in indulging the freedom to touch him.

"My grandmother always talks about magic and the power of it," she said softly. "But I never believed in it. Until now."

"Magic?" Jake shook his head, covering her hand with his, bringing it to his mouth. With infinite slowness, looking into her eyes, he kissed her palm, letting his lips linger in the sensitive hollow of her hand. "This isn't magic."

"Isn't it?" she asked, her breath breaking as he nibbled lightly at the pulse point of her wrist, tasting her skin.

"No," he murmured and Isabel felt the sound as a heated breath against her neck.

Jake tangled his hand in her hair, the bewitching slide of gold and silvery satin through his fingers, watching the play of firelight on each strand. It held him in thrall to her. The small breathy sound she made when he brushed his mouth against her cheek twisted him so tightly inside it became torture not to let loose the desire clawing at him.

Tasting the corner of her mouth, her lower lip, he whispered so close she breathed with him, "I don't want magic. I want you. I want this."

He brought his mouth down on hers, and Isabel opened to him, willingly falling into the tempest, into him. Desire beyond understanding made her bold, made her want, made her need what only Jake could give. She forgot they stood together in her bedroom, with her family asleep down the hall, and his duty waiting for him outside her door.

Old fears murmured in her mind. But she refused to hear them. Jake's temptation called stronger. And right now she could only listen with her heart.

Perhaps it could never be more than this: one midnight, one forever kiss, one timeless enchantment when she felt she would never be alone. She feared a lifetime of loneliness. But she was more frightened of never chancing her heart again, of never knowing the full power of love.

"This is magic," she whispered, almost to herself. She slipped her hands under his shirt and ran her fingers over his chest, liking the feel of unyielding strength and the quickened pace of his breathing. She felt a rich delight in knowing she could rouse him with so simple a gift as her touch. "We are magic."

"No, angel." One hand curved around her nape, Jake gently bent her body back, arching to his. Making every motion forever, he unfastened the buttons of her blouse. "This is stronger."

Very softly, savoring her scent, her taste, he kissed the silken flesh he had uncovered.

It felt to Isabel he poured living light onto her skin and she trembled as it spread through her, into her.

"This is passion..."

Two more buttons gave way to Jake's persuasion and his mouth followed, lingering in the hollow between her breasts, tracing the outline with his tongue.

"And promise..."

Watching her, holding her gaze, Jake opened the rest of her buttons and spread the material wide. Pressing light kisses where his fingers led, he slipped the blouse free and unfastened her skirt. It fell away, leaving only the barest wisp of a cotton shift between them. Firelight spilled over her skin. But he felt the heat, burning him alive.

"And madness," he said hoarsely, his restraint seared and scorned by his need for her. He looked at her, bathed in flame and flushed from his touch, her body begging his kiss, and suddenly seduction became an uncontrolled hunger.

He shrugged out of his shirt and Isabel muffled a little cry with the wonder of the feeling as he gathered her against him, his skin coupling with hers. His hand moved in a silken slide down her spine, drawing her closer so his hardness pressed against her, seducing her even nearer, intoxicating her with the knowledge he wanted this and only this.

Out of patience, Jake helped her strip off the rest of their clothing, then drew her down with him to the soft rug in front of the fireplace, pulling her atop him.

Isabel's soft whimper when they came together nearly drove him over the edge. He gripped the tattered edges of his control and steeled himself to move slowly, to draw out the pleasure for her until she drowned in it.

For a long, lingering moment, she only gazed at him with eyes that saw straight into his soul. She searched the ripples of his muscular chest with her fingertips, toying with the mass of dark, silken hairs. Then she began to move with him, urging him into the rhythm that drove him on a wild careen toward a pinnacle of pleasure that left him gasping for breath, his heart thundering in his ears.

Isabel dug her fingers into his arms, the light inside her shattering into a million shards of white-hot brightness that made her bury her face in his neck to stifle the joy surging to her lips from the wonder of it.

She collapsed against Jake's chest as the world settled around her again, bringing her back to her room and the feel of Jake's arms wrapped around her, holding her as if he never intended to let her go.

She nearly told him then she loved him. Together like this, it seemed right and certain.

But some instinct held her back, a fear he might not welcome such a confession.

Instead, she held fast to him as he gathered her close and stroked her hair, memorizing each feeling, each touch with her heart so when he was gone, she would always have her memories to treasure.

With Isabel in his arms, her body still fitted to his, Jake was reluctant to move and break his fragile sense of peace. Tranquillity was something he hadn't felt since long before his family's death. He never expected to know it again.

She stirred, drawing a little away from him to look into his face. "I seem to be keeping you from your duty again." she said, her voice uneven, with laughter or tears Jake couldn't tell.

"I'm beginning to believe duty is highly overrated," he murmured, "especially when you're near. Isabel…"

She had no idea what he wanted to say to her but the expression in his eyes, both warm and tender, left her fumbling for words.

"Jake? What is it?"

"I— It's nothing," he said, pulling her back against him fully once more. His need for her washed over his reason, his pain, his deepest fears, drowning them in desire. "Or maybe it's everything. But not now. It's late. I've got to get back to the jail and…"

Isabel barely heard his last words, muffled as he started to kiss the curve of her throat. She tried to think, to remind him of his job, and her reputation, and the danger of making love on the floor of her bedroom.

But as his caresses grew bolder and more demanding she gave up any attempt at reason and abandoned herself to Jake.

It wasn't until later, when the flames in the fireplace like the fire burning hot and wild between them settled to embers, that he carried Isabel to her bed and her dreams.

It was then Jake regretted not telling her he loved her.

There was no use denying it any longer, though Lord knew he'd tried. He gazed down at her sleeping peacefully, looking like an angel.

His angel.

*So much to gain in loving you,* he told her silently, *and oh, so much to lose.*


An urgent banging on the jail door jerked Jake upright in the chair he'd been dozing in, bringing him to his feet in one swift motion.

He'd been back at the jail for a couple of hours, trying to settle into a fitful sleep without much success. The unexpected noise brought him fully alert, hands sliding to his hips to check the position of his six-shooters.

"Who is it?" he called out, moving close to the door.

From the back of the jail Jake could hear shuffling and murmurs as Digger, his son and Daniel woke to the commotion.

"It's Chessie. Elish sent me. There's an awful fight

goin' on at the Silver Rose. One fella's already been cut pretty bad and Elish is afraid they're gonna start shootin' up the place.''

Digger, coming up behind Jake, glanced out the window. "Yeah, it's Chessie all right and it looks like she's alone.''

Jake cursed. "I'll be right there," he called out to Chessie. Checking to see his guns were fully loaded, he grabbed his hat and shoved it on.

"Don't unbolt the door again unless it's for me," he said to Digger. "If Grey is behind this, he'll make a try for the gold as soon as I'm gone.''

"We'll hold our own here," Digger said as he readied to lock the door behind Jake. "Just don't go gettin' yourself shot up again. I don't want to be the one to tell Isabel.''

Jake started for the Silver Rose at a run, leaving Chessie to trail behind. He got to the saloon doors just as a cowboy came hurtling out of them backward. The man landed flat on his back on the porch, tried to get up, then fell against the planks.

Dragging the man out of the doorway, Jake bent to check him.

"I'll do that.''

His head jerked up. "You—"

"Don't say it," Isabel warned off his protest. She knelt beside the man, dropping her basket next to him and running her fingers over a welt on his temple in one graceful motion.

"What the hell are you doing here?''

"What does it look like? Elish sent for me. It's not the first time I've done this.''

"It's going to be the last. You can just turn around and go back home.''

A chair crashed through one of the front windows and they both instinctively ducked the flying glass and wood.

"I think you have more to worry about than me, Sheriff."

Jake swore violently. He admired her calmness in the midst of chaos, but her stubborn determination to go anywhere, help anyone in need drove him crazy. How the hell could he protect a woman like her, especially from her own good intentions?

"Stay out here," he commanded, heading for the saloon doors.

"Jake—"

He glanced back. She looked at him, worry showing through.

"Be careful."

"Aren't I always?" Grinning at the exasperated look she gave him, Jake shoved open the doors of the Silver Rose.

The doors slapped into two men swinging fists at each other just inside. Before Jake could get between them, one man's fist was already balled up and aimed at his face. Reacting out of instinct, Jake moved fast, landing a punch square to the man's left jaw that threw him flat on his back.

The other man took one look at Jake and dived past him out the doors.

Shielding his face from the mayhem of glass shards, bottles and splintered wood peppering the air on every side, Jake gave the room a quick scan, looking for Elish.

Chessie crept in around him, seeking shelter at Jake's back. The labored sound of her breathing near his neck brought his head around. "Did you see who started this?"

"Sort of." Chessie practically clung to Jake, using his large frame as a barrier. "It's strange," she shouted near his ear. "Some fella I seen in here a couple of times just went crazy 'cause Zeke told Anita she was pretty."

A foot from them a man's body crashed onto a table, cracking it in half.

"Son of a—" Jake shoved Chessie out of the way. "What's his name?"

"Don't know. But soon as he got everyone all riled up, I saw him duck outta here like he didn't want no part of it."

Elish caught sight of Jake then and forced his way through the chaos to him. "You're the sheriff now. I don't know what the hell started this, but I'm countin' on you to stop it. And fast, before they take the whole place apart!"

"I was about to do just that."

Yanking out one of his Colts, he shot twice into the ceiling.

The bedlam in his immediate vicinity came to an abrupt stop. Several of the brawling men took one look at the gun in Jake's hand and the look on his face and started fast for the doors.

Shoving around them, Jake holstered his weapon and waded into the remaining fray.

After breaking up a half dozen fights, bruising his knuckles confiscating a drunken miner's pistol, and locking in Elish's back room one man who insisted on trying to crack a full whiskey bottle over his opponent's head, Jake finally got the pandemonium under control.

He was ready to congratulate himself on getting out of the Silver Rose with nothing more than a knife slash to his upper arm when Chessie let out an earsplitting scream.

Jake whirled, hand moving to his hip, just in time to see Elish collapse. A crimson blotch stained the front of his shirt. He looked surprised just before he slid back against Chessie.

"Hurry!" she cried. "Find Isabel, somebody stabbed Elish!"

"I'll get her." A kid with a thatch of red hair popped up from behind the bar and made a beeline for the doors.

Jake knelt down beside Elish.

He didn't want Isabel in here, of all places. But, taking one look at Elish, he knew no one else could help.

"Who did this?" he asked.

But Elish's eyes had already closed, his face drenched in sweat. Only a weak moan answered Jake.

"I didn't see nothin'," Chessie wailed. "All of a sudden, he just fell."

Getting to his feet, Jake kept one hand to his gun as he faced down the remaining men in the saloon.

"There's been enough damage for one night. Clear out, or the whole lot of you will be sleeping it off in jail."

A general muttering and shuffling answered him. A few of the men and most of Elish's girls began setting chairs aright and picking up broken glass and wood. Few dared leave for they'd have to walk right by Jake to get out.

And one merciless look from the town's new sheriff

was enough to convince anyone with half a brain to keep as far away from him as possible.

Jake looked back at Chessie. "Where's Anita?"

Chessie swallowed the sobs turning her eyes to watery red pools. "Don't know. I ain't seen her since this started."

With that, Jake stormed through the bar straight to Anita's lair. He burst in, and found her lounging on her red satin bedspread. Striding straight over, he dragged her up by her shoulders. "You're coming with me and you're going to do a lot of talking on the way."

"How dare you!"

"Elish may be dead thanks to you."

"Elish…?"

"At least try to pretend you give a damn. Did you plan that, too? Do your ambitions include taking over the Silver Rose?" He yanked her with him back out into the bar.

"I—well, I have no idea what you're talking about—"

"Save it for someone who'll listen. I'm sure you'll find quite an audience in jail." Jake pulled her through the wreckage in the saloon toward the doors.

Anita dug her heels in then. "You're not taking me there!"

"The hell I'm not, woman." Refusing to waste a second on her stubborn resistance, Jake whisked her off her feet and slung her over his shoulder like a sack of flour.

"What's the matter, Miss Devine," he growled, "isn't the jail a safe place to be tonight? You managed to stay plenty safe during the brawl here."

Jake, the wriggling, cussing woman pounding on his back, reached one door and shoved it out just as the other door swung in. The basket on Isabel's arm swiped Anita's backside as she brushed past.

Both Jake and Isabel stopped and stared.

"The witch! Always the damned witch!" Anita screeched.

Isabel's eyes flew wide open. "Jake?"

"I'll explain later. Promise me, whatever you do, don't go to the jail tonight. I don't care who sends for you this time."

Catching a glimpse of the ruined barroom, of Chessie sitting on the floor with Elish's head in her lap and the battered and bruised strays left in the saloon, Isabel's eyes narrowed in suspicion. "What happened here?"

"I don't have time to explain! Promise me, Isabel. Now!"

"Fine, I promise," she returned. "It looks like you have your hands full."

"More than you know."

Isabel hurried to Elish's side.

She set aside her questions, promising herself she'd demand an explanation later. Elish needed her now. And from the looks of him, he would take all she had to give.

Despite Anita, Jake picked up his pace out in the street as he strode toward the jail. He had a bad feeling about the fight, Anita and the reason for it all.

Digger's son met him halfway there, panting, his shirt smudged with blood. He barely glanced at Anita.

"Grey hit the jail. The gold's still there, but Daniel's been shot. Pa sent me to get Isabel."

"She's at the Silver Rose, with Elish," Jake said,

keenly aware of telling her just minutes ago to stay
put. "Someone stabbed him."

The boy hesitated at Jake's darkening expression.
"Should I—"

"Go tell her. But be careful and watch your back."

With a quick nod, the boy raced off in the direction
of the Silver Rose. Jake headed for the jail.

Digger waited at the door, his face grim. "My boy
tell you?"

"Yeah." Jake glanced at the front door, hanging
askew, acrid yellowish smoke belching out the opening. "What happened?"

"Your instincts were right. You'd been gone only a
few minutes when we first heard 'em outside. Then the
cell wall blew and they were on us. It was Grey and
two others, near as I could tell. I got one of 'em right
off, then my boy managed to hit another of 'em,
couldn't tell if it was Grey or his friend. They took off
after that, one draggin' the other." Shaking his head,
Digger spat at the ground. "I'm gettin' too old for
this."

"And Daniel?" Jake asked.

"Took a shot in the ribs. Looks bad, but then I'm
no healer. I do know one thing, though," Digger said.
"You were right in thinkin' they had help from someone."

"You're looking at her backside now."

Anita screeched an obscenity at him. Jake ignored
her and hauled her inside, depositing her, kicking and
clawing, into a cell. He clanged the door shut on her
screaming and strode back to the front to check the
damage there.

Daniel lay on a makeshift pallet in the front office,
Digger bending over him. Digger straightened to face

Jake. "He's passed out, good thing I'd say. I hope my boy gets back with Isabel soon."

"He should. I met him coming here. Isabel's at the saloon. Elish was stabbed during the fight our visitor managed to start."

"Anita?"

Jake nodded. "The timing of this whole mess along with a lot of other things leave me no doubt of it. That woman has a hell of a lot of explaining to do. And I'll bet my bottom dollar she can take me straight to Grey."

Digger's son burst into the jail then, chest heaving. He struggled to catch his breath enough to speak.

Jake shot to his feet, alarm turning his veins to ice. "Where's Isabel?"

"Sheriff Coulter," the boy gasped, "she's gone. She's just gone."

# Chapter Eighteen

The shatter of glass against stone echoed in Isabel's head. She shifted a little and pain stabbed her temples. What had happened? She'd been at the Silver Rose, tending Elish's knife wound, then...

Experimentally, she moved her fingers against the surface beneath her and felt the scratch of a rough wool blanket. Not her bedroom. The stench of old whiskey and dirt confirmed that.

"She's awake," a raspy voice said somewhere behind her head. "'bout time."

"You better hope she stays that way, *amigo*."

A cool, damp cloth touched her face. Isabel forced open her eyes and looked into the face of Jerico Grey. She jerked up with a cry of surprise, regretting it as pain flooded her head.

Jerico pressed her back against the narrow bed. "Easy, Bella, go slowly."

Isabel drew a deep breath, reaching deep for some measure of calm. She looked at him fully, the first time in years, since he'd ridden off with the law on his heels. The time had weathered him, hardened him, but he still had that wild dark look that had once seemed so exciting to her.

Now, it only made her afraid.

"Where am I?" She forced the words out. Jake, what had happened to him? If Jerico had the gold it meant— She pushed the thought aside, made herself focus on her immediate problem.

"What, no greeting for an old friend, Bella?" Jerico said. His eyes wandered over her as if he were remembering the times he had held her in his arms.

Isabel fought the urge to rub her hands over her skin. "We have very different ideas of friendship. I don't have friends who knock me on the head—" she fingered the painful bruise near her temple "—then abduct me."

"That was Ray," he said, nodding to the man slumped in a chair behind Isabel. "I would never have hurt you."

"But you would have forced me to come here against my will." Steeling herself against the wave of pain, Isabel slowly pushed herself to a sitting position, sliding as far as she could away from Jerico.

He smiled faintly at her attempt, not moving from his seat on the bed's edge. "Well, Bella, you'll have to forgive me that. I need your help."

Isabel stared incredulously at him. "My help? You can't be serious!"

"Oh, but I am." He shifted and opened one side of his duster, revealing a large blackish patch staining the side of his shirt. "Another old friend's work. Unfortunately I didn't get a chance to return the favor."

"Jake?"

"No, old Digger Parker. I got your lover out of my

way. No use courtin' a showdown with him if I didn't have to. But I didn't count on Parker's move.''

Relief swept through Isabel. Jake was safe. ''And the gold?''

''My gold, you mean. I have you to blame for not having that now. If you hadn't come into the barn when I was digging it up, I would have had it and been long gone.'' He reached out and fingered a strand of her hair, ignoring her flinch. ''Of course, if your husband hadn't double-crossed me, I never would've come back at all.''

''Are you telling me Douglas helped you rob that mine?''

Jerico gave a short, derisive laugh. ''Douglas did have his uses. He always knew how to find out when the gold was being moved and where the payroll was kept. Trouble was, he started to believe he was important. I should've killed him then but I never thought he'd be so stupid.''

Isabel tried to pull her hair free of the snare of his fingers, but Jerico held fast.

He rubbed the strands between his thumb and forefinger, eyeing her with a strange intensity. ''You should never have left me for that fool Douglas. We were good together, Bella,'' he said, sliding a finger down her cheek. ''Real good.''

''You loved danger and gold,'' she countered. ''There was never room for anything else. We never loved each other.''

''No, Bella, we loved the excitement of you and me. That's what matters, isn't it?'' He shrugged away her denial. ''And now you have a new lover.''

''Jake won't stop until he finds you,'' Isabel said

unsteadily. The way he looked at her made her skin crawl. "He'll come looking for you."

"No, Bella," Jerico said, his voice cold. "He'll come looking for you."

"He'll kill you."

"He won't get the chance. I'll be gone before he gets here." Taking her chin roughly in his hand, he forced her to face him. "Fix me up, Bella. I need to go get my gold."

Isabel jerked away from him. "You're crazy."

"Told ya she wouldn't do it," Ray drawled from the chair. Isabel darted a glance at him. He grinned, showed a row of crooked brown teeth.

Isabel fought the panic that rose up in her throat. She tried to muster a bravado she was far from feeling.

"You'll never get away with this," she snapped, when Jerico leaned back on the bed.

"Shut up and listen to me, Bella. I want this damned bleeding stopped. Now. *¿Comprende?*"

"I understand your life is in my hands."

Jerico grabbed her wrist, squeezing hard. "Let me make something clear. I don't have my gold—yet. And you have the only other thing Ray wants. Now, you were always a smart girl. I think you'll want to make sure I get my gold first. If I don't make it, Ray'll have you and the gold. In that order."

Isabel swallowed hard. "That girl has grown into a smart woman, Jerico. I promise you, I haven't lost my edge."

Jerico laughed. "You were a hellcat, that's for certain. And from the way you fought me in the barn that night, I know you still are." His expression swiftly darkened. "But you're too softhearted to just let me die."

*Don't count on that,* she thought to him silently.

She stood up and looked down at him, wondering if she could kill him outright and find some way of escaping Ray as well. At the same time she prayed Jake was looking for her and that he would find her before she had to make the choice.

"Your medicines are there—" Jerico flung a hand in the direction of the rickety wooden table. "I already cut the bullet out. I don't trust you with a knife, no matter how devoted you are to healing."

Isabel walked slowly to the table and picked up her pouch. She held it between her hands, looking at it, then to Jerico.

She had to take the chance. She believed Jake would look for her, but without knowing where she was, it could take him hours, even days. She couldn't wait.

Steeling herself, Isabel gripped her pouch and moved toward the bed.

Jake finished reloading his six-shooters, shoved them in the holsters, then grabbed up his rifle.

He'd left Digger in the back, making certain the jail was secure again. Digger's son had gotten a few of the men still at the Silver Rose to help carry Daniel to Isabel's house, where Esme and Katlyn were tending to him. They'd left Elish in one of the rooms at the Silver Rose with Chessie at his side—after Esme had looked him over.

He hoped Esme had more than her witch's spells to help Elish and Daniel. *If Isabel had only been here—*

With a vicious curse under his breath, Jake cut off the thought. He had to stay focused or Grey would win and he would lose everything.

He would lose Isabel. Lose his love again. Only this time the loss would be the other half of himself.

His past had stopped him from risking loving Isabel. And now, when he was ready to chance everything with her, fate taunted him with a repeat of the nightmare behind him.

*Not again, dammit! I won't lose her. Now or ever.*

He turned to Digger when he finished with his guns. "Keep the guard here. Grey might not be in any condition to come back here, but then he also might have given someone else an idea. I'll be back as soon as I find Isabel."

"You can't just ride off, not knowing for sure where she is or if Grey even took her," Digger protested. "He could be halfway to the Colorado line by now."

"Not without his gold. He's out of time, and he's out of money. And he does have Isabel. I found a blood trail leading out of town. He needs her."

Even as he said the words, Jake prayed it was true. If Grey needed Isabel to patch him or one of his men up, he wouldn't hurt her—yet. It bought him time to find her.

He had to find her. And if Grey so much as touched her... His hand fisted around the rifle so tightly his knuckles bleached ice white.

Digger put a heavy hand on his shoulder. "I hope the map Anita drew is right. If I were you, I wouldn't bet your life on it, or Isabel's."

"Oh, it's right, don't worry. Anita and I understand each other now. Don't we, Miss Devine?" he shouted back to where Anita paced her cell like a caged wildcat.

"Go to hell, Jake Coulter!"

"So she was feeding Grey information all along." Digger scratched his head. "I'll be."

Jake started out the jail door but Digger stopped him. "Isabel needs you alive. Grey ain't alone so don't go ridin' yourself into trouble. We don't want to be losin' two sheriffs in one week," he said gruffly.

"I don't plan on dying any time soon. You just keep everyone away from that gold."

Jake unhitched his horse and mounted, headed for the steep, winding mountain path that led to the abandoned mine Anita described. Fury ran hot in him. He let it have full rein; he drove his horse harder than he ever had, leaning his chest almost to the saddle as they climbed up into the dense evergreen forest.

Fear for Isabel mounted in him in equal measure with raw hatred for Grey. He'd left Isabel vulnerable when he'd rushed back to the jail after Grey.

Since the day he'd told her never to count on him, for anything, she'd never asked once for his help or protection.

Now his words rose in his throat in a bitter mockery.

At the same time, Jake knew she trusted him, without question. She'd given freely of herself, and never asked for anything in return, though he knew deep down she feared he would walk out of her life just like her husband and her father had done. Knowing that, he'd ride to hell and back to find her.

And when he did, this time, he wouldn't let her go.

Isabel sat back on her heels, hardly daring to breathe. She'd spent most of the last hour tending to Jerico, managing to staunch the bleeding from the bullet wound in his side and stitch up the gaping hole. Ray had taken one look at the blood and, with a grunt of distaste, retreated with his bottle to a corner of the room while she worked.

She sent up a prayer of thanks Jerico had willingly gulped down nearly a half bottle of whiskey before she started sewing him up. With Ray distracted by his own whiskey and Jerico by pain, she managed to pour in a good measure of one of her grandmother's elixirs into Jerico's bottle. It was a mixture she rarely used, because of its potency and its tendency to produce waking dreams. This time, she didn't hesitate.

He'd guzzled it so quickly, he'd never noticed the slight alteration in taste and, after about ten minutes, had slipped into a fitful sleep. Isabel fervently prayed he would stay unconscious long enough for her to find a way to escape Ray.

She began gathering up her pouch and the used poultice, giving her hands something to do while her mind furiously worked on a way out.

"Did ya kill him?" Ray drawled from the corner.

Isabel fought to keep her voice level, devoid of the fear surging up inside her. "Did you want me to?"

"Would've saved me the trouble later. He ain't gonna last long. But I am." Pushing out of the chair, he came toward her, lurching a little. "Now then, little lady, let's see what Grey liked so much he had to come back for it."

Scrambling to her feet, Isabel ducked his lunging hand. He laughed and circled around her. His bulk blocked her path to the cabin's only door.

Isabel took her eyes off him long enough to judge the distance. When he grabbed for her again she ran straight for him, twisting under his arm and sprinting for the door.

Her fingers closed around the handle just as Ray caught a handful of hair and yanked her backward.

Isabel cried out at the pain. Ray held fast, his fingers

closing around her throat. "You like it rough? Fine with me."

He dragged her toward the table, clumsily forcing her back against the splintered wood. His hand pushed up under her skirt and a fresh burst of fear gave Isabel new strength.

She wrenched her head around, biting down hard on his hand.

"Why you little—" Ray jerked back his fist.

The blow she expected never came. Before he could complete the motion, the door to the shack crashed open.

A huge hand on Ray's collar snatched him backward. Isabel dragged herself upright in time to see Jake drive his fist into Ray's face.

As the other man sprawled senseless on the floor, Jake yanked out his Colt and aimed it at Ray's chest. Isabel hoped never to witness such an expression of cold, pitiless rage on a man's face again.

"Jake," Isabel pleaded. "No."

She took a faltering step toward him, reaching out a hand.

For one terrifying moment, she thought he would pull the trigger.

Then he looked at her, slammed his gun back into its holster, and in two strides reached her side, running his hands over her in almost frantic haste to assure himself she wasn't hurt before pulling her into his arms.

Jake crushed her to him, not quite able to believe she was whole and safe. She trembled all over and clung tightly to him as if she feared he'd disappear at any moment.

"It's all right, angel," he murmured softly to her,

his voice roughened by a potent combination of relief and the residue of fury. "It's over."

"I knew you would find me. I—I just knew…" She gave a small, unsteady laugh.

"Sweet heaven, woman." He pulled back a little and looked at her with a mix of wonder and some fierce emotion Isabel didn't dare name. "Isabel, thank God you're safe. If anything had happened to you…"

Jake stopped, unable to give voice to the depth and strength of the feelings surging through him.

Laying her head against his heart again, Isabel listened to the ragged rhythm, comforted by the sound and the strong, solid feel of him. Then a sudden thought occurred to her, drawing her back from him again.

"Jerico—you didn't ask about him." When he looked at her blankly, she said, "I mean, it's why you came. To find him."

"I came to find you. You're all I wanted, all I want now."

He softly traced his fingers over her face before gently putting her from him, guiding her to sit in a chair. Isabel stayed there as he tied up Ray, shackled Jerico to the bed, then did a quick search of the cabin, collecting guns and Ray's knife.

But while her eyes watched him her mind and heart only heard his last words.

And try as she might not to give them more meaning than he intended, she couldn't quite quell the stubborn hope that she had somehow made a place for herself in his heart.

## Chapter Nineteen

"That's the last of my things," Cal said, flipping the leather cover over his knapsack. "You can move young Daniel in here this morning, Belle. I'm goin' home."

Isabel smiled. "You're the most determined patient I've ever treated, except for Jake." Her smile faltered, but she put it firmly back in place. "I'd almost given up hope. I've never seen anyone as sick as you recover. But look at you."

Cal returned the impulsive hug she gave him, then looked her over with a grin. "Always said your weeds were the best medicine. Esme and your mama taught you well."

"So, I guess you'll be going back to your job, now." Isabel made the comment more as a leading question than a statement.

She wondered desperately if Jake had talked to Cal before he'd left. After her ordeal with Jerico, Jake had brought her home in the early hours of the morning and tucked her gently into bed. He'd kissed her tenderly, touched her face, her hair.

Then he'd told her he was leaving to finish with Jerico.

But he hadn't told her what that meant. The last thing she'd heard before she'd fallen into a dreamless sleep was the sound of his boots walking down the hall.

The next morning he was gone.

Since then, she'd heard nothing from him and she hadn't worked up the courage to seek him out. Coward, she told herself. And it was true. Nothing frightened her more than imagining Jake saying goodbye and her knowing it was forever.

She'd heard goodbye before, but this time it meant everything.

Cal's voice drew her back to the present. "No, Belle," he was saying. "I've decided to leave it for good. Time I turned over my badge to a young fella with plenty of fight left in him."

Isabel bit her lower lip. She felt foolish asking, but she had to know if Jake had said anything to Cal about his plans. "Have anyone in mind?"

"Yep, sure do" was all Cal would say. "You go on and have those boys of yours bring Daniel up here. I know from experience your couch is about as comfortable as a pile of rocks."

Reluctantly, Isabel turned. She wanted desperately to ask if Jake had already left to take Jerico back to Texas for his trial. But a sudden burning in her eyes and throat stopped her.

She'd hardly slept or eaten the past two endless days, glancing out the window at every turn, running to the front door like a silly love-struck girl every time someone knocked.

The house was full of people, but without Jake it seemed empty. Where once her home, her family, her

work were all she needed to be content, now nothing
satisfied her. It all seemed incomplete without him.

She was incomplete without him.

Swallowing hard to force back the ache in her heart
that threatened to become tears, she headed downstairs.

It was no use. If Jake had offered to take the job,
Cal would have told her. He'd always wanted them
together. Now he didn't want to be the one to crush
her dreams.

Isabel paused at the base of the stairs, gathering herself. If he hadn't left already, Jake would be gone soon.

Standing there, alone, faced with the truth, Isabel at
last shook off the paralysis that had gripped her since
Jake brought her home. All these years, she'd been on
her own, stood up for herself, made her own way.

Jake admired that in her, she knew, yet at the same
time, he'd taught her the true pleasure of sharing the
troubles and joys of life with a man at her side.

She was still that woman who determined to meet
the challenges of life unafraid. And she was also
changed. Changed by loving Jake Coulter.

Once, the thought of losing her heart terrified her.
Now, she knew she could never live with herself unless
she found Jake and told him the truth. That she loved
him. That all he'd done for her boys, all the time they'd
shared, from the most intimate passion to everyday
household tasks, had given her more happiness than
she'd ever dared dream of.

Swiping away the wetness slipping down her cheeks,
she left Cal to finish his packing and walked into the
living area. She found Katlyn sitting at Daniel's side.

Daniel held Katlyn's engagement ring in his palm,
Katlyn's hand outstretched as if she had just put it
there.

Seeing Isabel, Daniel sat upright, coloring slightly.

Katlyn turned to her sister with a broad grin. "Daniel is doing much better this morning. Doesn't he look stronger?"

"Yes, I'm glad, but—" She couldn't help staring at the ring.

Daniel curled his fingers around it and tucked it into his shirt pocket. "The weddin' is off, ma'am."

"That's right." Katlyn stood and walked over to Isabel. She took her sister's hands in hers, her pretty face beaming. "We agreed. We're not right for each other. Are we, Daniel?"

"Yep. We should've known it from the start."

"But—I thought this was what you wanted, both of you."

"It isn't. I can't be a rancher's wife. It wouldn't be fair to Daniel."

"Or to yourself," Daniel added. "You're meant for bigger and better things, Kate. And there's nothin' else I wanna do for the rest of my days except raise longhorns."

"You made me think hard about my doubts," Katlyn said softly, squeezing Isabel's hands. "Daniel had them, too. But when I saw your face that morning, and knew how you felt about Jake, I couldn't marry Daniel knowing in my heart what we felt for each other would never be that powerful."

Isabel could only look at her sister. Katlyn gave her a quick hug, murmuring in her ear, "He'll be back, I know it."

Before Isabel could answer, the back door slammed and the boys rushed in, Esme slowly following them.

"Look, Mama," Matt said, rushing up to her. "I found a shell from a robin's egg, and one from a sparrow. Next, I'm going to hunt for a hummingbird egg. Mr. Coulter told me once they're so tiny they're hard to see, unless you know where to look.''

"They're lovely." Isabel admired the broken, dirty little pieces of shell as though they were priceless treasures.

"So, Señor Coulter has finished his work and now he is taking his prize back to Texas, eh?" Esme sought the rocking chair always reserved for her alone.

"That was his plan from the start, Nana. We all knew that." Isabel wished for once her grandmother would hold her tongue.

"I would not start counting the days without him just yet, Granddaughter."

Isabel looked at her in astonishment. She'd had enough surprises in the last few minutes to last a month. "Nana, you always said Jake would leave me in the end."

"Isabel, is it not clear to everyone now where he has left his heart? Besides—'' Esme fingered the beads around her neck, her smile satisfied ''—my magic is strong. He will not leave.''

Cal poked his head into the room then, rescuing Isabel from Katlyn's laughter and Esme's smug expression at her complete bewilderment. "Could I talk you into a ride back to my place, Belle? I don't think I'm up to the walk yet."

"Of course. Boys, go hitch up the cart. Katlyn, you'll stay here with Daniel, won't you?"

"Of course. Matt and Nate, I'll need you to help me move Daniel upstairs after you pull the cart around."

The boys nodded then trotted back outside.

Cal said his goodbyes, then added, "You come and visit any time. You'll find me on my front porch watchin' time go by.'' With a wink for Isabel, he gestured her toward the door.

Isabel went out into the sunlight, glad for the distraction, and resolving to use the time with Cal to persuade her friend to tell her exactly where Jake had gone.

Fifteen minutes later, Isabel was ready to strangle Cal.

To her blunt inquiries about Jake, he'd only smiled and shook his head, then made some remark about the fine weather or how well Elish was looking after Isabel's healing and Anita Devine's abrupt departure from Whispering Creek.

By the time Isabel guided the cart around the corner off the main street to where Cal's little cabin stood alone on the far side of town, she'd made up her mind he'd accidentally drunk locoweed instead of the teas and syrups she'd pushed on him.

But as they approached the cabin, Isabel suddenly fell silent.

An imposing figure of a man paced back and forth across the front porch. He turned as the cart slowed and stopped, his eyes going straight to her.

"Jake." His name felt like a prayer on her lips. She turned to Cal, questioning. "He hasn't left."

Cal set a hand on her knee, a warm indulgence on his face. "Well, what do you know? The devil's come a callin', just in time to save me from his angel's wrath."

Isabel's heart began to pound. She sat and just stared for a moment.

He looked magnificent. No black now. His white shirt and denim pants clung to him, the dark wave of hair that fell stubbornly over his brow making her fingers curl to brush it back and touch him. Oh, how she wanted to touch him.

He wasn't making it any easier for her to say what she had to say to him. It would be a bigger mistake than she imagined now to confess her love, knowing he was probably ready to ride out of town today.

And seeing him when she was unprepared made her suddenly self-conscious. She'd donned her same old yellow dress this morning since she'd planned to spend the day catching up on chores. Her hair hung in a haphazard braid tied with a string because she couldn't find a ribbon and everyone was already waiting for breakfast by the time she'd finally risen.

Feeling as plain and unkempt as the day they'd met, she tried to take an ironic sort of comfort in the thought that perhaps not much had changed after all.

Jake walked over to the cart and, surprising Isabel, offered Cal a hand down first. "Thanks, my friend," he said, slapping him lightly on the back.

"My pleasure." Cal turned to Isabel and, with a wink and a thank you, walked inside his house.

Isabel sat in silence, confused by both men.

"Mind if we go for a little drive?" Jake asked, motioning her to slide over so he could take the reins.

"A drive? Now? Where?"

Jake stepped up and moved beside her. "Oh, I thought we might go visit that spot near the lake. I told you I'd remember it for another day. And then later, I thought we'd do a little shopping."

"Shopping?" She gaped at him, not sure she had heard him correctly. "Are you all right?"

"Never better, angel." He tipped her mouth closed

with one finger and laughed, the deep, rich sound lifting Isabel's heart.

"Then—I don't understand."

"I was sitting here at Cal's place thinking this morning. All this time I've known you, we've never gone shopping together or much else, for that matter, that regular folks do."

"Well, those things didn't matter much, under the circumstances." Isabel felt more confused than ever. He hardly sounded like the same gunslinging Ranger who'd burst into the shack the other night and dragged a murdering thief off to jail.

This lighthearted man was someone she scarcely knew.

"That's my point exactly."

"I think the sun's gone to your head," Isabel said. "I don't understand any of this—or you."

Jake only glanced at her and smiled. He enjoyed the perplexed look on her face and drawing out the anticipation of finally having her all to himself. It had been too damned long, but he intended to remedy that soon enough. "Don't you?"

"No, but it doesn't matter. I'm glad you're still here. I wanted to talk to you, at least once more."

"Only once?" Jake turned to look at her, his grey eyes smoldering with an intense warmth that nearly stopped Isabel's heart. "I have a few things to say to you, too. And the first is you're the most beautiful woman I've ever seen."

Isabel had to laugh. "Oh, Jake, please. I wore this dress the first day we met."

"I know." He let his eyes graze appreciatively over her from head to toe.

Isabel felt her face grow hot. He wasn't going to

make this easy for her. They rode on in silence for some time and she was glad of the time to collect her thoughts.

"You're too quiet," Jake said finally, as the big cottonwood where they'd picnicked came into view.

"I need to tell you something that's hard for me to say."

"Then don't say it, not yet."

Jake slowed the mares to a halt and pulled the cart to a stop beneath the heavy boughs of the ancient cottonwood tree. He reached under the back seat of the cart to pull out the old green-and-white quilt she kept there.

"Come on, help me spread this out."

Helping her down, they smoothed the quilt out and sat down, each motion bringing back the memory of that day for Isabel. Had that happiness been an illusion?

Turning to her, Jake took her hands in his, his eyes changing to a gray as clear and sharp as the blue sky above.

Isabel braced herself. Here it comes. How can I listen? He tried to console me. Now he's going to tell me he's leav—

"I'm staying."

She blinked twice. "What?"

"I'm not going back to Texas. I've taken the sheriff's job, permanently. Cal and I made it official yesterday."

"But—what about Jerico?"

"I rode down to Taos the night we found Grey and talked to the county marshal. He's not sure whether Grey'll stand trial here or in Texas. He'll probably end up back in Texas since he's wanted for murder there, but the marshal insisted on taking Grey into his custody. I didn't argue. I'd wind up killing Grey on the way back, and we both know it.''

Isabel tried to make sense of his words but they seemed to jumble together in nonsense. Only one phrase seemed clear. She tried hold back the wild surge of joy in her heart long enough to make sure she'd heard him say the words.

"You're staying in Whispering Creek? You're not leaving?"

"Not even if you ask me to. I've taken a liking to this little town and to a lot of folks here."

Jake couldn't resist any longer. He took her face in his hands and kissed her. "One lady in particular has caught my fancy. I'm hoping she'll be happy I plan to stick around for the next fifty years or so."

"Oh Jake, I can't believe it."

"Does that mean you want me to stay?"

"It means if you don't stay now, I'm going to use one of Nana's spells to keep you here." Isabel threw her arms around his neck, laughing and crying at the same time. "I was so afraid you were going to walk away. But I didn't have anything to keep you here."

"You're wrong about that. You have everything."

Jake pulled back enough to take her hands and turn them over in his, lifting them to kiss the palms. "These hands healed me, body and soul. And now they hold my heart. I love you, Isabel Bradshaw. You're truly my angel, you've given me back my life. I can never live without you."

Tears ran unchecked down her face. Jake kissed them away, tasting their sweetness because he knew they were tears of joy, not sorrow.

"I know there aren't any guarantees and I could lose

you tomorrow. But if you'll stay with me, be my wife, I swear to you, I'll never leave you. We'll stay here, raise our children, be a real family. We've both wasted too much time without each other. Can you risk loving me?''

"Oh Jake, don't you see, I already have?" She kissed him, giving free rein to all the love and passion and need inside her that was for him alone. "I do love you. I'm only afraid I can never show you how much."

"I can give you a few ideas," he murmured, touching her in that way that started a slow, hot trembling inside her.

"I thought I heard you say something about shopping," Isabel said, even as she drew him into her arms and into her heart. "You know, one of those things regular folks do in the middle of the morning."

"Mmm…you know, I'm beginning to think nothing about our life together is going to be regular. In fact, I think you were right the first time." Lying back with her against the quilt, under the shelter of the cottonwood, in the wilderness they both loved, Jake smiled at his angel. "I think we're going to be magic."

\*     \*     \*     \*     \*

**Your Romantic Books—find them at**

# www.eHarlequin.com

## Visit the *Author's Alcove*

> Find the most complete information anywhere on your favorite author.

> Try your hand in the Writing Round Robin— contribute a chapter to an online book in the making.

## Enter the *Reading Room*

> Experience an interactive novel—help determine the fate of a story being created now by one of your favorite authors.

> Join one of our reading groups and discuss your favorite book.

## Drop into *Shop eHarlequin*

> Find the latest releases—read an excerpt or write a review for this month's Harlequin top sellers.

> Try out our amazing search feature—tell us your favorite theme, setting or time period and we'll find a book that's perfect for you.

All this and more available at

# www.eHarlequin.com
## on Women.com Networks

# HARLEQUIN
## SUPERROMANCE®

*You are now entering*

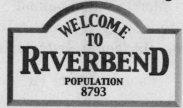

WELCOME
TO
**RIVERBEND**
POPULATION
8793

Riverbend...the kind of place where everyone knows
your name—and your business. Riverbend...home of
the River Rats—a group of small-town sons and
daughters who've been friends since high school.

The Rats are all grown up now. Living their lives and
learning that some days are good and some days
aren't—and that you can get through anything
as long as you have your friends.

Starting in July 2000, Harlequin Superromance brings
you Riverbend—six books about the River Rats and
the Midwest town they live in.

**BIRTHRIGHT** by Judith Arnold (July 2000)
**THAT SUMMER THING** by Pamela Bauer (August 2000)
**HOMECOMING** by Laura Abbot (September 2000)
**LAST-MINUTE MARRIAGE** by Marisa Carroll (October 2000)
**A CHRISTMAS LEGACY** by Kathryn Shay (November 2000)

*Available wherever Harlequin books are sold.*

# HARLEQUIN®
*Makes any time special* ™

Visit us at www.eHarlequin.com                    HSRIVER

Take a romp through
Merrie Olde England
with four adventurous tales
from Harlequin Historicals.

In July 2000 look for

**MALCOLM'S HONOR**      **LADY OF LYONSBRIDGE**
by **Jillian Hart**            by **Ana Seymour**
(England, 1280s)         (England, 1190s)

In August 2000 look for

**THE SEA WITCH**          **PRINCE OF HEARTS**
by **Ruth Langan**           by **Katy Cooper**
(England, 1600s)         (England, 1520s)

# Harlequin Historicals
## The way the past *should* have been!

HARLEQUIN®

*Makes any time special* ™